GROWING UP
DELICIOUS

70125890

Marianne
BANKS

Bella
BOOKS
2012

Bella Books, Inc.
P.O. Box 10543
Tallahassee, FL 32302

Printed in the United States of America on acid-free paper
First published 2012

Editor: Katherine V. Forrest
Cover Designer: Linda Callaghan

ISBN 13: 978-1-59493-264-9

PUBLISHER'S NOTE

Dedication

To Patricia Riggs for the loveliness of the day to day and Bubbles for teaching me how precious the day to day is.

To my family who taught me the cadence of storytelling.

Acknowledgment

Thanks to Leslea Newman who planted the seed that writing this novel just might be possible. I will always be grateful to the AWA method, Patricia Lee Lewis and Patchwork Farm. My heartfelt gratitude for the dedication, patience and good humor of the women of the Tuesday Night Manuscript Group: Jacqueline Sheehan, Ellen Meeropol, Rita Marks, Celia Jeffries, Lydia Kann, Brenda Marsian, Kris Holloway and Dori Ostermiller. Many thanks to The Great Darkness Writing Group for the creative alchemy they provide: Jeanne Borfitz, Jennifer Jacobson, Celia Jeffries, Lisa Drnec Kerr, Patricia Lee Lewis, Alan Lipp, Edie Lipp, Christine Menard, Patricia Riggs, Jacqueline Sheehan and Marion VanArsdell. A big thank you to Bella Books, Katherine V. Forrest, Karin Kallmaker and Nancy Heidenreich.

About The Author

I grew up in a town so small that reading was the only thing to do because television reception was so poor. My first job was mowing around the grave stones at the cemetery which offered a valuable perspective on life...we all end up dead. Growing Up Delicious, my first novel, took 25 to 30 years to write with time off for bad behavior, coming out of the closet and self doubt. I am under-educated but could muddle through butchering a cow or stringing a barbed wire fence if I had to though I haven't found much use for that in the suburbs. I can't put any letters after my name except PO Box and that's only if I'm writing out my address. The truth is I like writing stories because I like making things up. When I was growing up there were few stories for girls like me about girls like me and I wanted to write some.

CHAPTER ONE

My mother hung herself. Surprised the hell out of everybody. Me included. She always seemed to me to be a prime candidate for a murder victim. I spent years fantasizing ways to do her in. Electric razor into the bathwater. Mighty push down the cellar stairs. House fire. Mysterious car accident. Sometimes the fantasies were so real I'd have to go look for her to make sure I hadn't done the deed.

My sister Dorothy found her Saturday morning. Our mother was a human pendulum swinging from the crossbeam in the barn. Ticktock goes the mama clock. Blue chenille bathrobe. Funky rubber mukluks she'd had for the last hundred years. Was she wearing underwear? Did the police have to lower their eyes from the holy box she kept under lock and key? (I know I should watch my tone.)

They were going tag sale-ing. Dorothy had gone up early for a coffee and a mother-daughter chat. She freaked out and had to be sedated within an inch of her life. Or so she said when she finally "came to" enough to call me on Sunday night, half-way through *Sixty Minutes*. Though I still haven't figured out how she got my number. The wake's been planned for Tuesday and funeral for Wednesday, providing the coroner gets to the autopsy today. Which is Monday.

Before I could swallow my words I said "Of Course I'll Be There" in my best adult, mature woman voice. Grown-ups attend funerals. Grown-ups attend their mother's funeral. Even when their mothers have hanged themselves. Especially when their mothers have hanged themselves. The problem was I looked grown up but felt twelve years old.

The road to Delicious wound up through the gorge like a corkscrew. I downshifted the Toyota hoping that would help. Going home was like an Everest, air so thin my heart sprinted between my cervical vertebrae and my coccyx. I couldn't decide if it was a heart attack or diarrhea.

Just when the Toyota seemed to be clattering and wheezing its last, the road crested and evened out. Maple Street. The maples were gone, sacrificed for curbs and sidewalks. The clapboard houses looked basically the same, smaller maybe. The names on the mailboxes different from the ones I remembered. I passed the Delicious Public School. Its quaint little portico and front door were all that remained of the school I attended. It had grown several brick appendages, an unruly insect ready to devour the center of town. The village green. Picturesque New England. Public Library. Grange Hall that someone had turned into a day care center. Holy Roller Fry-Your-Ass-in-Hell Federated Church with a steeple high enough to skewer the heavens. The Delicious General Store. Max's gas station. The phone booth.

The Toyota needed gas. I needed something too. Water? Soda? A cigarette after more than ten abstinent years? I wondered if Auntie Rosie Potts who used to own Max's gas station was still alive.

She wasn't my aunt, wasn't anyone's as far as I knew. She was a character. The story went that she had been married, at one time, to a man named Max. Apparently, Max had resembled a barrel with legs, was very fond of sausages, sauerkraut and homemade root beer. Besides having breath as dank as a basement he was a genius with cars. Could fix anything and taught Auntie everything he knew, which proved to be prudent. Sometime in the late fifties or early sixties a Buick as big as an airplane rolled off its blocks and crushed him against the back wall of the garage. By the time Auntie found him he was flat enough to slide under the front door. Auntie never remarried but she did take to Max's business and began wearing his clothes. She had to gain a few pounds to fit into the chinos and T-shirts or flannel depending on the temperature. His large-faced Timex graced her muscular wrist. My father always said she became more Max than Max had been.

The screen door slapped shut behind me. A gray swirl of tobacco smoke greeted me before Auntie did.

"Hot enough for you?" Her voice was loud as though she'd grown hard of hearing.

"It'll do," I said, sliding my sunglasses down and peering over them at the old lady.

Auntie Potts sat in a rocker, which grew out of the floor like an old hickory tree between the counter and a picture window. Her position afforded Auntie a view of her gas pumps and the center of Delicious. She could see the comings and goings at the General Store, the literate among the townspeople who might be taking out or returning books to the library, and kids climbing the jungle gym at the day-care center. If Auntie hadn't been looking at me she would have been able to see the minister, the apparently immortal Pastor "The Antichrist" Jameson, crossing the common on his way to the Fry-Your-Ass Federated.

His was the one church in Delicious. It attracted Baptists and Congregationalists exclusively. Catholics, Jews and Methodists had to tuck their respective tails between their legs and go to

Equally Delicious (the name of the next and larger town to the west settled by a disgruntled Unitarian) to worship in their own peculiar manner.

I noticed the sign in the middle of the town green: "Welcome to Delicious. Home of The Biggest, Bestest Apples in Massachusetts." Because of the recent Fourth of July holiday, the posts were festooned with red, white and blue crepe paper. I looked back at Auntie.

"Bad perm." She caught me staring.

Auntie's hair was almost as short as mine and stood off her head in dozens of white, frizzled exclamation points.

I nodded, unable to remember why I had stopped in.

"What can I get you?" Auntie plucked an unfiltered Lucky Strike from a severely depleted pack on the windowsill and lit up with a wooden kitchen match.

My brain kicked in. "Five dollars of unleaded and a pack of...." What had I used to smoke?

"Salem Lights wasn't it?" Auntie said.

Time stopped just like my breathing. Why did I think I could skulk into town without being noticed? The only people who came to Delicious were the residents or the relatives of residents or the estranged daughters of mothers who ended up twisting in the wind. If there'd been any wind in that barn.

"Sooooo, you came back. I wondered if you would." Smoke escaped from Auntie's mouth.

"How did you know it was me?"

"Family resemblance."

I nodded, wondering if it extended beyond big noses, near-sightedness and high foreheads.

"Second, Gert's dead. Wasn't an easy way she picked neither. I can't help wondering why. Any clues?"

"You got me, Auntie. I haven't spoken to her for twenty-odd years."

"What do you suppose she'd think of your coming back?"

"If she was alive it would probably kill her. Maybe she'll sit up and spit in my eye." I opened my wallet.

"I'll have to be sure to go to the funeral." Auntie started to laugh.

At least it sounded like a laugh but could easily have been bronchitis.

"Keep your money, kiddo. It's nice to see you. Sorry for the circumstances."

"Thanks. You know I won't be here long."

"Of course not. There's nothing for you here." She flicked the Lucky Strike stub into a Maxwell House coffee can near her feet.

"There never was." I picked up the Salems and headed for the door.

"Don't be a stranger while you're here." Auntie followed me out the door. "You know your daddy used to stop by for a smoke once in a while."

I stopped in my tracks. My father. I was suddenly running in the dark. Blind. Heart pounding.

"It's been years since your daddy died but there ain't a Saturday morning goes by I don't think of him driving in here and..."

"Jenny?" My father shouts up the stairs. "You going to lay in bed all day?"

The brand-new AM-FM radio alarm clock I got last week on my twelfth birthday sits on my night table. Seven o'clock Saturday morning. Dump Day.

"I'll be right there, Dad," I yell, throwing back the covers and pulling on a pair of denim shorts and the T-shirt I'd gotten as a souvenir from the Catskill Game Farm. I raise the shade and see my father loading the trash barrels into the back of his pickup. No time for breakfast. Dad is in a hurry. Then I remember why. It is the second Saturday of the month. Dump burning day. I jerk open my underwear drawer for a pair of socks, pick up my sneakers and rush downstairs. I open the screen door and step out. The grass glitters with dew. My feet get wet. I hardly ever wear shoes in the summer but the dump is a dangerous place.

"Come on Jenny. I'll buy you a doughnut at Auntie's for breakfast on the way." My father opens the truck door for me. "Your chariot awaits." He always says the same thing.

The dump isn't much more than a hole filled with trash that always smolders and stinks a lot. I finish my doughnut before we get there. Any food left in my mouth tastes like the dump smells. There are other pickups already here, some empty and some waiting. My father backs up to the hole and sets the emergency brake.

"Don't want to fall in," he says. He hoists himself onto the back of the truck and empties the barrels. I kneel on the seat and look out the rear window and watch our trash join every other person's in Delicious.

Odie Burgess, the Dump Master, weaves up to the hole carrying two gallon jugs of gasoline.

"Had enough to drink, Odie?" one of the men yells.

He turns around to face the crowd and says, "Not yet."

Odie punctures the sides of the jugs and throws them into the rubbish. Nothing happens for a minute. No one looks anywhere else. With a great whoosh the smoldering gives way to fire. Leaping orange flames rise to the sky accompanied by roiling black clouds of smoke. The smell grows in the air until it is everything. My nose seems to get bigger, swelling like a tomato before it bursts in the sun. Suddenly the rats scatter out of the hole. It seems like hundreds rush from their flaming trash homes and run willy-nilly across the parking lot, scattering toward the men who are waiting to shoot them.

My father picks me up off the seat and boosts me into the back of the truck.

"Don't want to miss nothing, huh Jenny?" He reaches into the cab and takes his .22 out from behind the seat, loads it and climbs onto the back bumper.

He is a good shot, my father. One of the best. None of his rats suffer. They just explode like stepped-on grapes. Some of the other rats aren't so lucky.

Eventually the fire dies back. Odie meanders around the parking area pushing a wheelbarrow and shoveling rats into it. "Hell of a haul boys," Odie slurs as he shovels. "This here's a public service. Otherwise these sons-a-bitches would run over us in our sleep."

Someone offers my father a beer. I lie in the back of the

truck, my head on an old burlap grain sack, and watch the cloud of smoke drift away and disappear.

"You okay, kiddo? You look like you've seen a ghost." Auntie screwed on my gas cap.

"I did. This place is crawling with them." I started the Toyota and fastened my seat belt for the two-mile drive to my mother's house.

CHAPTER TWO

I pulled into the driveway and parked behind my mother's Gremlin. I couldn't believe it was still there. Apparently my mother's countless trips to the Fry-Your-Ass Federated rendered the car impervious to rust.

I took a deep breath, trying to screw up the courage to get out of the car. I played games with myself. Reminded myself I didn't have to stay. No one from Delicious expected me to be here. Only Auntie had seen me, and knowing her she might never let on to anyone else. Sure, I told Dorothy I would come, but I could break my word. She'd expect that from me, anyway.

Without permission, my hand opened the door and my body got out. Despite my mother's often repeated description of me, my head was attached and, so, there I was standing under the shade of the big sugar maple I used to climb when I was a kid. I looked at the bucolic utopia I grew up in. Maybe, if I hadn't grown up here, I might have felt differently. As it was, my stomach was a fist of anxiety.

Things were never what they seemed.

The house looked like a Currier & Ives print. White clapboard. Big four-over-four paned windows, half-lidded with the green room-darkening shades my mother preferred. Shade trees. Flower beds. Birds twittering. Bees drifting from daylily to daylily. The barn, red faded to shadow, stood behind the house. It looked empty.

The barn door screeched like a cat when I opened it. My eyes slowly adjusted to the murky half-light. I recognized the ancient, pointed apple-picking ladder leaning on its side against the wall. It was the balled up latex glove left behind by somebody, a medical professional or cop, that turned what had always been a comforting place into something else. What had possessed Gert to kill herself? Why couldn't I feel what my mother had done? Was it now haunted and unhappy rather than the place that had once held cows, hay, baling twine and pitchforks? Observing everything was the John Deere tractor: rusty, tires flat.

This place was a soundstage for the past. There used to be people here having lives. In the house my father was born in the downstairs bedroom. My cousin Jane and I used to jump in the haymow, echoes of my grandfather's warning in our ears to make sure we knew where all three pitchforks were. Big Thanksgiving dinners, dining room table extended with plywood and sawhorses, Grandma's gingerbread permeating the house like incense in a church.

If walls could talk, the stories they would tell.

I was a bad story. I joined my grandfather's heart attack. My grandmother's stroke. My Aunt Emily's scandalous marriage to a Catholic man. I joined my mother's shame at having her wedding day and my birthday only five months apart. I joined my father's need to drink a lake of Budweiser every night before the eleven o'clock news. I joined all the arguments and threats, swear words and ugly thoughts that oozed from our brains and stained the walls like nicotine.

"Jennifer?"

I whirled around at the voice behind me. "Mrs. Lewkowski?"

"Why, yes, dear."

She sounded the same. Suddenly I felt like the gawky twelve-year-old I'd once been. The one with Bat Woman horn rims and a more than substantial space between my front teeth. It was twilight on any one of a thousand evenings I crossed the street to knock on the kitchen door and ask Mavis to come out and play.

Ina Lewkowski couldn't believe her eyes. She squinted through the kitchen window. Yep. That was her. Jennifer. Jenny. Come back for her mother's funeral. Now, that was nice. How bad could a daughter be who came back for her mother's funeral? Especially that mother. Especially the way she died.

Ina still couldn't believe Gert had hanged herself being such a "Holy Roller" and all. That's what Ina's husband Earl called Gert. Ina thought "each to their own" but Earl didn't have much use for them Bible People since the preacher he grew up listening to had turned out a thief and had put in an in-ground pool with all the money he took from the Evangelical Outreach Fund.

Ina watched Jenny walk up to the barn and then come back to stand in the yard and look at Gert's house. Like a statue, barely breathing. Now, how long had it been since Jenny'd left? Let's see, Mavis was going to be a freshman at UConn that year. Jenny and Mavis were in the same class. So, land sakes, twenty-five years ago. Lordy. Hard to believe all that time had passed. Mavis had turned out good, thank heavens. Got that degree in landscape architecture, which truth be told, Ina didn't quite understand how a body could get paid for gardening. But Mavis was, and had that condo and new Volkswagen Golf to show for it.

Ina turned down the heat under the cabbage. It shouldn't be pulpy for rolling golumkis. Goodness, she hadn't made them since the last time Mavis visited on Mother's Day weekend. She'd wanted to take Ina out for Chinese food but that MSG business gave Ina a headache.

Mavis was coming up for Gert's funeral on Tuesday. Nice of

her. She and Jenny had exchanged a few Christmas cards over
the years, but, like Mavis said when Ina called her with the news,
"I know Jenny'd come to the funeral if you died, Ma, so I'll be
up." Earl liked her golumkis too. It was nice to make the family
happy.

Ina looked back out the window.

"Now, that was one unhappy home," Ina said aloud, surprised
she'd spoken. How many nights had that Jenny run over here
like she was being chased by bees. Can Mavis play? Can Mavis
play? Once she even came over when she knew Mavis was at Girl
Scout Camp and asked if there wasn't something she could help
Ina with around the house. They made Toll House cookies and
watched *The Brady Bunch*.

Ina decided she should go across the street and say hello.
Maybe invite her to dinner. Even if Jenny was one of those
lesbians now, she looked pretty much like she always had.

The years had been kind to Mrs. Lewkowski. Her hair was
grayer and the laugh lines had deepened, but, otherwise she
looked pretty much the same.

"How've you been, Mrs. Lewkowski?"

"Aside from a little diverticulitis, I've been fine." She wiped
her plump hands on an apron appliquéd with #1 Gramma. "I was
so sorry to hear about Gertrude's passing." She paused to cross
herself. "Never in a million years would I have imagined her...
well...taking her own life."

"Yes, I know. It took us all by surprise," I said, thinking that
had to be the understatement of the year.

"Surprise isn't the word. Why, Earl and I were having
breakfast Saturday morning and he noticed your sister pull in
the driveway, not that that was unusual. I often said to Earl how
I wished our girls lived close enough to stop by more often. You
know Mavis lives down in Connecticut and Roxie and her family
are all the way out in Eugene, Oregon. Anyway, it wasn't long
before we noticed Dorothy running up to the barn. Which was
unusual. Not two minutes later she came running out of that

barn like she'd seen a ghost...oh, pardon me. I didn't mean that, dear."

"That's okay." Now that was an unsettling thought. Gert the unfriendly ghost.

"Of course, Earl and I wondered what was going on. We were just having our second cup of coffee and thinking about going to see what was wrong when we heard sirens. I got a bad feeling then. I just knew something had happened to Gertrude..."

It was strange to hear my mother referred to by her entire name. She hated the name Gertrude. Almost everyone called her Gert. Mavis and I nicknamed her Gert The Alert. Mrs. Lewkowski and my mother didn't exactly get along.

"Why do you have to play with that Mavis?" my mother would ask every once in a awhile.

"Because she's my friend," I said, trying to sidle out the door before I had to hear what I knew was coming.

"She's Catholic. You know that, don't you?"

"Yes, Mom."

"You realize she's on a fast train to hell."

"Yes, Mom."

"Papists are no better than those Canaanites dancing around the Golden Calf."

"Yes, Mom."

"What with their praying to all those saints and kow-towing to the pope. They're nothing short of pagans."

"Yes, Mom. Can I go out and play now?"

"Just so long as you remember where you come from, young lady."

I'd never been able to forget. Where I came from followed me like a very long shadow. I suddenly realized Mrs. Lewkowski's lips were moving and I had no idea what she was saying.

"...covered with a sheet. Just like one of those crime shows on television..."

It was difficult to reconcile the Currier & Ives picture of where I came from to include this latest image.

"...tomorrow night."

"I'm sorry, Mrs. Lewkowski, did you say Mavis was coming up tomorrow for the wake?"

"Yes, dear. Well, I've got to get back to my golumkis. Mavis' favorite. Why don't you consider coming for dinner tomorrow night. I know Mavis would love it. We all would." She squeezed my shoulder and hurried across the street.

I watched her climb her front steps. She'd think I'd lost my mind if I followed her home and begged her to read me a story and put me down for a very long nap.

I turned and felt the pull of the house—a nasty undertow.

The key was under a pot of geraniums on the front porch. The first place anyone would look, including a thief. The door unlocked with a resounding click and swung open with a stuttering squeak. I stood on the threshold, greeted by the smell of Pledge, Spic and Span and Comet. The Seth Thomas, which, no doubt, still took its leisure atop the mantelpiece, welcomed me with measured cadence. Even though my mother was dead, I found myself straining to hear her efficient footsteps and the roar of her ever-present companion, the ElectroLux. I wondered what it would be like to hear "Hello Jennifer, it's so nice to see you after these long and many years."

I was losing it. My mother never welcomed me home. Not from school. Not from anywhere. She never liked me. She put on a show of it once in awhile, depending on who was around. But, that's all it was. A show.

When I thought of all the money I spent in therapy trying to figure out why Gert hated me, I could have afforded a 5,000 square foot home with landscaping and the visit of a professional masseuse twice a week.

I remembered taking a poll when I was a kid. "Excuse me, but do you have any idea why my mother hates my guts?"

Dorothy's advice was to try to be more like a girl. My father told me that my mother didn't like anybody so why should I be any different. Pastor Jameson said that my mother loved me but hated my sinful ways. I even asked Mrs. Lewkowski. All she could do was tear up, kiss me on the forehead and offer me a chocolate chip cookie.

Of course, now I'd never know. The only reason I was standing on the threshold of my mother's kitchen was because Gert The Alert had transformed herself into Gert The Inert.

Inert on a slab in some autopsy room in Pittsfield. Slit from pubic bone to sternum. Innards weighed and measured. The medical examiner wondering why some nice little old lady from Delicious had killed herself.

Gravel crunched in the driveway. A lumpy blue Prism clattered to a stop behind my Toyota. The door opened, a head appeared over the roof. Blond highlights. Very bouffant. Big round sunglasses. Pursed pink lipsticky lips.

Dorothy.

CHAPTER THREE

Dorothy was not looking forward to seeing her sister. She felt bad about that, she really did. She wanted to love Jennifer but all she felt for her was shame and embarrassment. Dorothy knew that wasn't right. Pastor Jameson had preached countless times on loving thy neighbor as thyself. She felt sure that "thy neighbor" also meant "thy sister." Everyone knew God was all about love. Dorothy knew God thought she should love everyone. Even sinners. Or people who weren't necessarily bad but weren't Christians either. Jennifer fell into that category.

First and foremost there was the "gay" thing. Dorothy couldn't bear to use the word Lesbian. It sounded so ugly. At least gay had a happy, harmless sound to it. Though it wasn't harmless. It was an abomination to the Lord. It was hard having a sister everyone, including God, didn't approve of. "Love the sinner, hate the sin," Pastor Jameson was always saying. Jimmy said that was because his daughter had straightened up and now flew right.

What a scandal that had been.

Dorothy shuddered when she thought about Jennifer and the pastor's daughter Ruth having a...what was the word...affair. Not that anyone ever said anything. But, everyone knew it. All because of how Jennifer had behaved at Ruth's wedding. Ugh. It was sickening. Pastor Jameson had been a saint. Even after Jennifer had tried to kill him. He'd refused to press charges and forgave her publicly from the pulpit, saying Jennifer was possessed by Satan and wasn't really responsible for what she was doing.

Dorothy still wasn't sure she bought that explanation. She figured it had much more to do with Jennifer drinking too much beer, coupled with the fact that Ruth was getting married. In any case, Jennifer wasn't charged and came skulking home after they let her out of jail. Dorothy thought their mother was going to have a stroke. She'd yelled and waved around the huge King James family Bible with such a vengeance that she ended up tearing a ligament in her shoulder and needed a sling for six weeks. Mother had taken a permanent magic marker and crossed out Jennifer's name in the family tree.

Mother was such a righteous woman. That's why it was so hard to understand why she had done what she'd done. Dorothy always knew Mother would pass away before her. That was the way of the world. But, not like this. Tears stung Dorothy's eyes. No. She would not give in. It was important that Jennifer see her like she usually was. A together person with her own day-care business and a happy marriage.

Dorothy squinted into the rearview mirror. It was really amazing how normal she looked considering that her whole world was going to "you-know-where" in a handbag.

I watched Dorothy's head swivel like a jack-in-the-box. She looked like she didn't know what to do with herself. That made two of us.

"Hey Dorothy, long time no see." Another understatement.

"Hi." Dorothy pushed her sunglasses onto the top of her head and crossed the lawn toward me. We met at the porch stairs wondering if we should kiss, hug or shake hands.

"Jennifer, what did you do to your hair?"

That surprised me. I don't know why. But, Dorothy had always been concerned with hair, makeup and coordinated outfits. Even today she was wearing lime green plaid Bermudas, lime green tank top and espadrilles.

"It's my summer 'do." I ruffled my very short hair.

"But, you're so gray."

Oh yeah. Forgot about that. "I've gotten older, Dorothy."

"Well so have I. I'll have to introduce you to my best friend, Miss Clairol. Jimmy just would not tolerate a gray-haired wife..." Her voice trailed off.

Amazing. Our mother was dead and we were talking about hair. We hadn't seen each other in forever and we were talking about hair. Not that I minded but I knew it couldn't last.

"How are you, Dorothy?"

"Okay I guess. How about you?"

"Okay. It's weird being here after all this time, to say nothing of why." How could I ever say everything I needed to say to someone I haven't seen in so long and hadn't exactly gotten along with for most of my life?

"It is weird. I've been running errands all day." Dorothy lowered herself, like she would shatter, to the front step. She sat with her knees up around her shoulders.

"I had to take an outfit down to Healey's for Mother to wear. Then I went to Stop & Shop to order deli platters for the reception or whatever they call it after the funeral. Then I stopped by the church and spoke to Pastor Jameson about..."

So, he was still alive. I hadn't imagined things when I saw him through Auntie's window. The Antichrist. I felt my heart beat in my ears.

"...hymns and using the fellowship hall afterward..."

I was crazy to have come. Delicious closed around me like a tight overcoat on a warm day.

"...I went, people were very nice. Sympathetic. But you could see everyone wondering. Why would Mother do such a thing?" Dorothy's lower lip began to tremble.

I sat next to her. If she were anyone else I would have put my arm around her. But, we'd never had the arm-around-you kind of relationship. Maybe things could be different now that we were both adults.

"Do you know why, Dorothy?" I squeezed her shoulder and felt her flinch.

"No. I've been thinking about it a lot since Saturday morning."

"I'm sure you have." I patted her thigh and watched her leg jerk away. Maybe I was generating electricity.

"And, well, I just feel guilty. Like I should have guessed and done something about it before it happened."

Leave it to my mother to make other people feel guilty about something she had done. I touched Dorothy's hand, which she quickly pulled away and used to root around in her lime green straw bag. So much for adulthood and things being different.

"Pastor Jameson told me to turn it over to God. That this was between Mother and her Maker."

"I never thought he'd say anything I could agree with." I considered touching Dorothy again just for the fun of it. But, that would make me a sadistic cat torturing the beleaguered mouse.

"Now, Jennifer, don't start. I know you have never liked the pastor."

"Hate, Dorothy. I hate him."

"All of that was a long time ago..."

"I'm going to go out with him, Jenn." Ruthie turns her head away from me toward the wall.

Anger rushes through me like I stuck my hand in a wall socket.

"Why?"

"Because I don't want anyone to find out about you and me."

I sit up and scoot toward the foot of the bed. Our jeans

make two puddles of denim where we left them twenty minutes ago.

"You don't mean anyone, Ruthie, you mean your father."

"Okay. I do. But, it's not like you want your parents to find out either." She rolls toward me and traces my spine with her finger.

"Yeah, I know. But, I'm not going to date the missing link to put them off."

"He's not the missing link, Jenn."

"He's got one eyebrow."

"He's not so bad, Jenn."

"One brain cell."

"I know he's not going to be voted class brain…"

"And a penis."

"I don't have to have anything to do with that. After all I am the minister's daughter…"

"A minister's daughter who kisses girls."

"David will keep my father happy."

"Goodness knows, we have to do anything we can to keep Daddy Pastor happy." I feel tears prick my eyelids. Sometimes everything seems so hopeless.

"We'll still be able to see each other, Jenn. You'll see. After school. Weekends. I'll just have to see David on Saturday nights. Maybe we can double-date."

"Double-date, my ass." I push her back on the bed. "How long before the Holy Roller gets home?"

Ruthie glances at her alarm clock. "About an hour."

She pulls me to her.

"Jennifer?" Dorothy's voice crackled through the haze of memory. Suddenly I found myself back on my mother's front steps.

"Jennifer? Are you all right?" Dorothy patted my shoulder. It was my turn to jerk away.

"I guess." Breathe, I told myself. That was the last thing Estelle said to me when I left our little house in Northampton earlier today.

This morning seemed like a century ago.

Delicious was a time warp.

"Listen. I've got to get home. Jimmy must be thinking I've fallen off the edge of the earth." Dorothy inhaled deeply.

I watched Dorothy open and close her mouth several times. Like people do when they aren't sure if they should say what they're thinking. Finally she spoke.

"Why don't you come for supper tonight. About six o'clock?"

I wasn't expecting that. Wasn't sure I'd be able to spend an evening making small talk with my sister and brother-in-law. But, an evening alone in Gert's house seemed worse.

"Okay, Dorothy. Thank you." I glanced at my watch. Four thirty. Just enough time for a shower and a cup of tea. Providing I was able to force myself inside the house.

CHAPTER FOUR

Having to pee was what did it. The bathroom gleamed. Pink tub, toilet and sink, relics from the fifties, managed, with the relentless ministrations of Gert, to look showroom-new. Everything seemed the same, even the smiling ducks swimming in little puddles all over the shower and café curtains looked suspiciously like the ducks that swam around my childhood. I wondered if, before Gert took the final plunge, she gave any thought to me, the handmaiden of Satan, returning. Returning to pee. Shit. Shower. Use the teakettle. And if I could get up the guts, rifle through the closets and drawers.

I took a cup of tea and the cordless phone out to the porch. I wanted to call Estelle and let her know I'd arrived. I wanted to hear her voice and imagine her sitting next to me, her curly red hair with more than a few silver threads and blue eyes crinkling at the corners because she's smiling at me.

Her eyes weren't crinkling last night. More like squinting. What a fight we had when I got off the phone with Dorothy. It was one of our worst.

"What do you mean, that was your sister? You told me she was in a mental institution. You said she was hopelessly psychotic." Estelle looked at me like I was the one who was hopelessly psychotic.

What could I say? What should I have said when we first met? Estelle fresh from divorcing a Kansas corn farmer. At the time, I didn't want to get into a long explanation. That's how it is in the beginning of a relationship. You want to make a good impression. Where my family was concerned, anything was better than the truth.

"Your mother is dead? Of course she's dead. You said she died when you were in high school. A fiery car crash, wasn't it?"

More like wishful thinking I wanted to say but didn't. Estelle continued staring at me like she didn't know who I was.

"Well, she wasn't dead when I told you she was, but she is now. She hanged herself. My sister isn't crazy. Not noticeably anyway. She's married to Jimmy, or was the last time I saw her, and has children I'm sure. Though I don't know their names or even if they exist." I wished I could shut up. "My father is dead and has been dead for about twenty years. Though he didn't die of lung cancer like I said he did. He drowned in Trout Sussmann's bullhead pond. It's assumed he was drunk." I felt like a pile of dirty laundry as I settled onto a kitchen chair.

"Why did you lie to me?"

I looked up at Estelle. Her hair was pulled back. She was making cookies when the phone call had come through. The Phone Call. That is how I would always think of it. "I don't know. We had just met and I didn't want to get into it."

"Okay, Jenn, I'll buy that. But, why didn't you clue me in later? After things had started to happen between us?"

"What was I supposed to say? 'You know that lie I told you when we met? Well, let me tell you the truth. My mother hates my lesbian guts. She is a testament-toting, Bible-quoting, born-again Christian who—did I mention—hates my lesbian guts. My sister is a younger, less bitter-but-only-because-she-married-a-goofball-she-loves-rather-than-the-alcoholic-my-mother-married, version of my mother, Saint Gertrude of the ElectroLux.'

"My father is dead but not because of something as benign as lung cancer. Oh no, he drowned. Snatched by the hand of God. Or so they said at his memorial service. Knowing my father, God didn't have anything to do with it."

I realized I was shouting.

"I'm sorry, Es, it just didn't seem important. I never thought I would hear from those people ever again."

"Not important! The truth is always important. A good relationship, which I thought we had, is always based on honesty." Es filled the teakettle and slammed it onto the stove.

"It is a good relationship. I don't usually go around lying."

"How would I know that?"

"You'll just have to trust me." Which sounds lame even to me.

"If I weren't so angry that might actually be funny."

Things went downhill from there. We settled into the "You Always" and "You Never's" like it was a comfortable couch. After midnight we surrendered to fatigue and went to bed.

At that point, I was grateful for the dark. I wished I could turn myself toward Estelle's back. Feel her warm skin and smell her smell where it rises off her neck. But I lay there, reluctant to move a muscle. Visions of my dead mother lurked behind my eyelids. Except she wasn't really dead. She kept talking. A ventriloquist's dummy scolding me for not picking up my room. Lecturing on the importance of cleanliness and how everything in her house would be clean, clean, clean. Why memorizing Genesis was necessary. The whippings, with a switch I cut myself from the apple tree across the yard, when I didn't comply. A malicious cuckoo clock marking the dark hours. Finally exhaustion hit me like a truck.

NPR jerked me awake at six thirty. I automatically rolled to the right to curl into Estelle for a pre-shower snuggle. Except she wasn't there. The sheets were cool. She'd been gone awhile. Fortunately, I knew where to look.

The back door was open. The tea tray, teapot and two cups sat on the top step. My eyes filled at the sight of two teacups. I hoped it was more than polite routine. I hoped it was forgiveness. Estelle, flannel robe flapping loosely around her calves, wandered around the flower gardens.

I screwed up some courage and stepped onto the porch.

"Is the tea ready?" My voice, low in the morning, carried easily across the backyard.

Estelle looked up. Smiled. My stomach relaxed.

"Good morning, babe."

I was babe today. Last night I was Jennifer: my identity only at banks, accountants and lawyers' offices. Never at home.

We sat side by side on the top step holding our steaming cups of tea.

"Are we okay?" I had to ask.

"Yes."

Relief washed over me. "How come? You were so mad at me when we went to bed."

"Angrier than I have ever been I think. Nana came to me in a dream."

I was used to Nana showing up. Estelle said she saw more of her grandmother since she'd passed away in 1988 than in all the years before. "What did she say?" I asked, hoping Nana was on my side.

"She reminded me of my Uncle Jasper. He and my father owned a trucking business. They called it Brother and Brother Trucking. Anyway, Uncle Jasper had a heart attack on Route 50 just east of Hutchinson, Kansas. He must have felt it coming and managed to pull over before he died."

I had never heard of Uncle Jasper.

"Aunt Maureen was devastated. He left her with my cousins Jasper Jr., Darlene and Bobby all under the age of twelve, a new three-bedroom ranch and a very meager life insurance policy. A woman nobody knew showed up at his funeral. The mystery woman had three kids in tow, all around the ages of my cousins, each the spitting image of Uncle Jasper. Turned out he had another family in Ponca City, Oklahoma."

"Now that's a story." I sipped my tea and wondered what a mystery woman had to do with me.

"Everyone thought Aunt Maureen was going to die of apoplexy then and there. But, she rallied and went to speak to the woman. Janet was her name. Apparently Janet knew all about Maureen and the kids. She had met Uncle Jasper at a Rexall Drug in Ponca City when he stopped by, on his way through town, to purchase Maureen's birthday gift. One thing led to another and Janet found herself with three children. For years Janet had entertained the hope that Uncle Jasper would leave Maureen, though he always said he never would. After a while Janet stopped caring because she was stuck loving Uncle Jasper."

I thought Uncle Jasper was a pretty slick operator.

"Of course, Aunt Maureen had to agree with that. Uncle Jasper was lovable even though at that moment, if he had been alive, Aunt Maureen would have sliced off his pecker. In a strange way, Janet and Aunt Maureen hit it off. Eventually Janet and her kids moved to my aunt's house in Wellington. Janet got a job behind the cosmetics counter at Newman's Department Store and Aunt Maureen went to work with my father driving a truck. She often joked with my father that they should rename the business Brother and Sister-in-law trucking." Estelle smiled and poured us each another cup.

I waited a decent length of time. "What do you suppose Nana was getting at, Es?" I loved Estelle's family stories. They made me feel that her family was even stranger than mine.

"Well, Uncle Jasper was a liar. To Aunt Maureen anyway. When she found out about Janet and Janet's Jasper Jr., Suzie and Patty, she could have freaked out and focused on Jasper's dishonesty. She could've gotten bitter and wondered about their life together and if it had meant anything. Instead she chose to look at the positives and make the best of things."

"So, your uncle was a liar but that wasn't all he was."

"Exactly."

"So, I am a liar but that's not all I am."

"Right, except your lying pales next to Uncle Jasper's. Though you are, like him, very lovable." Estelle leaned in to kiss my neck just below my earlobe.

Goosebumps. "What happened to your aunt and Janet?"

"As far as I know they still live in that same three-bedroom ranch."

"Really? That's interesting."

"It sure is. I always wondered about them."

We sipped and watched the mourning doves do their hurdy-gurdy dance under the pine trees. I invited peacefulness to seep into me like dye. I'd need it where I was going.

"I've got to go to Delicious."

"I know you do."

"I'm scared, but I have to go. I'm not sure why. I haven't spoken to my mother in eons."

"How long is eons?"

I did the math in my head. "Somewhere around twenty-four years give or take an eon."

"Wow."

"Yeah."

"What happened?"

"Not that different from your story. Girlfriend. Sex. Scandal. Leave. You know, the stuff novels are written about."

Estelle smiled into her tea.

"Maybe death brings out propriety. Maybe I have to go and make sure she's really dead. Maybe it's time to slam a car door on my hand to remind me that it really hurts."

"When are you going to leave?"

"Later this morning after I rearrange my appointments, pack a few things and have my head examined."

"You know, babe, I have that conference in Hartford today and tomorrow..."

Thank God I thought, surprised at my sense of relief. This was a solo odyssey.

"That's okay. I'd rather go alone."

Estelle looked at me. Blue laser beams. Heat. Light. "Are you sure?"

"Positive." My voice sounded tentative even to me.

Before I could call Estelle the phone in my hand rang. I knocked over my teacup and dropped the cordless. The battery pack popped open and the battery skittered across the porch and disappeared in the shrubbery. I hoped it was clumsiness and not some message from across the great beyond.

CHAPTER FIVE

Dorothy's split-level ranch rose out of a meticulously manicured lawn like an exotic mushroom. Unlike my mother's house, Dorothy's had undergone some changes since Jimmy built it for her as a wedding gift, in 1975.

Gert had been happy with Dorothy's marriage. Jimmy and his family were members of the Fry-Your-Ass Federated. Big Bill, Jimmy's father, was a deacon and his mother Francine, or Frannie as everyone called her, was in charge of the Ladies' Aid Little Evangelicals Choir.

Gert was mighty relieved that Dorothy managed to avoid getting pregnant before the wedding. Exactly the opposite of her own situation. Apparently Grandpa Spencer had to threaten my father with a deer rifle before he agreed to accompany my mother down the aisle. She never got over it. My father delighted in reminding her of it after imbibing a few Budweisers. "Yep, ol' Gertie," he'd say, eyes glittering with beer and mischief, "your daddy told me my head would be on the wall hanging beside his five point buck if I didn't make an honest woman of you." Then he'd laugh like it was the funniest thing he'd ever heard.

Dorothy was a flat-stomached size eight on her wedding day.

I parked the Toyota behind Dorothy's car. There was a giant plastic jungle gym on the side lawn, a wading pool and a few thousand Tonka trucks engaged in a road building project in what had once been a flower bed. Some valiant marigolds and black-eyed Susans hung on amid the front-end loaders and bulldozers. These couldn't be Dorothy's kids' toys. Probably grandkids.

I noticed Jimmy's Ford 250 pickup parked under an apple tree beside the garage. The kitchen door opened and he leaned out.

"Hey sister-in-law. Long time no see."

"Hey Jimmy. How're you doing?"

"Just fine. Sorry about your mother."

"Thanks." I gestured toward the Ford. "I see you've changed your theory."

"How so?"

"Remember that black Camaro you used to have?"

"A course. She was a beauty."

"I remember you telling me that if you parked under a tree it raised the likelihood of a bird shitting on your car."

"Did I also tell you what oxidizing bird shit can do to a paint job?"

"You sure did."

Jimmy held the door open as I stepped into the kitchen. "Well now I'm more interested in keeping the interior cool. Guess I'm getting old, huh?"

"It's not just happening to you."

We chuckled at each other. I'd probably just exhausted all my ability to be polite in these last few minutes. It promised to be a long evening.

"Let's go see what's keeping Dorothy."

I followed Jimmy through the kitchen and dining area and out onto a deck. The smell of charcoal briquettes burning off was overpowering. It was probably too much to hope for grilled salmon or tofu pups. Dorothy was nowhere to be found, though there was a tray of snacks on the table.

"I'll go see what's keeping the little woman." Jimmy ducked back into the house.

Grapes, Velveeta cheese, saltines and green olives with pimento. It had been a long time since I'd seen Velveeta.

From my vantage point in the barn I watch Jimmy drive his black Camaro into the driveway and maneuver it so it isn't parked under any trees. Not an easy feat in a yard as shady as ours. The goofball lopes across the lawn toward me. His legs start at his armpits and are topped by an Adam's apple and an unruly mop of orange hair. He is dressed for the unveiling of Dorothy's Dream House.

"Hey little sister-in-law." He adjusts the cummerbund of his rented powder blue tuxedo.

"Hey brother-in-law. What are you wearing a tux for? You said you'd never get in a monkey suit again after your wedding."

"Yeah, I know, but this is a special occasion and I want Dorothy to be happy."

"And seeing you in a tux will make her happy, huh?"

"She thinks I'm cute." He shines his shoes on the back of his pant legs, standing on first one foot then the other. The Goofball bird.

"Anyway, what'cha doing up here in the barn?"

"Hiding out from Gert. She's got her tits in a wringer over the party at your place this afternoon."

Goofball chuckles. He once told me, while under the Genesee beer glow, that he thinks Gert is a hard-ass. Hardly a revelation to those of us who know her best.

"Would you do me a favor, Jenny? Drop me off at the Dream House and go pick up Dorothy at the apartment?"

"You're letting me drive the Camaro?"

He grins at me like the goofball he is. "Yep, I'm going to trust you with my two favorite things in all the world."

"Far out. Do me a favor and clue Gert in. Otherwise she'll call the cops."

After I drop him off I drive the long way around to Dorothy's. I get the Camaro up to sixty-five on the straightaway between Arlis Branson's junkyard and the stop sign at the end of Cemetery Road. If I had any idea that Jimmy was going to let me drive the Camaro I would have been better prepared. Taken my savings out of the bank. Put a couple pair of underpants and a toothbrush in my knapsack and headed for Boston or San Francisco.

"Jennifer? Are you all right?" Dorothy touched my arm.

I practically jumped out of my skin.

"Yeah, you look like you've seen a ghost," Jimmy said as he poured some murky sauce over a pile of hamburgers.

"I'm fine. I was just remembering the unveiling party for Dorothy's Dream House."

The smell of grilling meat filled the air.

When I get to Dorothy's I blast the Camaro's horn. Goofball has replaced the normal car horn with the fanfare played at the beginning of a horse race. He and Dorothy have been living in a furnished room over Big Bill and Frannie's garage since they got married, while Goofball completed the Dream House.

Dorothy sticks her head out the door. "Come on up, Jennifer. I'm just finishing my makeup."

Frannie waves from her place at the clothesline. She uses five clothespins to hang one of Big Bill's plaid sport shirts.

"Hey, Jenny. You here to pick up Dottie?"

"Sure am, Mrs. Fifield."

"Now if I've told you once, I've told you a thousand times to call me Frannie." She hangs a sail-sized pair of boxers. "We're family now."

"Okay Frannie. I sure am looking forward to eating about a ton of your deviled eggs."

Frannie laughs and disappears into the house. No doubt to put the finishing touches on her award-winning deviled eggs. A recipe she refuses to share with anyone, including Gert. No matter what Gert does she cannot duplicate those eggs and has resorted, in her frustration, to a few "sin of pride" and "unchristian" comments directed Frannie's way. The deviled egg tug-of-war will no doubt continue until we all get high cholesterol and die.

Dorothy waves me inside.

"Are you almost ready, Dottie?"

"Shut up Jennifer. Frannie thinks I like to be called Dottie and I haven't the nerve to tell her I don't, especially because they aren't charging us rent while Jimmy's building the house." Dorothy shakes a bottle of foundation and applies three dots across her forehead, two on her cheeks and one each on her nose and chin.

"Jimmy will have a shit fit if we're late. Gert will think I stole the Camaro."

"I know. I know. I'm going as fast as I can." Dorothy smears the dots to cover her face with a perfect Barbie Doll tan. "I don't know what color eye shadow to wear today. The blue I usually wear or the green to go with my dress. What do you think?"

"Jesus, Dorothy, I don't know anything about makeup." I slump onto the loveseat.

"Honestly, Jennifer, can't you at least pretend to care about me for once? I'm so nervous I could throw up."

I look at my sister. Hair recently permed. Anxiety thick as Maybelline. "Go with the blue. It'll bring out your eyes."

We look at each other and burst out laughing.

"That's a good one, Jenn." She paints blue carpenter's chalk on each lid.

"You must be pretty excited about moving, huh?"

"I can hardly wait to see it. I've always wanted to live in a brand new house after growing up in that drafty farmhouse."

"You really haven't seen it yet?"

"Of course not." Dorothy looks at me over the top of her makeup mirror. "Why?"

"Don't you feel weird moving into a house that is supposed to be yours but you've never seen?"

"What do you mean, weird?" Dorothy dusts her face with powder.

"Strange. Odd. Peculiar."

"No. I feel really lucky. Jimmy is just so wonderful to surprise me like this. We've only been married a year and already we got our house. You know my best friend MaryEllen? Well, she and Jeff are still living in that trailer with no hope of getting out. She says it'll take a miracle for Jeff to get his act together and get them their house. Don't tell her I told you this, but Jeff is a lazy slug. He's more interested in Pabst Blue Ribbon and keeping that car of his running." Dorothy lines her left eye.

"I hope you like yellow."

"Why?"

"Because it's the color of your kitchen."

"Jennifer! Don't you go and spoil everything for me. It's just like you to ruin someone else's happiness." The right eye is next. "What color is the bedroom?"

"Dorothy! I'm shocked! How can you ask me to spoil your happiness? To ruin your life? To dash your hopes and dreams?"

"Normally, I would never ask. But, I was reading an article in *Good Housekeeping* at RaeLynn's Beauty Salon; you know how time consuming a perm can be. Anyhow, the article said the color of your bedroom affects your love life." Dorothy applies mascara, thick as tar, to each and every eyelash.

"What did the article say about red?"

"That it creates passion."

"Gert reads *Good Housekeeping* too. She painted the bedroom blue. You know how she is about sex. The only thing worse is a dirty oven."

"What about the living room?" Dorothy's applies blush to each cheek.

"I don't know if I should tell you. Gert threatened to pull my fingernails out if I said a word."

"If you don't tell me I'll tell her you did." Dorothy smirks, hand poised over a shoebox brimming with lipsticks in varying shades of red and pink.

"Don't threaten me, Dottie, or I'll tell Gert you had sex before you got married."

"I did not."

"Dorothy, I don't care if you went down on every guy in high school."

"Jennifer! What a thing to say. Jimmy and I waited until our wedding night."

"Yeah. Sure."

"We did!" She digs frantically through the shoebox. I watch her decide on a tube of something peachy. Her hands shake so badly she messes up her lip line. "How'd you find out, Jennifer?"

"I overheard you telling MaryEllen."

"Were you eavesdropping?"

"I didn't need to. Your volume control knob wasn't working."

"Oh my God! Do you think Mother knows?"

"No. If she did she'd have painted the living room black and hung sack cloth in the windows."

"I suppose you're right." Dorothy turns off the makeup mirror. "How do I look?"

"A bit like Barbie's friend, Midge."

"Can't you say something nice for once?"

"I did. Midge is cute."

"I looked like such a fool in that dorky tuxedo." Jimmy laughed.

"You were cute, honey." Dorothy kissed his cheek.

I struggled to focus my eyes on the present. Somehow the three of us were grouped cozily around the patio table and I was eating a slab of Velveeta.

"Remember when Dad fell off the front step into that laurel bush? He was so fat I thought we'd never get him out." Jimmy sipped his lemonade.

"Goodness, yes. He lost all that weight after the triple bypass. That massive coronary was the best thing that ever happened to him, right honey?"

"Absolutely. Remember that cake your mother made, Dorothy? Shaped like a split level?"

"I sure do, Jimmy, chocolate with green frosting. And those darling little windows she made out of Necco wafers."

I smiled. I had no memory of what they were talking about. Conversation is tough when the only thing people have in common is the past.

CHAPTER SIX

Jimmy took himself and a copy of the Burpee's Seed Catalogue off to the john. It was a well-known signal that he and the master bathroom were going to be off limits for a while. The bathroom was really the only place he got left alone. Sometimes he found himself going in there when he didn't have to take a crap. This wasn't one of those times. Since Gert hanged herself, Jimmy had had diarrhea. For the past three days he'd found himself hunkered down on the pot several times a day. He didn't know what the deuce was wrong. Stomach virus? Gall bladder? Nerves? It almost felt like Gert was lodged sideways in his colon. Jimmy winced as another cramp grabbed his guts. If this kept up he would have to ask Dorothy to pick up some Keopectate.

Dorothy really was a great wife. God knows he was blessed starting the day he married her. She still looked as good as the day they got hitched. Better. He sure as heck looked better since he got caps and a decent haircut. There were times, though, that Dorothy stuck to him like static cling. She always expected him to know the answers to everything. Most of the time he liked being in charge. He was the man after all and men were ordained by God to be the brains of the family.

Since Gert did herself in, Dorothy cried almost constantly and asked him question after question. What should they do about the funeral? What would people think? Should they serve ham salad or turkey sandwiches afterward? Did he think they should have an open casket? Baby gerkins or bread and butter pickles? Jimmy wasn't a detail man; he was a broad thinker.

He tried to cut Dorothy some slack. It wasn't every day you walked into the family barn and saw your mother dangling from a rafter. Jimmy would never forget climbing the ladder and cutting her down which he got in a world of trouble for doing by the state police. Evidence they said. What evidence? He'd be damned if he'd let Gert dangle up there one minute longer than she had to, even if she had been a royal pain in the butt. Gert had always acted like she had a direct pipeline to God.

Then she goes and hangs herself. How holy was that?

When Dorothy first called to tell him what she had found in the barn, Jimmy figured she was pulling his leg. He would've sooner believed Jesus Christ sitting down with him for Sunday barbecue. Jimmy wondered how much one man could shit as he felt another cramp shoot through his guts.

Yep, this thing with Gert was downright shameful. And now, on top of that, Dorothy's queer sister Jennifer has shown up. Was, right now, sitting in a lawn chair on his back deck sipping lemonade, soon to eat one of his world famous boom-a-rang barbecued one hundred percent sirloin cheeseburgers.

Jimmy had told Dorothy not to call Jennifer. Nobody had seen hide nor hair of her in years. But, Dorothy felt it was the right thing to do and Pastor Jameson had agreed with her. Jimmy was outnumbered and deep down he knew it was the right thing to call her even though it wasn't the least bit convenient. Lesbians were okay in a movie but he sure didn't want to see one eating off his dinner plates.

And, if all this wasn't bad enough, in about an hour the pastor was coming over to discuss funeral music. Ever since Jennifer had tried to kill Jameson, well let's just say, they didn't exactly see eye to eye. This promised to be a very uncomfortable evening. But, he would be polite and extend Jennifer his best Christian fellowship, which would make his little woman happy. And with any luck they'd all leave early and he'd be able to catch the end of the Red Sox game. Well, he better get out there and deal with the barbecue. Jimmy could handle anything with a cheeseburger under his belt.

"Jimmy, honey, tell Jennifer why you call this boom-a-rang barbecue." Dorothy put a bowl of potato chips in the center of the dining room table.

"Because it's so spicy it boom-a-rangs inside your mouth and threatens to come back out." Jimmy layered his cheeseburger with a thick slab of Bermuda onion and a drippy glob of coleslaw.

Whatever, Goofball. It's still some poor under-exercised, hormone-and antibiotic-laced bovine who got its brains blown out and throat slit in some midwestern cow concentration camp, then shipped to Stop & Shop where assholes like you buy it up and incinerate it on your Weber grills.

"Do you make it yourself?" I asked. Not that I cared, in fact I didn't care so much I wondered why I was bothering to talk about it. But, I was determined to be polite and get through the evening as smoothly as possible. I could see the dark circles under my sister's eyes.

"Sure do, sister-in-law. It's good on chicken too, right Dorothy?"

"Sure is, honey." They smiled at each other. "Jimmy, would you say grace?"

Uh-oh.

"Dear Lord. Make us better people as we digest this bounty and help us know your will and behave in a Christian way even though we don't always understand your plan. Help us to trust you know what you're doing. In your son Jesus Christ's name, Amen."

"Amen." Dorothy winked at the Goofball and he winked back.

I was amazed to see how in love with each other they still were. Just the same as they were on their wedding day, a day when they both wore white. False advertising, but folks down at the Fry-Your-Ass Federated were big on that. Our father was alive then. He refused to wear a tuxedo, no matter how much Dorothy pleaded or Gert browbeat him. Jimmy's father, Big Bill, even tried to have a man-to-man chat, the gist being "buck up and wear the stupid midnight blue tuxedo with crushed velvet lapels if only to make the kids' wedding day a little slice of heaven on earth." My father said he wasn't going anywhere looking like an idiot before he'd had even one beer. Besides, had Big Bill even considered how someone as fat as he was would look wearing a paisley cummerbund? They settled on navy blue suits.

I hated that wedding. All of Delicious was there, especially those citizens who were members of the Fry-Your-Ass. Dorothy asked me if I minded horribly not being her maid of honor because her best friend MaryEllen would be devastated if she couldn't be. Dorothy had been MaryEllen's wedding attendant and this way everything would be just perfect. I said I would rather have both knees broken with a softball bat than be expected to be in Dorothy and Goofball's wedding. She punished me by making me a bridesmaid.

I had to wear a dress, crushed velvet in midnight blue with an empire waist and puff sleeves, from nine a.m. until three p.m. By then, I had consumed enough beer from the coolers my father and other wedding attendees had stashed in the back of their various pickups to puke my guts up and ruin my dress and my mother's mood.

"Jennifer, is something wrong with your burger?"

"Yeah, sister-in-law, is it too rare for you?"

I didn't tell them I was a vegetarian. That the blood pooling on the plate reminded me too much of those November mornings when my father went off on the butchering circuit knowing that eventually he and his friends would make it to our barn and Moo

Moo or Ruby or Hannibal would soon bite the big one. Our freezer would be full of steaks and roasts and hamburger for another year. My father often asked who our meatloaf was made with.

"Oh, I'm not very hungry. Maybe I'll just take it back to Gert's." And throw it out the car window on my way. "My stomach isn't itself."

"I know what you mean, sister-in-law." Goofball took another handful of chips.

"Ummm, I don't know if I mentioned it, Jennifer, but Pastor Jameson is stopping by to go over the funeral arrangements." Dorothy dabbed at her lips with a napkin.

Thank God I hadn't eaten anything. "Maybe I should leave."

"Now, Jennifer, you're going to have to see him sooner or later. You might as well get it over with before we get out in public." Dorothy scootched back her chair and leveled me with a gaze that reminded me of Gert.

"Dorothy, don't look at me like that."

"I don't mean to butt in little sister-in-law, but the pastor is a man of God and I'm sure he has forgiven you your little transgression."

Transgression. That was one way to put it.

The church sits on a slight hill in the center of town, a huge, white monstrosity with twelve-foot leaded glass windows and a portico entrance. There are twelve granite steps leading to heavy double doors with shiny brass knobs. Off the main building an L had been added which houses the kitchen and fellowship hall, bathrooms and the Antichrist's office. The foundation is of granite blocks with small windows set in the granite every ten feet. There is a back door that enters into the basement where all the classrooms are located and a large supply room. It is the morning of Ruthie and the Missing Link's wedding. I lie on a pile of choir robes in the supply room that the Young Seamstresses for Christ were supposed to turn into curtains for the Sunday school classrooms. I am drunk.

On my way out of the house that morning I took a six-pack from the stash in the barn left behind when my father died, which Gert had never found, along with the blackberry brandy she kept in a soup tureen in the china cabinet. I drove to the church in my father's pickup an hour and a half early for the ceremony, which was scheduled for eleven a.m., allowing plenty of time to drink enough to be able to get through the day's festivities.

I start with the Budweiser. Sip slow and steady and stash the empties in the costume boxes for the annual Christmas pageant.

After the beer, I drank the brandy. Sweet, but as Gert so often says, you have to make do with what you have. I squint at my watch and see that it is ten forty-five. Time for a trip to the bathroom before things get started. In the corner of the supply room is a little bathroom the handyman uses. It's not as nice as the ladies' room upstairs but I can't risk running into anyone. I pee with the satisfaction and relief of beer-drinkers everywhere. My father always said that you only borrowed beer.

The bum-bum-bum-bum of the wedding march begins as I wash my hands. Euala Brown has the bass turned so low on the organ that the water in the toilet bowl vibrates. I make my way to the back door and ease it open. Glance to the right and left. No one. I sprint to the corner of the building and peek around the side. No one. I run toward the front of the building under the cover provided by the hedge of burning bush planted three feet in front of the foundation. I edge carefully around the corner. Everyone is inside. Delicious is deserted.

I run up the stairs and into the vestibule. No one. I sneak toward the door into the sanctuary and listen for an appropriate time to enter.

"Dearly beloved, we are gathered here on this glorious day the Lord has made to celebrate the marriage of David Alan Bishop…"

Missing Link.

"…to my daughter, Ruth Esther Jameson…"

Ruthie.

I know the sanctuary is decorated with lilacs and apple blossoms. Everyone is dressed to the nines. Candles flicker on the altar. White. White everywhere. Antichrist really pulled out all the stops. Ruthie said yes to everything.

"If anyone knows of any lawful reason why this man and this woman may not be joined in holy matrimony, speak now or forever hold your peace."

My cue.

I jerk open the vestibule door and run down the center aisle. The look on Antichrist's face is positively heartwarming. I am dimly aware of people in the pews turning around to look at me as I speed by. I hear the murmur of voices, Gert's ringing out above them all. I run fast and yet it seems to take forever to reach the happy couple.

"What the hell..." Missing Link grabs my arm.

"Fuck off, monkey face." I shove him into the pulpit.

"Jenn, don't..." Ruthie's eyes are round in her head.

I don't look at her. I can't. The white gown and veil make my stomach queasier than the beer and brandy. It's not her I want anyway. I tackle Antichrist and push him back until we are both teetering on the edge of the baptismal font. He pushes back trying to get a purchase on the edge. Wounded anger has made me strong. I shove with all my strength and back he goes, splashing water all over the place. I jump on top of him and push his head under the water. I feel him struggle. I lean all my weight on his head and shoulders and wait for him to stop moving.

I cry. Snot runs from my nose. I wonder if I am going too far. I wonder if I can live in a world where Missing Link can fuck Ruthie whenever he wants to.

"Die, you fucking bastard, die!" I scream it over and over.

"Right, my transgression," I said, thinking that Christians specialized in two things, hyperbole and euphemism or some combination thereof. Just as I was trying to think of an excuse not to eat the congealing hamburger on my plate there was the sound of a car pulling into the driveway. The three of us looked at each other, eyes wide.

"Excuse me, I need to use the..." I jumped up.

"The powder room is just off the foyer," Dorothy said, craning her neck to look out the window and make sure it was who we all knew it was.

I lurked in the hallway listening to Antichrist's gear-oil voice as he gave his condolences "once again" and offered up a prayer for Gert's departure and destination. His basic rap was that Gertrude was now with Jesus Christ, a roommate she had wanted as long as I could remember and though her exit had been "premature and reckless," the perfect love of the Lamb of God would heal her and she would be welcomed into the kingdom of heaven. I heard Dorothy sigh with relief. Amens all around. My sister mentioned key lime pie and would the pastor like some. Of course he would, my dear, with a nice cup of coffee if there is any brewed and the admission on his part, with a diabolical chuckle, that he had a bit of a sweet tooth.

My body vibrated with the effort it took not to rush into the kitchen and snatch him baldheaded. But, I needed to remain civilized. Not doing so always landed me in trouble, like that night I spent in Delicious Jail.

I am without shoelaces and bra and hope the day never arrives when I want to hang myself with the 18-Hour number Gert makes me wear because my tits are too big. Constable Bergeron told me that no way was I going to do anything hinky on his watch. Do you mean string myself up, I asked him. He looked embarrassed though I tried telling him I was too angry to kill myself. He didn't get that. The craziest thing he's ever done is get drunk and shoot at stop signs with his deer rifle.

Even I know that death will be preferable to the wrath of Gert when I get out. If I get out. Bergeron and I have a friendly bet about that. He says I'll be out tomorrow providing you-know-who comes around enough to be released from the hospital. I say the Antichrist will take this opportunity to get rid of me. All bets are off if he dies.

The Delicious jail shares space with the police department in the firehouse. It's an old two-story barn converted to house a couple of fire trucks and a tanker truck. Behind the firefighting equipment is an office, which at one time was a very nice tack room, and behind that is a big cage with bunk beds. Across the hall's a bathroom and a toilet and sink used by the volunteer firemen and police constables as well as any prisoners in custody. As jail goes this probably barely qualifies but it has bars and a locked door.

Bergeron checks on me every fifteen minutes. I suggest he wheel his chair back here so we can play cards but he says it wouldn't be proper police procedure. This is Delicious, I tell him, have you forgotten where you are? He says police procedure is police procedure so he sits in the office drinking coffee and playing solitaire while I sit on a bunk and listen to Bergeron slam his cards down in frustration and wish for a radio. I have trouble being alone with myself. I have to read or do something so I don't start thinking too much, otherwise I feel desperate. My heart will pound and I'll have trouble catching my breath. Especially tonight. I know I went too far. I knew it while I was doing it but I couldn't seem to stop myself. I feel like a rock rolling downhill except I am both the rock and the thing it hits when it stops.

About six a.m. Bergeron gets a phone call. Thanks holy shittin' Christ, I hear him mutter on his way to unlock the cell.

He drops me off at my house wishing me good luck, which I know I'll need once Gert catches on that I'm home. I stand in the road hoping a gigantic bird will swoop down, grab me by the collar and lift me away to a nest of young ones screeching for their breakfast. I notice my father's truck and wonder who drove it home after yesterday.

"How dare you show your face back at this house," Gert hisses across the Sunday-still lawn.

I had expected her to slam out of the house, waving her suitcase-sized King James, wailing on about the devil's handmaiden, me. Beseeching God to deliver her from her Jezebel daughter, me. Offering to cut off her right arm and beat herself to death with it if only she could be washed with enough Holy Spirit to be able to forgive Satan's spawn. Me.

"Here's the keys to your father's pickup, two-hundred dollars, your birth certificate, bank book and some clothes. You get out." Gert throws a garbage bag, keys and an envelope at me.

"Don't call and don't come back." She turns and goes into the house.

I hear the key turn in a door that is never locked. This isn't what I expected but it is what I have always wanted. I put my things in the truck and start the engine. The gas tank is full. I guess that's my going away present.

"Hello, Pastor." I stepped into the kitchen and glared at him.

"P...Pastor, you remember Jennifer..." Dorothy's voice vibrated with nerves.

How could he forget?

"...in town for mother's funeral." Dorothy spilled coffee on the counter.

He looked up at me, his eyes clouding over. Cataracts? No. Hatred.

Though I wanted to launch myself on his desiccated, decrepit body and dig his eyeballs out with my thumbs I thought better of it. Hatred is like ragweed. Every summer I forget about ragweed until my eyes start to water and mucous runs from my nose like an erupting volcano. I was surprised at my hatred for this man. I knew that coming to Delicious was a mistake. I felt myself slipping away. The me who happily lived with Estelle. Owned a home. Had a backyard and a lawnmower. Was a successful massage therapist. I was melting. Hot wax without a bowl.

Would the past ever stop mattering?

I thought I had escaped years ago. At first Delicious followed me like a loyal dog. I drank and smoked dope trying to forget where I came from. I slept with any woman who would have me, not caring if we even liked each other, hoping to outrun Gert. I drifted from job to job trying to find something to take the place of my past. I finally found my way to The Third Eye Ashram and Organic Egg Farm deep in the Adirondacks, where meditation and whole food helped. While I was trying to achieve selective amnesia at The Third Eye, two things happened. I learned about alternative protein sources, a welcome relief after years of seeing a little face on every bite of meat that came my way. I also met a massage therapist named Julia Whitcome. I learned a lot from her, mostly how to breathe. I went to massage therapy school and after graduation moved to Northampton, Massachusetts—a mecca for lesbians, massage therapists and psychotherapy, my new holy trinity.

"Would you like some coffee, Jennifer? It's decaf."

I felt Dorothy, Goofball and the Antichrist staring at me, waiting for the next thing to happen. Suddenly my fingers tingled almost like a carpal tunnel flare-up. Power flooded through me. They all assumed I'd fly off the handle and act like a drunken maniac. Who could blame them? That's exactly what I was the last time they saw me.

"No thank you, Dorothy. Thank you for the dinner invitation. I'll leave you all to discuss the funeral without me. I'll see you tomorrow at Healey's Funeral Home."

And I left. I didn't rush. I didn't kick the chair out from under the pastor's bony ass. I just left. Like a grown-up.

CHAPTER SEVEN

I drove out Mountain Road toward the state forest. It was way too early to even think about going back to Gert's. If there had been a motel in Delicious I would have seriously considered checking in. On the hills that rolled away on my right and left were long, neat rows of apple trees, lined up, marching like soldiers toward the horizon. Macintosh. Delicious. MaCoun.

Apples grew just fine in Delicious.

When I was seven I saw my first black man at Stub Olsen's orchard. My father did weekend work for Stub during the fall. They were cousins by some convoluted marriage arrangement common in places where no one new has moved into town for generations. Bill was from Jamaica. He was black as newly harrowed earth. He wore a kerchief tied around his head and a pair of too-big Levis with sweat-stained suspenders. His voice was deep and kind of sing-songy.

When my father introduced me, Bill reached inside his pocket and gave me a quarter. It shone in his pink palm. Pink as mine. I asked him if he was black underneath his clothes. Stub and my father laughed. Bill didn't. I didn't mean to make a joke, I said. I had never seen anyone with black skin before. Bill looked serious when he hunkered down on one knee and looked me in the face. I could see his eyes were dark and liquidy like molasses. It felt like he was looking inside my head.

"Yes," he said, "I am black all over. And so is my wife and three children back home on the island."

"You live on an island?" I asked.

"Yes," he said, "surrounded by the ocean."

"Why doesn't your family come with you, don't you miss them?"

Stub spoke up then and said he could get more work out of a colored man if he was alone and didn't have anything else to do.

But, Bill must be lonely, I said. Stub and my father started laughing. Bill shrugged and stood up. I knew something had happened but I didn't know what. I went and sat in my father's truck and waited for him. Bill went back to work fixing Stub's spraying machine.

I continued up Mountain Road. I couldn't seem to stop myself from looking for that old access road that used to run between Marvin West's orchard and Stub's place for about a half mile or so, providing each access to his land. The road ended in the deep woods that surrounded a reservoir another mile up the mountain.

I slowed down and saw a hint of where the road once was. I felt like a criminal returning to the scene of a crime. I parked the Toyota and gazed into the woods, almost as dark as my own mind is with memory.

Ruthie pedals ahead of me. I watch the muscles work in her

legs. I know it isn't right the way I think about her. The way I think about running my hand along those muscles. We have just been released from vacation Bible school. Gert believes in vacation Bible school which means I go. Every summer. This year is a bit better because we were finally old enough—thirteen and going to high school in the fall—and had memorized the required one hundred Bible verses, to teach vacation Bible school to the next unlucky generation. Ruthie and I work with the youngest kids in the Genesis Group. They are four-and five-years-old and can't really read yet. So, we spend three hours each morning watching them coloring in the Moses coloring book, playing hopscotch across a pretend Red Sea and having snacks of graham crackers and lukewarm Kool-Aid while pretending we're stopping for a lunch break during our wandering with Moses out in the desert.

We have the afternoon to ourselves.

Ruthie thinks we should try out for the freshmen field hockey team. It is important to make our mark early, she says, especially because it is a regional high school and prone to cliques. Consequently, we are in Ruthie's boot camp to increase our lung capacity and strengthen our thigh muscles. Today's torture is a bike ride up Mountain Road.

"Hey, Ruthie, hold up will you?" I gasp for air. What saliva I have in my mouth is thick. "I need water." I get off my bike.

"You are such a sissy."

I watch her keep going. I slide off my knapsack and get my thermos of water. The cool wet unglues my lips from my teeth. "Want some?" I yell, pushing my bike up the road behind her, confident she'll give up in a minute. Even trucks downshift climbing Mountain Road.

Finally she can't take it anymore and wobbles to a stop. I hand over the thermos when I catch up. She takes a big drink. Head back. I watch her throat work up and down.

"Look there." She points. "I never noticed that road before."

"That's just a woods road that goes up to the reservoir."

"Really?"

"I've been up there with my father. It's pretty. Want to go look?"

"Jennifer, you're trying to break training."

"Come on. A little break won't hurt. My legs feel like jelly." I push my bike across the ditch and leave it in the tall grass. It is dim on the road. Maples, oaks and birches join arms over our heads. It is instantly cooler. I hear Ruthie following behind me, hoping she is watching me like I watch her.

"Wow," she says. "This is neat. It seems like we've crossed into a secret place."

That's exactly how I feel. "We have. Just a little ways up here is this rock that looks like a giant's bed." Almost as soon as I say it, it appears in front of us.

We stretch out side by side. Nature is subdued. I hear the occasional car whoosh by on Mountain Road. I drink it in and think that my life would be perfect if this moment could last forever.

"I'm getting kind of nervous about going to high school, aren't you?" Ruthie sits up and gazes down at me.

"Yeah. Mavis's older sister says it's not so bad. She's a cheerleader. Dorothy wants to be one too. Gert likes that idea, thinks it's almost as good as being filled with the Holy Spirit. I think that little skirt looks idiotic."

"You know, Jenn, you have to wear a skirt for field hockey."

"Are you kidding?"

"Nope. You'll have to show off those legs of yours." She rubs her hand over my knee.

I feel like there is an electric current running up my leg and ending at my crotch. I know I am in big trouble. Why do I have to feel this way? All my friends, Mavis next door and Dorothy, everyone talks about boys the way I feel about Ruthie. I know what I feel has a name. The same name everyone at school calls Miss McLarren, who works in the cafeteria. She wears a hairnet and has a mustache. Miss McLezzie.

"Jenn? Earth to Jenn."

"Sorry."

"Sometimes you get this weird lost look on your face."

I close my eyes. I know what I feel will show. And then the worst thing happens, tears leak from my eyes and fall back into my ears. Maybe she won't notice.

"What's wrong? Did I say something?"

"No. It's not you. Believe me. It's just...I...you won't understand. No one will understand. Sometimes it's just too hard to keep it in." I sit up quickly. "Let's go, Ruthie. Remember training."

I feel her hand on my shoulder stopping my progress across the rock and out of this quiet, dark place.

"Tell me."

"I can't." But, how I want to. How I want to say I love you. And what if I do? She will scream and run away and never speak to me again and I'll watch her every chance I can and wish I had never said anything because to be with her this way is better than nothing.

"Tell me." Ruthie's eyes are brown. I look into them and watch them warm as she looks back at me.

"I love you, Ruthie." I feel myself turn tight inside. Waiting.

"I love you too, Jenny. You know that. We're like sisters."

"No, Ruthie. Not like sisters. Like girls usually like boys."

I watch the confusion on her face fade to surprise and then go blank. Smooth river stone. I wait. Wait for the sun to crash out of the sky. Wait for the darkness growing inside me to spread out and cover me like a heavy woolen blanket.

"Why?" Ruthie's eyes glitter.

Why? Because I have known you forever. I don't remember ever not knowing you. But knowing someone doesn't make you love them.

"I don't know if I can explain it."

"Try."

"When I walk in the woods I feel calm inside, like everything is perfect. I never feel like that when I'm inside, at home or school or anywhere else. Only when I'm outside in a place like this."

Ruthie nods for me to continue.

"Being with you makes me feel the same way. I think that feeling is love." I look down at my hands. I am afraid to meet her eyes. The ages seem to pass while I wait for something to happen.

"No one has ever said they loved me before."

"I know it isn't right, Ruthie, and I've tried to stop myself. But, I can't."

"That's okay, Jenn." She takes my hand and holds it in both of hers. They are hot.

The phone rang as I let myself into Gert's house.

"Babe?"

"Estelle?"

"Now, who else calls you babe?"

"No one here, that's for sure."

"Where've you been? I've been calling for a while. I was starting to wonder if something had happened."

"Nothing's happened except dinner at Dorothy's. Remind me to tell you about Jimmy's boom-a-rang barbecued cheeseburgers—"

"Cheeseburgers?"

"Yeah, and dare I forget, an unwelcome, though hardly unexpected visit with Antichrist—"

"Antichrist?"

"My pet name for Pastor Jameson. I almost drowned him in the baptismal font at Ruthie's wedding."

"Jenn, are you okay?"

"Surprises you, doesn't it Es, to have a girlfriend who almost committed murder by baptism? All for Ruthie…"

"Who is Ruthie?"

"The Antichrist's daughter and my first lover."

"Wow. It sounds like a movie."

"It was a movie with a plot no one would believe. I could barely follow along and it was my life."

"Was your life, babe. *Was.* Not your life anymore." Estelle's voice crackled through the phone like peanut brittle.

Suddenly I could breathe again. "It's hard to remember that. I feel myself regressing by the minute. Like I'm on some backward escalator to the past and I can't get off."

"You know, babe, I've been thinking and I've decided to cut my conference short and come to Delicious."

I sink to the kitchen chair with relief and dread. Relief makes sense. But dread?

"The wake is tomorrow night, right?"

"Yes."

"I should get there midafternoon, okay?"

"Sure it is, Es. Are you positive you want to come? This is one shindig worth missing."

"Yeah, but you're not."

That brought me up short. I am always surprised by how much Estelle loves me.

"Meet me at the funeral home. Healey's is easy to find. It's right in Delicious' center."

"Okay. I love you, Jenn."

"Love you too. See you tomorrow."

The phone rang again almost as soon as I hung up.

"Hello. This is...ah...Herlick Healey down at the funeral home."

I remembered Herlick from high school. He blended with the off-white walls.

"Hello, Herlick. This is Jennifer. You were ahead of me a couple years in school."

"Ah...yes. Yes. I remember. Well, I called you by mistake. I ah...meant to call Dorothy."

"Oh. I can look up her number for you."

"Ah...perhaps you could help me. It seems your mother is in need of a scarf. The dress has a nice high collar but not high enou...ah...your mother looks a bit severe and a scarf might soften things up. If you know what I mean..."

I thought it would take more than a scarf, even if you covered her face with it, to hide Gert's severity.

"...something dark. Maybe a navy blue paisley would be nice."

"Okay Herlick. I'll go upstairs and look. Should I bring it by now?"

"Well...ah...I still have quite a bit of work to do. Your mother just arrived so to speak. I'll be here until midnight."

"Okay."

"Come to the back door. Ring the bell." The phone clanked in my ear.

This changed my plans for the rest of the evening. I was hoping for a cool shower, a cup of tea and a mindless television show. Now I would have to go upstairs, behind enemy lines, and infiltrate Gert's bedroom.

CHAPTER EIGHT

Herlick Healey specialized in messy deaths. Car accidents. Deer hunting mishaps. Anything involving farm machinery. He also took care of the run-of-the-mill: old-age-die-in-your-sleep deaths, slip and falls, which could be categorized as messy if the fall involved distance and something hard or pointy at the end of it. Cancer could be a challenge. Not the quick ones, fine one week and gone the next. Those were a breeze. But, the long involved cancers that left a body looking old and worn down to a nub. Those fell into the challenging but not necessarily messy category.

Herlick had an extensive filing system. Who died and when, the cause and any special procedures or techniques he might have used. These were color-coded. Red for messy. Green for challenging. Orange for messy and challenging. Blue for run-of-the-mill. Black for cancer. Purple for cancer and challenging. He was thinking of adding yellow for suicide.

Suicides were good for business. People who would never ordinarily come to a wake always showed up for a do-it-yourselfer. The more gruesome the better. Not that he did many of those or if he did they were disguised as something else. Gertrude Andersen was a make-no-mistake type of suicide. Somewhat challenging. Maybe yellow with a green stripe. Herlick was running out of colors.

The rope had done a lot of damage and, of course, she'd hung there for a few hours before she was found. Heck of a thing really. He felt sorry for Dorothy. Walking in and seeing your mother dangling like a frost-killed tomato must have knocked her for a loop. Though she'd held up pretty good when she brought in her mother's clothes. Pale and a little weepy, but not too bad. Herlick was determined to do a nice job for the daughters' sake. He would use a lot of that thick foundation to help Mrs. Andersen along.

Not that she deserved it, mind you. If the truth were told, Mrs. Andersen had been quite a trial when she was alive. He remembered the night her husband had drowned. Herlick wasn't a mortician then, just a kid a couple years out of high school learning the ropes of the family business from his father, Harrison.

She'd stormed in the private back door entrance. Not even pausing to ring the doorbell which gave a heads-up to anyone working in the embalming room to cover things up quick so no one walked in and saw something that would make the average citizen an insomniac. She demanded to speak to Harrison pronto. Herlick was mopping the floor with a bleach solution. His father was a regular Mr. Clean about the embalming room. Herlick's father was upstairs finishing a bowl of beef stew before getting to work on Mr. Andersen. She made such a racket that Harrison came downstairs, napkin still tucked into his collar, and took her into his private office.

It wasn't that Herlick meant to eavesdrop. It was just that his floor mopping happened to take him in that direction.

"Harrison," she said, "I'm paying and I want Robert to have an open casket."

Herlick listened to his father's murmur and wondered why anyone would want to look at a man who had spent the afternoon facedown in Trout Sussman's bullhead pond.

"I don't care how he looks," she said, "I want everyone to see what happens when a man drinks himself into a stupor and falls into a fishpond."

Herlick gave up any pretense of mopping and listened to his father's answering murmur. Harrison went on for some time and then there was a long moment of silence, which led Herlick to believe his father had persuaded Mrs. Andersen to have a closed casket.

"I don't care if he's bloated. Do something to deflate him."

Murmur. Murmur. Murmur.

"Cover up that part with a hat," she said. "He always wore that gosh forsaken John Deere cap when he was alive he might as well take it with him to the grave."

Herlick had seen the rather large contusion on Mr. Andersen's forehead. The police figured he had hit his head and knocked himself out. That was really the only explanation for drowning in eighteen inches of water.

"I don't hold with protecting children," she said, "especially from the wages of sin. I want Dorothy and Jennifer to remember what became of their father."

Herlick remembered, and he had seen countless bodies since. Fortunately the Andersen girls were spared the sight because his father refused to open the casket. He had offered to take Mr. Andersen to Dolan's Funeral Home in Equally Delicious free of charge if that was what Mrs. Andersen wanted, but by God, he would not be party to opening a casket that should remain closed.

Herlick was proud of his father that night and worked hard to become half the mortician his father was. Harrison was now retired and lived in a condo on the intercoastal waterway in Boynton Beach, Florida. And here was Mrs. Andersen. Brought in feet first this time and a good deal quieter for certain.

CHAPTER NINE

I tiptoed up the stairs. The second and seventh step squeaked as they had every day of my childhood. The hall light illuminated little, creating more shadow than it relieved. The wallpaper had faded and yellowed along the seams. I stood on the landing working up the guts to open one of the three bedroom doors. Sweat crawled along my neck. I decided to start with the relative safety of my old bedroom.

Hot mustiness greeted me. The room was stripped. Peter Frampton gone. Tie-dyed curtains gone. Only the furniture remained, dust like a gray sweater on top of the desk.

It was surprising to think that Gert could close her eyes and sleep in the next bedroom with so much dust and grime accumulated in here.

The light pools on my desk blotter. Warm. Almost yellow. The rest of the room is dark. My long division homework is done and I am saving my English homework, chapter 5 of *Tom Sawyer*, for bedtime reading. The Revised Standard Version of the H.B. is open on my desk to Luke, or what is left of Luke.

Suddenly my bedroom door slams open and hits the doorstop so hard it vibrates. I look up, heart pounding in my throat. Gert. Her eyes narrow as she looks at me. Snake eyes. I swear I see her tongue slither from between her lips and disappear back in. Tasting the air.

"What are you up to?" Gert demands. "You wouldn't be reading the Good Book unless I forced you to."

"Actually, I'm doing my Sunday school homework." I push my desk drawer shut, hiding my X-Acto knife.

"What does Mr. Phillips have you studying?" Gert takes a step closer.

I want to slam the book shut but I know that will make Gert wonder what I'm hiding. "You mean besides his dandruff and nervous twitch?"

Gert glares at me.

"Chapter four. The part where Jesus comes down out of the wilderness after forty days and wants something to eat and the Devil says if he's so hungry why doesn't he turn a hunk of rock into some Wonder Bread?"

Gert steps closer. I feel my innards turn to water. It's stupid of me to work on my little editing project when Gert is anywhere near.

"I doubt Mr. Phillips or the Good Book mentions Wonder Bread, Jennifer. You need to have more respect or one of these days God will take all those smart words and scour your mouth out with them." She snatches up the Bible before I can stop her. "What are all these holes?"

I push my chair back wishing the wall would give way and I could fall from the second floor into the rhododendron bushes. With any luck I'd break my back and end up in an iron lung or something. "Nothing. Some kind of paper eating bug, maybe."

Gert fans back through the book with her thumb. "You have defiled God's Holy Word."

Which was true. It needed defilement. The thing was a piece of trash. Ever since my favorite Aunt Lil had died last September I figured God and Jesus were figments of somebody's imagination. So, I decided to X-Acto-out all reference to either. The Confetti Edition of the Revised Standard Version of the H.B., edited by Jennifer Andersen, otherwise known as smart-mouth.

"You demon!" Gert screams and swings the Bible back, like a home run hitter, and slams it into the side of my head.

My glasses fly off and crash to the floor. Little explosions of light flash in my nearsighted eyes. Gert is a blur as she swings to send another one out of the park. Crack. This one knocks me off my chair. I am grateful for the floor because I know that it isn't spinning. Not really. It's just my head on its own carnival ride.

I opened the door to Dorothy's room and was faced with a shrine to the Good Daughter. Cheerleader pom-poms. Sappy pictures of Dorothy and Goofball. David Cassidy and Jesus side by side over her bed. The cross given to her by Gert on the occasion of the Mother-Daughter Christian Quilting and Devotional Weekend. Large enough that Gert could have used it to crucify herself instead of choosing the noose for her getaway.

Okay, now for the reason I climbed the stairs. Gert's room.

I stood there waiting for the ability to open the door. A fool on her errand. Stuck in that absence of space between the rock and the hard place. My heart raced in my chest. The oxygen grew thin. I watched my hand gain on the doorknob. Fingers closed around it. Brass cool to the touch. Wrist turned. Click. Latch released and with the merest of pushes, the door opened.

The smell of Gert washed over me. Something between Lemon Pledge and Secret deodorant. The double bed was gone, replaced by a twin. Otherwise the room was the same: the persistent hum of the electric clock, alarm set for five a.m.

and turned off before it ever had the chance to ring. The sun only rose because Gert did. King James and concordance shared space with a box of Kleenex on the nightstand. Lavender chenille bedspread.

I had always been told to stay out of her dresser drawers. Which, when I was a kid, made them all the more attractive. I remembered sneaking in, using a hand mirror to peek around corners, a trick I learned from Mavis's Dick Tracy comic books. The only mysteries the drawers ever produced were underwear. I remembered thinking at the time that grown-up women required a lot of it. Slips. Big white underpants with elastic waistbands. Bras with pointy cups and lots of hooks on the back. Stockings. Girdles. Sanitary pads the size of blackboard erasers. Nothing of interest. Just additional reasons to not grow up to be a woman.

I mentally shook myself. Get the scarf and get out. Herlick was waiting. I tiptoed to the dresser and slid open the top drawer. Underwear. The second drawer held sweaters and turtlenecks. The third drawer squawked when I opened it. There was an array of socks and several scarves. I rifled around until I found a navy blue one with a geometric pattern that made my eyes cross. Hopefully this would not clash with the dress that Dorothy had dropped off earlier today, the one with a collar not quite high enough.

I nearly made the threshold before I stopped. There was a fourth drawer. Might as well have a look while I was here. It had always had photo albums in it. My favorite was my parents' wedding album. My father looked constipated in all the pictures and Gert looked like she had a smoked oyster in her mouth and couldn't decide whether to spit or swallow.

The drawer was heavy as I pulled it out. Photo albums. Dorothy and Jimmy's wedding pictures. Even though I had been there I couldn't resist flipping through. Dorothy looked so young and hopeful. He looked nervous. Gert beamed as though she were plugged in. My father looked drunk, but handsome in his blue suit. I wasn't all there. Gert had carefully removed my head with one of my favorite tools, the X-Acto knife. My body remained. A headless dyke in a dress.

Underneath all the memorabilia were three thick manila

folders. One contained medical reports from Albany Medical Center. Another held information printed from the Amyotrophic Lateral Sclerosis website. The third had various tracts on suicide methods. "How to Tie a Hangman's Knot" was highlighted in yellow.

CHAPTER TEN

Healey's Funeral Home was opulent by Delicious standards.

Mr. Herbert Robinson built the original house for his daughter Eleanora on the occasion of her wedding to an Irish Catholic boy named Patrick Healey. The Robinsons were Episcopalian. To a Delicious Baptist or Congregationalist there wouldn't have been much difference between an Episcopalian and a Catholic. But, to an Episcopalian there was every difference. Initially, Herbert ranted and raved and threatened to disown Eleanora. Until Herbert's wife, Eleanora's mother, reminded him that his people had changed their name from something decidedly Middle-European and non-Episcopalian when they set foot on Ellis Island, and perhaps he should consider the merits of a compromise. Herbert built Eleanora's house with guilt, anger and the money he had made in the fabric mills of Springfield. It was, however, eighteen miles from his own home. Distance was his compromise.

I drove around behind Healey's and parked next to a hearse. My heart was pounding, which it had been doing almost constantly since my arrival in Delicious. Quite the stress test.

I rang the bell and waited. It was almost dark. The moon peeped through the trees. It looked like a paper plate with food stains on it.

The door opened. Herlick stood there as pale and thin as a #10 business envelope.

"Hello, Herlick," I said. "Here's the scarf you asked me to bring."

"Ah...thank you. I'm sure she will appreciate it." He slipped it into the pocket of a very white apron.

"I doubt it, Herlick. She's dead."

He looked at me. "Well, yes, you're right. I...ah...suppose. But, I think they know if they look nice."

I gave that a moment's thought. "If she had cared about that she would've taken some sleeping pills rather than hanged herself."

Herlick raised one eyebrow. "Would you...ah...like to see her?"

Now there was a question.

"It's okay...ah...Jennifer. She is presentable."

To whom, I wanted to say. "Sure."

Even as I followed Herlick down a short hallway I wondered why I had agreed. I didn't have to do this. I could have waited until tomorrow when that navy blue, geometric patterned scarf was firmly knotted in place. That would've been soon enough. And yet, here I was in the back room of a funeral home about to see Gert for the first time in twenty-odd years. At least I had the advantage this time around.

The hall emptied into a larger room, which was painted white. The windows were hung with red and white gingham café curtains, and a scented candle, something sweet like a baking dessert, burned on the windowsill, but underneath that was a hint of chemical and bleach. A jazz CD was playing. It was cozy for an embalming room.

"She's over...ah...here," Herlick said as he led me toward a cubicle and whisked aside the curtain.

The woman laid out under a sheet with curlers in her hair didn't look like Gert. I wondered who it was.

"I apologize for the...ah...curlers. Her hair wasn't quite dry." Herlick rocked back and forth slightly, in time with the music.

"You wash their hair?"

"Of course. It livens them up, so to speak."

I stepped closer.

"Don't worry, Jennifer. She...ah...won't bite." Herlick smiled. At least it seemed like a smile.

"Are you sure? She's been biting all her life." I stared into her face. She looked older and like she was made of plastic.

"I'm sure. Their mouths are glued shut..."

Now that was more than I needed to know.

"...can't have them popping open during the proceedings."

Especially Gert's mouth.

"I think she needs more rouge and, of course, lipstick."

"I never remember her wearing any."

"Everyone gets...ah...lipstick. Even men..."

I stood there, torn between the fascination of seeing a dead body and the feeling that I should be more disgusted by the whole thing.

"...reading glasses on the chain around her neck..."

Where were my feelings? Why did this feel like something I was watching rather than doing? A situation comedy: Meet the Mortician.

"...a bit too...ah...symbolic if you get my meaning. So, I left them aside. What do you think about your mother holding them?" Herlick raised his eyebrow at me.

"Holding what?"

"Her glasses."

"I didn't know she wore them."

"Oh, well, the...ah...deceased holding a personal item is nice. Reassuring, if you know what I mean."

"The only personal thing Gert had that I knew about was her King James Bible. That's probably too big for the coffin. And her cleaning products. Pledge and Comet were her favorites."

Herlick raised his eyebrow. His face as devoid of emotion as a CPR mannequin.

"Just kidding, Herlick." Though I wasn't. Not really. "Ask Dorothy. She knew Gert much better than I did."

"Of course." He stepped back.

"Well, I've got to be going," I said, suddenly eager to be gone.

"It...ah...will be crowded tomorrow." Herlick shut the curtain on Gert.

"What do you mean?"

"The...ah...wake. It's been my experience that suicides have high volume attendance."

I'd forgotten about that. All of Delicious trooping by. Dressed up like they were going out to dinner.

When I got to the Toyota I ripped open the pack of cigarettes I'd bought at Auntie Potts's earlier that afternoon. This had to be the longest day I had ever lived through. I pushed in the car lighter and waited for it to ping out at me. When the cigarette was smoldering I put it into the ashtray. Anything to take the smell of Healey's out of my nose.

I rolled down all the windows and drove through Delicious screaming at the top of my lungs.

Auntie Potts wondered why someone hadn't opened a pizza place in town. She even had a name for it. 'Delicious Pizza.' It worked on a lot of levels. She could almost smell the double cheese with pepperoni, hot sausage and mushrooms. Could see the steam escaping from gaps on the sides of the box. Taste the tang of peppy tomato sauce. Yep, a pizza would be nice. Especially with a Pepsi. Poured over ice in her Boston Red Sox commemorative beer stein. Nothing cleaned the tongue of pizza grease like the sweet snapping fizz of Pepsi. And not diet either but full strength.

Auntie had just finished sweeping around her gas pumps, emptying the trash and refilling the paper towel dispenser. She had turned off her GAS sign and sat in her darkened store enjoying her fifteenth Lucky Strike of the day. She inhaled, sat back in her rocker and put her feet up on the windowsill. Auntie allowed herself twenty cigarettes a day. It was mighty hard, at first, cutting back. But, now she was used to it and even felt a little better though she wouldn't admit that to Dr. Delerzon. He was after her to quit, take up tai chi at YMCA in Westfield and eat a "plant-based" diet. Whatever that meant. She was seventy-six, for God's sake. Old enough to decide how many smokes would kill her and how many wouldn't. Her father, Horace Tatro, had smoked up until the day he died. In fact, a freshly lit Chesterfield was smoldering between his fingers when they found him next to the car crusher at the junkyard.

Auntie listened to the bells at the Federated Church bong once. She glanced at her watch. Eight thirty. The lights were still on at Healey's across the street. Herlick must be over there finishing up Gertrude. He was a good boy. Hard working just like his father Harrison. But, peculiar. Maybe a person had to be to do that sort of work. She always suspected the Healeys to be drinkers. Not bleary-eyed drunks. Just people who kept themselves in a constant state of relaxation.

Tomorrow Auntie planned on closing the gas station early. Herlick would need extra parking with the overflow crowd that was sure to attend Gertrude's wake. And she wanted to go too. Not so much to see Gertrude. Auntie hadn't liked her. But, because she figured Jennifer would need to see a friendly face. Hell, most folks wouldn't be there because they thought so much of Gertrude. They'd be there because they'd never seen anybody who'd hanged themselves before. There couldn't be any other reason because Gertrude wasn't that popular. All that piety made people nervous. And then hanging herself like she did. Well, it was too good to miss.

Auntie watched a car leave Healey's at top speed with someone screaming out the windows. It looked a lot like the car Jenny had driven in with this morning. That didn't make sense. Why would she be over there before she had to? And if she was, well, it was no wonder she was screaming. No, it was probably just some kids out cruising with nothing better to do. Yep. Auntie wondered if Gertrude was making some kind of joke. A last laugh-type of thing. Except Gertrude had about as much a sense of humor as a flat tire on a dark road.

CHAPTER ELEVEN

I couldn't bring myself to close my eyes in Gert's house even though I'd seen her dead body. Knew that if somehow it was a wax dummy and she was still alive, by this time she would have hunted me down like a dog. So, it wasn't that. Perhaps it was my bedtime reading. I had scanned Gert's medical records. She was diagnosed with ALS in January. Then I read the information sheet some thoughtful doctor had put together for her. If I lived forever I would always remember that little pink sticky note.

Dear Mrs. Andersen, here is the information per our discussion of January 8th. If I can offer any further information please give me a call. Your records have been forwarded to Dr. Wilbourne at Baystate Medical Center. Good Luck. Frank Allen, MD

Good luck? The sheet on ALS read like a recipe for hell.

ALS, or Lou Gehrig's disease, was fatal, eventually, but before a person died they became paralyzed. Most people died within eighteen months. If a patient used a ventilator they might live for many years.

I looked up from my reading—I could swear I could hear Gert muttering that living in a wheelchair wasn't living. I actually turned my head to make sure she wasn't in her easy chair.

The good news was a person with ALS retained control of their mind, bladder, bowels and, usually, eyeballs. Until the end, which needn't be bad. Hospice and the buildup of carbon dioxide in the body made death painless and peaceful. Gert was impatient. She wasn't a fan of eventually. That's why the creation story appealed to her. She liked a world that was created in six days.

When I finished reading the medical records and literature from the ALS Foundation, it was too late to call Dorothy. Too late to call Estelle. I took a cool shower and gave TV a whirl. Gert had no cable and minimal reception so I was stuck with a movie about a woman who had a perfect husband, perfect children, a perfect house and still she drank several jugs of vodka every week. When I found myself offering suggestions to the woman on screen I decided to turn out the light and try sleeping on the couch.

It was stuffy. Even with the fan blowing on me.

I took off my T-shirt and tried naked. Naked didn't work. Especially in Gert's house.

I wrapped myself in a summer blanket I'd found in the linen closet and went out to the backyard. The moon threw silvery light across the yard. I settled into a chaise lounge and looked up at the sky. Delicious was dark at night, even with an abundance of moonlight. The Big Dipper tossed a waterfall of stars across the darkness. I stretched out, wiggled my toes and felt the cool of the cushion soak through the blanket and touch my skin. I watched the moon. Couldn't take my eyes off her. Imagined her light burning Delicious off me.

"Make me new," I whispered. "Like you do yourself, twelve or thirteen times a year."

I opened the blanket. Felt the light on my skin. Inhaled

the light. It moved through me. Made the fillings in my teeth sing. Made my throat burn like Szechwan wontons. My nipples hardened. Belly expanded. Intestines unclenched.

The stars glittered around me. I looked down on myself. Saw a woman on a chaise lounge. Naked. I watched myself watch me. I was everywhere. Saw the deeper darkness inside each chimney. Watched the roofs begin to glisten with dew. Peeked though Venetian blinds and watched the unsuspecting sleep. And some not sleep. Skimmed down Cemetery Road, slipped through the wrought iron gate, stood close to the newly dug grave. It was bottomless.

CHAPTER TWELVE

A robin woke me up. He looked like Alfred Hitchcock. His spindly legs were poor scaffolding for his body. He studied his situation in perfect silence. And he took his time about it. His situation was the peak of Gert's roof. He stood at the point where a lightning rod would be, cocked his head as though he was listening for something. Occasionally he looked at me, like Alfred might, wondering how he could work me into his story.

"My situation is worse than yours, Al," I murmured from my spot on the chaise lounge, wrapped in my blanket like a sausage in puff pastry. My hips ached from the night spent in the sway-backed chair. There was a constellation of mosquito bites around each ankle.

It was the thought of that first sip of tea that got me up. I clutched the blanket, groaned to my feet and staggered through the wet grass. I thought I'd left the door open last night and maybe I had, but now it was closed. And locked.

Shit.

My next thought was Dorothy, a sorry state of affairs thinking of her and her perfect hair and makeup first thing in the morning. Pre-tea. She only lived a mile away but, I knew I didn't have the emotional wherewithal to walk that distance adorned in a blanket. Summer-weight, as it was, with little lavender flowers. Though it might almost be worth it to see the expression on Dorothy's face.

I next thought of Mrs. Lewkowski. She had a sense of humor. More than most people. Of course, she would have to, being married to Earl Lewkowski who taught science at the Delicious Grammar School. I remembered one science class when he brought all of us out to his pickup where he had a gutted deer tied to his rear bumper. We had an anatomy lesson and helped him quarter the carcass. Little Al Phelon, who had a weak stomach anyway, threw up and had to be taken to the nurse's office.

I sneaked across the street to Mrs. Lewkowski's house. Her kitchen light was on and I could see her little gray head bobbing around like a dashboard ornament. Strains of polka music escaped from her screen door. I knocked.

"Goodness, Jennifer, you scared me." She bustled over and unlocked the door. "Come on in, dear. You look nice and summery this morning. You caught me doing my morning exercises. I do them to the Eddie Grametka's Accordion Orchestra CD that Earl got me for my birthday. I'm in cool down. Help yourself to some coffee. I just have to get through Babci's Golumki Polka and then I'll heat up some cinnamon rolls and we can have a nice chat."

I watched Mrs. Lewkowski swivel her hips and wave her hands over her head.

"I'm not usually up this early but Earl wanted to go to Otis's fishing so I made him some nice bacon and eggs for breakfast." She did two deep knee bends. "He was disappointed there was no rye toast. He's partial to rye, with seeds or without, he doesn't care."

I held tight to the blanket as I poured myself a cup of some of the thickest coffee I'd ever seen. "Do you have any cream, Mrs. Lewkowski?"

"Of course, dear. In the fridge between the farmer's cheese and that tub of the new-fangled olive oil spread Earl's heart doctor wants him to eat. He's got the angina." Mrs. Lewkowski sashayed to the oven and set the temperature to three hundred. "Between you and me, Jennifer, I can't abide it. I sneak a little of the Land O'Lakes when Earl isn't looking."

I lowered myself into a kitchen chair. Any sudden moves would bring on an unwanted disrobing. Though I wondered if Mrs. Lewkowski would even notice.

"What got you up so early this morning, dear?" She dabbed her forehead with a paper towel.

"I couldn't sleep last night so I went outside and fell asleep in a lawn chair."

"Well, that's no wonder, dear. You've got a lot on your plate at the moment."

That was true. It felt like I was carrying around the two-plate breakfast special from the Miss Florence diner. "Somehow I locked myself out of the house."

"Gracious sakes, Jennifer. Lucky for you I've got Gertrude's spare. She changed that lock last year to the automatic kind. Just before her trip out west."

"You have a key? That's great. I thought you two didn't get along." I grimaced as a sip of coffee made the glands in my cheeks ache.

"We didn't but we are...were...neighbors. Besides last year she and Dorothy and Jimmy went on vacation to Utah and the Grand Canyon. So, I had to water her violets." Mrs. Lewkowski slid two cinnamon rolls into the oven and set the timer for eight minutes. "Would you like some eggs, dear?"

"No, thank you. The coffee is great." For stripping furniture, I thought. "I appreciate you letting me in dressed like a Hare Krishna."

"Well, I wondered about that, dear. But, sometimes we do things when we're stressed out that we normally would never do. Like when I had my mastectomy. When my hair fell out from that chemo business, I bought a blond wig. Earl said, 'why a blond one, you've always had brown hair.' But, there was something inside me needed to be a blonde." Mrs. Lewkowski took a sip of coffee. "Earl liked that wig. Once in a while he still asks me to put it on. He says it's like taking another woman to dinner."

"Are you all right now?"

"Oh yes, dear. I only had the cancer in one breast but I decided to have them both taken off. It wasn't like I needed them anymore what with the girls all grown up. And I wanted to be around for my grandchildren. And Earl. He's a smart man but he can't seem to run the dishwasher."

We both sipped our coffee.

"Mrs. Lewkowski, I think Gert was sick."

"Really? What makes you think that, dear?"

"I found some medical reports. It seems she had Lou Gehrig's disease."

"Land's sakes. That's terrible. I just saw a TV movie about that not too long ago. Earl said if he ever got that he'd be sure to shoot his head off with his hunting rifle."

We both looked at each other. I watched Mrs. Lewkowki's eyes widen with alarm.

"Oh, goodness, Jennifer. I can't believe I said that. I'm sorry. It just flew out of my mouth." Her eyes filled with tears and she reached for a tissue from a box next to the lighthouse salt and pepper shakers.

"It's okay, Mrs. Lewkowski." I felt tears prick my eyes. I hadn't cried over Gert and I didn't want Mrs. Lewkowski's kitchen to be the place it happened. If the floodgates were going to open I wanted to be by myself. Just in case I started howling like a dog or something.

"Sometimes I just say things and then I'm stuck with having said them." Mrs. Lewkowski dabbed her eyes.

"I know what you mean. Sometimes I have social Tourette's myself."

"Is that what they call it?"

"It's what I call it." I sipped some coffee.

"Have you told Dorothy about what you found, dear?"

"Not yet. I think she'll flip out, especially after finding Gert and having to arrange for the funeral. I almost wonder if I should wait..."

The oven timer buzzed.

"Excuse me, dear, while I get those." Mrs. Lewkowski put on a pair of oven mitts shaped like two-pound lobsters. The smell of cinnamon filled the kitchen. "Land O'Lakes for you, dear?"

"Yes, please." I was definitely in the mood for a little cholesterol.

"Dorothy and your mother were very close, Jennifer. Cut from the same cloth almost. Except that Dorothy's nicer. She's forever taking in those foster kids. You know, she couldn't have any of her own. A heartbreaker, but she made the best of it and started that day-care down in town. And Jimmy is a good man and they seem happy together, not like Gertrude and your father, what with his drinking and...oh, excuse me, dear. I shouldn't have said that. It was another of those social tumors you were talking about." She dropped a glob of butter the size of a golf ball on each cinnamon roll.

"You're not telling me anything I don't already know." Except about Dorothy's not having children, something I knew she'd always wanted.

"Well, you may know it dear, but you don't have to hear it too." She set the roll in front of me. It smelled like that candle at Healey's.

"Anyway, if you don't mind my saying so, Dorothy deserved better than she got from Gertrude."

Didn't we all. "What do you mean?"

"Well, like I said to Earl, why would any mother want her daughter to find her the way Dorothy found Gertrude? She had to know it would be Dorothy who'd find her. They always got together on Saturday morning." Mrs. Lewkowski took a dainty bite and blotted her lips.

"I was wondering the same thing," I said, thinking my cinnamon roll was starting to look more and more like a cow patty on a plate.

CHAPTER THIRTEEN

Dorothy lay in bed waiting for the alarm to go off. She had been awake since the sky first lightened. Four a.m. She hated being awake in the middle of the night. Too much time to think. Was ham salad the best choice for the finger sandwiches they'd have at the reception tomorrow? It was between that and tuna. But when the deli manager at Stop & Shop said they used chunk light instead of albacore, Dorothy knew she couldn't go down that road.

A bigger problem was what to wear to the wake and funeral. Should she wear a different outfit to the afternoon viewing hours and the evening hours? It went without saying that she couldn't wear the same black suit to everything. What would people think? Perhaps the cornflower blue linen pantsuit would be all right for the two p.m. to four p.m. session. Pants were appropriate for afternoon. She could always change before evening, which would probably be necessary. Linen wrinkled horribly. Even if she didn't sit down she would still end up looking like she'd slept in it.

As if she could sleep. Even with a Tylenol P.M. and the shot of Harvey's Bristol Cream Jimmy gave her, all she could see every time she closed her eyes was her mother dangling from that rafter in the barn. The same one her father used for hanging the butchered cows until Teddy Morgan came by with his refrigerated truck and took the carcass to his apple storage for aging. The forest green gabardine might be nice. Jimmy didn't really like her in it but if she explained her wrinkle problem he might see it her way.

She would have to wash and set her hair this morning because she wouldn't have time on Wednesday morning before the funeral. What had possessed her to schedule it for nine o'clock? Because Jimmy had suggested it, that was why. He didn't want to spend the whole day at a funeral and who could blame him. She knew he was hoping to tinker with that 1952 Chevy he'd been fixing up for the past couple years. He was hoping to have it finished for the Delicious Labor Day Parade. He wanted them to dress up like the Clampetts. Ever since they'd got that satellite dish, Jimmy watched nothing but re-runs of *The Beverly Hillbillies*. Jimmy wanted to be Jed and wanted Dorothy to be Elly May. After all these years of marriage she could read him like a book. This business with her mother was hard on him. He hadn't told her but Dorothy knew the whole thing embarrassed Jimmy.

Suddenly she remembered her gray polyester pantsuit. It was a little warm for July but she knew Herlick would keep Healey's as cold as a meat locker. She could wear a scarf to brighten things up a bit. The paisley would be nice with her pearl earrings and add-a-pearl bracelet. Dorothy smiled to herself. She would look like she just stepped out of the JC Penney catalogue.

Ruthie positively hated the drive from Albany to Delicious

to visit her pastor father. Oh sure, it was pretty enough, the hills rolling away so green and lush on either side of the van's windows as she drove Route 57 east from New Boston. Especially early in the morning. The fact was, she disliked going home, disliked even thinking of Delicious as her home. Her husband and sons were in Albany, which was home. But, she couldn't seem to grasp that inside where it really counted.

Why did Daddy want her to attend Mrs. Andersen's funeral? The pastor had called so late last night, after he'd helped Dorothy plan the funeral and had key lime pie for dessert in spite of his borderline blood sugar. He wouldn't explain himself either. Which infuriated her. Daddy always expected his requests to be obeyed no matter how inconvenient. And somehow she always did. Which made David unhappy. She hated feeling in the middle.

Ruthie popped a TheWay motivational tape in the cassette player to calm herself down. She enjoyed listening to TheWay success stories. This tape was one of her favorites. It was by Mary Pat Monaghan and her husband, Terry. They were real go-getters who had come from nothing and reached the highest level of the business in only two years. Ruthie's breathing slowed as Mary Pat's voice filled the Chrysler. Of all the things Ruthie had had to do in her life, at least she'd never had to cut meat, like Mary Pat once had, at a Von's Supermarket in Long Beach, California.

Listening to the tape helped to keep Ruthie's fear of meeting up with Jennifer Andersen to a manageable level. One of Daddy's reasons was clear. He had finally admitted on the phone last night that Jennifer was in town, he'd seen her at Dorothy's, and he wanted Ruthie to come so Jennifer would see how happy Ruthie was. He wanted Jennifer to see that Ruthie had a perfect Christian marriage blessed with two handsome, athletic boys and a husband who made a good living at his Chrysler dealerships. God had blessed Ruthie and it would do Jennifer Andersen good to see what was possible with the perfect love of the Lord.

It made Ruthie very uncomfortable to be Daddy's object for show-and-tell. But that's what she had always been to him. The good daughter who grieved in the right way when Mommy died, who'd got straight A's all through school and who'd made the right choice. It was a part she could play in her sleep.

If Gert weren't laid out at Healey's she would have killed me for daring to unlock the antique slant top desk that had been in the Spencer family since rocks roamed the earth. Gert kept the key in her sewing box. It was an ornate, filigreed thing that looked too frail and delicate to unlock anything material. It was stuck to a tomato pincushion with a straight pin.

After my morning coffee klatch with Mrs. Lewkowski, I was looking for information. More than the medical information I'd already found. Like why did she choose hanging? Especially when she knew Dorothy would be the one to find her. Dorothy was a major pain in the butt but even she didn't deserve to have that image burned into her retinas for the rest of her life. Why not a few sleeping pills washed down with vodka like any self-respecting suicide? Gert was making some kind of statement and there had to be a clue somewhere.

I wondered when it was going to occur to Dorothy that she had been set up. I'd be pissed off if I were her. Hell, I was pissed off and I wasn't her. My insides felt like kerosene-soaked rags stuck in a bucket.

The desk cubbyholes held stamps, envelopes, boxes of paper clips, pens and pencils, paid and unpaid bills. Nothing interesting. Though I wondered where all the medical insurance statements were for all the medical appointments Gert had to have had. Unless she didn't keep the paperwork. Which didn't seem likely. While I was growing up she was a stickler for keeping every receipt and canceled check for seven years, "Just in case." Or maybe she stopped going to the doctor once she got the bad news from the guy in Albany. That seemed more like Gert.

In the last cubby I found a diary, red leather with a strap and lock. I checked the sewing box for the key. Underneath the tape dispenser and the desk lamp. Nothing. I was getting impatient. Gert's bread knife might take care of the strap. The lock would probably give way with a little urging from the hammer in the toolbox under the kitchen sink.

Just as I was ready to swing the hammer, the phone rang.

"Hey, babe."

"Estelle." I imagined her sitting on the edge of a double bed, the covers messy and bunched at the foot in a hotel room decorated with inoffensive mauves and pale greens. Bleary watercolors bolted to the faux paneling. I imagined her wearing her ratty, lavender terry cloth bathrobe she took everywhere. No matter that its bulk required its own suitcase.

"God, it's good to hear your voice." I put down the hammer and took the phone out to the porch.

"Yours too. I think I miss you more knowing you're in Delicious and not home."

"Really? Why?"

"I know it's silly. When I'm away and I miss you I just think of you at home, making tea or sitting on the couch reading. You know, all that day-to-day stuff. But, I can't picture you in Delicious." Estelle sipped something. Probably tea. She always traveled fully equipped to make a proper pot of tea. Estelle did not subscribe to the throw-a-few-things-in-a-bag-and-let's-go school of travel.

"I am on Gert's porch about to beat a diary to death."

"Why do you have to kill a diary?"

I filled her in on what had happened since our last phone conversation.

"Wow. Well, hopefully you won't have to kill anything else before I get there."

I examined the pot of geraniums on the top step. Plucked off some dead leaves, stuck my finger in the dirt. The thing was dry as dust.

"It might be nice to burn the house down. But, I promise to wait for you."

"And don't kill too many diaries."

"I haven't found many. Just the one."

"There must be more. If I was a gambling woman, I'd bet this isn't your mother's first." Estelle took another sip. "I'm thinking of leaving early. I can pick up my CEUs after the morning session.

Why stay for conference chicken with bland cream sauce when I could come up there where all the excitement is? I'll be there around two o'clock."

"I can't wait to see you. I'll be at Healey's, pacing the front porch and gazing to the horizon, hoping to see a charcoal gray Nineteen Eighty-seven Nova. In mint condition."

"And I'll be the one in the charcoal gray Nineteen Eighty-seven Nova, in mint condition, looking for the cute dyke in a tastefully cut linen suit."

Tears stung my eyes. "I love you, Es."

"I love you, too, babe. See you later."

We hung up.

Estelle had to be right. There must be other diaries. People always keep their diaries. And journals. My journals were stored in a giant plastic tub in the basement. Gert's had to be somewhere. The attic? The cellar? Buried in the yard? Maybe I could interest Estelle in a treasure hunt. First, I had to crack the one waiting for me on the kitchen counter.

CHAPTER FOURTEEN

"I don't know what I was thinking, letting that girl go there without me." Estelle spoke to the muted Katie Couric as she folded her clothes and jammed them into her suitcase.

"Every time I talk to her on the phone she sounds less and less like the Jennifer I know."

Katie, on TV, looked alarmed.

Estelle remembered how Jennifer looked all those years ago when they met at the tea dance at the old Depot Restaurant. Those black jeans and red turtleneck. Her moth-eaten tweed blazer, which was way too big, with the sleeves pushed up. Very kissable lips. The men's wingtips. They were both wall-leaning on opposite sides of the room. They met at the cheese table, over smoked Gouda.

Going back home to the place you were raised is hell, Estelle thought, stomping into the bathroom to pack her toiletry bag.

She was moving quickly and knocked over the mouthwash. It spilled all over the counter and dripped onto the floor. She got a towel and wiped it up. It left a green stain. She had been in the middle of brushing her teeth when something told her to call Jennifer. She had learned long ago not to ignore those thoughts that appeared out of the blue. Real trouble resulted when she didn't listen. Her marriage had been a prime example of that.

Tom was a nice enough guy. He'd inherited a Kansas farm from his folks, who had retired and moved to Arizona. Tom was looking forward to growing corn and maybe soybeans for the rest of his natural life. He spent months wining and dining her. They went to pig roasts and square dances. Barbecues and turkey shoots. He toured her around his parents' farmhouse, the one they would live in. She looked out the dormer windows and saw nothing but flat. He promised to remodel the kitchen and bathroom as his wedding gift to her. His parents promised a new washer and dryer. Her parents said she was a fool not to marry a good-looking guy with acreage and ambition. Finally Estelle got worn down. Not because she was so enamored of him or the Maytags or the new laminate countertops and stainless steel sink, but because she was twenty-four and thought her life had to start sometime.

Tom wanted to have kids, and though they worked on it diligently it never happened. Estelle kept secret the relief she felt each and every month when she saw the red stain on the toilet paper. Tom's little wigglers, his term for them, had not taken root in her womb. Tom couldn't understand how a man could grow a bountiful corn crop but couldn't grow a baby. Each month, after Estelle stopped bleeding, Tom vowed to redouble his efforts. He bought an electronic thermometer and got in the habit of taking her temperature four times a day. He contemplated the merits of the missionary position over woman superior position. He considered having sex only during ovulation. That way his little wigglers would be all the more ready to jump the cervix and latch onto the uterus for the nine-month ride home. Her vagina was starting to feel like an overly plowed field.

Seven years passed in a blur of meatloaf Tuesdays, roast beef

Sundays and complicated ovulation calendars. Then, late one winter while thrusting his "ever-ready love-tool" in and out of Estelle's "baby canal," Estelle lying there, simultaneously patting his butt to urge him on and planning the menu for Easter dinner, he gave a strangled yelp. It wasn't the usual sound he made when he shot his "mother-load."

"Are you okay, honey?" Estelle asked.

"No," he said. "Something's wrong with my back. And I can't move my legs, either."

They both lay there waiting for something to happen. Finally she had to crawl out from under him, which wasn't easy because for some reason the ever-ready love-tool remained as rigid as a length of copper piping. Tom eventually ended up in hospital traction. Estelle spent a lot of time in town visiting him and a 24-hour diner a couple blocks from Saint Mary's Hospital. That's where she met Tina. She worked the three-too-eleven shift serving patty melts and chicken fried steak to truck drivers passing through town, and a great many nurses, physicians and visiting families who couldn't abide hospital cafeteria food anymore.

Estelle was never sure how it happened but one night she found herself in Tina's wide body pickup, kissing Tina's cigarette-stained mouth like a bee drinking at a honey suckle flower. When Tina snaked her hand into Estelle's jeans and stroked her "love-button," something Tom had never managed to locate, Estelle felt like fireworks had exploded out her ears.

So this is what I've been missing, Estelle had thought and may even have said aloud. She fell in love with Tina right then. But, for Tina, the women she took to her pickup were just a hobby: she wasn't planning on leaving her husband, Scott, or her two kids.

Estelle got the picture.

She divorced Tom. When her family found out why they told her she was, at the very least, courting eternal damnation and at the most making a big mistake separating herself from all that flat Kansas acreage. Estelle knew Tom would have no trouble finding a woman who could make meatloaf on Tuesdays and spit offspring out of her "baby-canal" like a combine spits corn.

She called her friend Cheryl who had gone to Smith College somewhere in Massachusetts and had stayed, after graduation, in a place called the Happy Valley. Cheryl offered her a spare room for as long as she needed.

And then she found Jennifer.

Estelle picked up the TV remote and snapped off Al Roker in mid-weather map. She couldn't wait for this morning's lecture to be over.

CHAPTER FIFTEEN

For all the hours I spent walking the woods and pastures growing up, I always felt as though I would never be able to escape. Someone, somewhere, would always know who I was and to whom I belonged. It made me angry. And it wasn't just Delicious. It was my entire family. I always felt like an alien and Gert always treated me like one.

I grew up wanting to drug them all, my beer guzzling, ineffectual, yet amiable father, my Bible-verse spouting, Jesus-is-mercy-but-I'll-make-your-life-a-living-hell   mother.   My perfectly dressed, always appropriately behaved younger sister. Then, while they slept in a drugged stupor, I would sprinkle gasoline throughout the Currier & Ives house and burn it down to the field-rock foundation.

Just kidding.

One day I was looking through the medicine cabinet for my father's razor. Gert had said, "You may not shave your legs, young lady. Only the whore of Babylon and Jezebels shave their legs. Besides you're only thirteen." I decided that there were a lot of whores and jezebels hanging around Delicious because almost every grownup woman I knew shaved her legs. Just not Gert.

My father's razor had shaving cream with little spiky hairs embedded in it dried around the edges. I turned the bottom of the handle and the razor opened like the double doors at the Delicious Public School. When I removed the razor I cut my finger and thumb. Just a little nick. It bled a lot. Like fingers do. I licked off the drops. Salty. And something behind it too. Like how metal smells when it's wet. I stood there watching the blood bead up and licking it off until the bleeding stopped. I made another cut in my finger. It didn't hurt. Just stung a little. More blood. It felt like something was escaping. Like I wanted to.

I couldn't help wishing I'd had a family I didn't want to kill. Like most people have. A fact I didn't realize until not that long ago. Estelle had been working late and my friend Vicki's girlfriend was working late so we decided to meet downtown at The Brewery for dinner. Vicki was having barbecued spareribs with rail-spike ale. We laughed about the name saying how the brewmaster must be some gay boy. I was having grilled mahi-mahi and iced tea. I'm not much for beer. My father and the fear of inheriting his two six-pack a day beer habit made me a tea drinker. We were perched on bar stools eating and talking when I casually mentioned all the fantasizing I did growing up about murdering my family.

"Familicide," I had said and laughed.

"What are you talking about?" Vicki said, putting aside the dessert menu and peering at me over her tortoiseshell reading glasses. She looked surprised.

"Oh, you know," I said, "burning down the house while they slept. Tampering with the brakes before a Sunday drive," (As if we ever went on those with a drunk for a driver and an over-bibled co-pilot.) "You know what I mean," I said. "No big deal."

"Actually, Jennifer, I don't know what you mean. My parents drove me nuts, but I never thought about killing them. My big fantasies involved moving out or short of that, making a room for myself in the basement." Vicki fluffed her short, spiky hair. A nervous habit.

I was dumbstruck. I had heard about Vicki's family. Her mother smoked, read romance novels and did crossword puzzles. Her father worked late at Mass Mutual Insurance Company. It came out, eventually, that her mother was agoraphobic and couldn't leave the house at all. She bribed the owner of Stan's Super Duper Shopper to bring over groceries when everyone was out so no one would know that she couldn't go out to her own mailbox. Her father was having an affair with the secretarial pool. Turned out he knew about Vicki's mother's problem and didn't do anything to help her because he liked boinking all those secretaries in the copy room and at motel rooms up and down Riverdale Road in West Springfield. The kind that can be rented by the hour.

After that dinner with Vicki I began to wonder about my own mental health. Even with all the therapy I'd had. Maybe I really was crazy. Or, perhaps, I'd just owned up to something that most everyone thought but didn't admit to. Like farting in the aisles at Whole Foods.

I started polling people I knew. My neighbors Steve and Justin had good relationships with their respective parents. There had been rough spots when they came out. But, like Steve said, no one wants their kids to be queer.

I asked Luanne, the massage therapist I shared an office with. Her father had died of colon cancer when she was nine. Luanne's mother worked a lot. When she was home she was tired and didn't bug Luanne about much except eating enough fruits and vegetables.

I asked the woman who cuts my hair. Queenie. She operates Queenie's Hair Palace, downtown. She's a lesbian who came of age during the butch-femme era of the sixties. She is one of the femmiest femmes anyone has ever seen. She looks like Mary Tyler Moore. Her parents were devout Catholics who came from Poland. They barely spoke English and drove Queenie, who was Helen then, nuts with their fears and worries about what would happen to her in America.

America, the land of opportunity and premarital sex. Opportunity was good. Premarital sex wasn't. The Holy Mother of Jesus was a virgin, after all. They loved Queenie and gave her piano lessons, dance classes and lots of clothes. Her mother cooked her favorite foods and taught her to polka in the kitchen. They didn't give her the opportunity to date because she'd have time for that later, after she'd made her mark on the world. Little did they know that Queenie had no interest in penises or the men they were attached to. That's when her girlfriend, Maxine, who does hair waxing and has arms the size of Virginia hams, waggled her eyebrows and said they should rename the salon The Virgin Queen's Hair Palace.

"What about your parents, Maxine?" I asked.

"My parents were assholes," she said.

Great, I thought to myself. Here was my ally. I waited to hear Maxine's grisly fantasy.

They did nothing but work, Max said. Seven days a week in that little mom-and-pop store they owned. Work. Work. Work. Save. Save. Save. It was always the future with them, always when they retired.

"Well," Maxine said, "they never got a future because my father died of a heart attack at fifty-nine and my mother had a stroke the next year. She wasted away in a nursing home for a couple years, which ate up all the money they'd saved. So, yeah, I want to kill 'em. The assholes." Maxine stalked into the hair salon's back room and slammed the door. I hoped she didn't have anymore hair-waxing appointments that day.

That was the end of polling my friends and acquaintances. It became very clear to me that my growing up had been terrible. More terrible than I understood while it was happening. Most families were not like mine. Most mothers didn't hate their daughters like Gert hated me. Maybe Gert's diary would tell me more than the mystery of her suicide. I just hoped I could stand it.

"Yoo hoo, Jenny."

Now what? I carried Gert's hammer to the screen door and looked out. A tall woman wearing Levi cutoffs and an oversized "10K Make Breast Cancer Run" T-shirt was crossing the lawn.

"Mavis?"

"Yep. How're you doing? Sorry to hear about your mom."

"Thanks." I held open the screen door. Mavis gave me a bone-crushing hug.

"It's good to see you, Mavis. Your mother told me this morning over cinnamon rolls that you were coming."

"I was hoping you'd be here. Gosh, what's it been? Twenty years?"

"Around that. Hard to believe isn't it?"

"You can say that again. Seems like just yesterday that we were riding our bikes, building that great fort in the apple orchard and eating bologna sandwiches." Mavis laughed. "I wouldn't eat that stuff now if you paid me..."

The late June sun is bright in the sky. It is Saturday. School vacation is only one week old. Mavis and I have just completed the fourth grade. Fifth grade seems like a long way off. We spent the morning constructing a tree fort in the apple orchard across the road down by the old well house. The orchard is old and looks more like arthritic hands sticking out of the ground than apple trees. My father says some day he's going to cut the trees down and use them for firewood. I figure it's one of his talking ideas rather than his doing ideas. Our tree house is safe, at least from my father. He's letting us use wood scraps for construction and all the nails we can hammer. He's got two rules, we can only use the hand saw and we have to put all the tools back, where they belong, when we're done.

"Here's your lunch, girls." Mrs. Lewkowski bustles out the kitchen door and across the lawn to the picnic table. The tray is stacked with bologna sandwiches on Dreikorn's white bread with the crusts removed. Dill pickles. Potato chips. Oreo cookies. A pitcher of lemonade with lots of ice.

I feel my stomach growl at the sight. "That looks great, Mrs. Lewkowski."

"Yeah, Mom. We're starving to death." Mavis grabs for a chip.

"I don't care if you are starving, you both better go wash your hands. And not in the house either, I just washed the kitchen floor. Go use the outdoor spigot. And use the Ivory soap I put there..."

Mavis and I rush off.

Mrs. Lewkowski is still talking when we get back to the table.

"Isn't it nice under this maple tree? I'm tempted to sit out here and have my lunch with you girls..."

Mavis and I look at each other with alarm. Who wants to eat lunch with your mother? Even if Mrs. Lewkowski is one of the nicest mothers around.

"...out of the oven. There is nothing worse than rubbery layer cake. No amount of frosting, even if it is chocolate, will cover that up. Anything else I can get you girls?"

"We're all set, Mom." Mavis crosses her eyes at me. It's the same expression she uses when she wants Stanley Shaw, the biggest cootie-carrier in school, to leave us alone.

"What did you say your mother was doing today, Jenny?" Mrs. Lewkowski nibbles on a chip.

"She's at some Baptist Bible Retreat with the ladies from her Bible study group."

"Are they down at the Federated Church?"

"No, they went somewhere else. All I know is she won't be home until late."

"Well, why don't you plan on having supper with us? Mavis's Aunt Ro is coming for dinner but that's no big deal. The more the merrier I always say."

"Okay. Thank you for inviting me."

"You're welcome, dear. You could learn a lot, Mavis, about manners from Jenny, here."

"Mom!" Mavis sticks her tongue out at me and crosses her eyes. I roll mine back at her.

"Just be sure to let your father know. Okay, Jenny?"

I nod. Mrs. Lewkowski makes her way back across the lawn. Mavis and I pounce on the bologna sandwiches.

"Why does your mother cut off the crusts?" I take a massive bite. The bread sticks to the roof of my mouth.

"I guess because I don't like them." Mavis opens her sandwich up and carefully lays down a layer of potato chips. If I ever said I didn't like bread crusts my mother would fill up a bowl with them and make me eat them at gunpoint.

"Ugh, gross, that's as bad as mayonnaise with bologna."

"I like the crunch. And mayo is great with bologna. How can you stand mustard? I don't even like it on hot dogs."

"Dorothy always puts mayo on her scrambled eggs. She likes her eggs really wet so the whole thing ends up looking like a pile of puke."

"That's as gross as the sardine sandwiches my father eats." Mavis takes a bite of her sandwich. It sounds like she is chewing rocks.

"The grossest thing is when Julie King makes those weird mashed potato sandwiches at school. Have you seen her do that?"

"Yeah. But, I have to leave the table when she starts eating it. She puts ketchup on it."

"A lot of ketchup." I take a long drink of lemonade. It is so cold it makes my teeth hurt. "It looks like her gums are bleeding or something."

"She is really gross. My mother always says I have to be nice to her. But, it's hard. She's in my catechism class."

"That's like Sunday school, right?"

"Yeah, and a total waste of time. And really boring. I hate it, but my mother makes me go. When I get confirmed in a couple years, I won't have to go anymore."

"Really? I'll probably have to go for the rest of my life." I unscrew the top of an Oreo and lick out the creme.

"Oreos are my favorite cookies." Mavis opens her cookie and puts a layer of potato chips on the crème. "I've never done this before. You try it, too."

"Okay." I break up a chip and make a little mosaic design, pushing the chips into the crème.

We click our cookies together and say in unison, "A toast." Just like they do on *General Hospital*, which we are addicted to. I have to watch it at Mavis's house because my mother thinks soap operas are a vehicle for Satan to invade your heart and turn you into a sin machine.

Just as we take our bites, a gigantic cornflower blue car with shiny chrome bumpers and shark fins slowly cruises down the street. The left turn signal suddenly comes to life and blinks at us like a lighthouse beacon.

Mavis jumps up and screams, "Aunt Ro is here." She drops her cookie and rushes the car, which stops in the driveway. The driver's door is yanked open and Mavis falls on the driver, hugging and kissing and squealing. I don't know what to do so I finish my Oreo-Wise potato chip sandwich. It is good. Maybe Mavis is right about potato chips. She says they go with everything.

I watch Mavis. She usually doesn't behave like this. Aunt Ro must be something special. Maybe she gives presents or can do magic or fancy yo-yo tricks.

Mrs. Lewkowski comes slamming through the screen door. "Earl, hurry up and get off the john. Ro is here."

Ro finally shakes off Mavis and gets out of the car. She is about five feet tall. Her hair is curly and cut shorter than I've ever seen on a woman. Her plaid sport shirt looks like the kind my father wears except it is wrinkle free with a crease on each sleeve. Her khaki trousers are also creased. Cuffs rolled twice. White socks with little red and black diamonds running up the side. Her loafers gleam in the sun. Nickels not pennies tucked into the little envelopes across the top of the shoe.

Ro hugs Mrs. Lewkowski and gives her a kiss on the cheek. Mavis grabs her hand and yanks her toward the picnic table.

"Come and meet my best friend, Jenny." Mavis tows her toward me.

I stand up and make sure I don't have any crumbs on my shirt.

"Jenny? This is my Aunt Rosemary Lewkowski. Aunt Ro? This is Jennifer Andersen. She lives across the street and is my best friend. We go to school together and are building a fort this summer."

Ro sticks her hand out and I know I should shake it. Most adults don't shake hands with kids. "Hi, Jenny. It's a pleasure to meet you."

"Hello, Miss Lewkowski." I shake.

"Goodness, girl, call me Ro. All my friends do." She sits on the bench and eyes the lemonade. "That looks good enough to drink."

"Mavis, run inside and get your aunt a glass." Mrs. Lewkowski loads up the tray with the empty dishes from our lunch. Mavis makes a mad dash for the door.

"Hey, Ro." Mr. Lewkowski yells from the kitchen door. "You want a Schlitz?"

"Yeah, Earl. Thanks."

"Mavis will bring it out. Do you want a sandwich or something?" Mrs. Lewkowski asks.

"No thanks, Ina. I'm skipping lunch today. I know you've made something delicious for dinner and I want to save room."

"Oh, it won't be anything special. Just some cheeseburgers on the grill and some of my potato salad."

"With that sour cream dressing?" Ro winks at Mrs. Lewkowski.

"Oh, you." She shoves Ro in the shoulder, picks up the tray and takes off toward the kitchen at full speed. "And chocolate cake." She calls over her shoulder.

Ro laughs and takes a packet of unfiltered Camels out of her shirt pocket. Shakes the pack. Dislodges one cigarette. Taps it against the back of her hand, puts it in her mouth and lights up. The lighter is the silver kind with a flip top. Butane smell fills the air. The drag she takes would kill most people. Exhales through her nostrils. Spits little bits of tobacco off her tongue.

I have never seen anything like it. A woman without a pocketbook, dressed in men's clothes, driving a huge car. Aunt Ro looks like a grown-up tomboy.

I knew what I wanted to be when I grew up.

"Jenny? Are you all right?" Mavis touched my shoulder.

"Yeah. I was just remembering your Aunt Ro."

"She was a hot ticket, wasn't she? I thought she was the coolest thing."

"Me, too."

"She died just a couple years ago."

"I'm sorry to hear that."

"She got Alzheimer's. Her 'lady-friend'..." Mavis made little quotation marks in the air, "...Aunt Ducky, took care of her to the end."

"Aunt Ducky?"

"Aunt Ro always called her Ducks. So, we called her Aunt Ducky. Her name was actually Doreen. Somehow, I never got out of the habit."

"You know, Mavis, she was the first lesbian I ever saw. Not that I knew then what it was all about."

"What about Miss McLezzie in the school cafeteria?"

"Okay, let me rephrase that. Ro was the first cool lesbian I ever saw. When she drove in your driveway that day, I knew if I could survive childhood, I might find a place for myself. Of course, surviving Gert was a tall order."

Suddenly there was a big elephant in the corner of the room.

"When my mother called to tell me about your mother's death—"

"You mean, suicide," I interrupted her.

"I'm sorry, Jenny. It's hard to think about suicide let alone talk about it. I just couldn't believe it. Does anyone know why?"

"There was no note. I found some medical records which seem to point to Gert having Lou Gehrig's disease."

"That's nasty."

"Yeah. So, I figure she checked out early. Hopefully, the answer will be in that diary over on the counter."

Neither of us can think of anything to say.

"So, my mother tells me you're coming over tonight for golumpkis."

"Yes. In between afternoon and evening visiting hours."

"Great. Well, I guess I'll see you then."

"Thanks for coming by, Mavis. We'll catch up more at

dinner." I walked her out to the porch. "Oh, and tell your mom that my partner Estelle might be with me. She's coming in later this afternoon. Hopefully, she won't mind an extra."

"Of course she won't. She's probably made enough golumpkis to feed all of us for a week. We'd love to meet her. See you later."

"Bye." I watched Mavis skip down the stairs. She waved as she crossed back to her mother's house. I waved back.

For probably the thousandth time in my life, I wished I had been born across the street.

CHAPTER SIXTEEN

Herlick Healey adjusted his dark maroon tie tight against his throat. He owned seven maroon ties. It wasn't his belief that funeral directors should wear black ties. Too gloomy. Maroon gave a nice contrast to his black suit or his charcoal gray suit or his navy blue suit. Yessiree. Maroon was versatile and since all his ties were identical, he wore a different one each day and then rotated it to the back of his tie caddie. Same with his black socks, boxers and T-shirts for that matter. A very workable system. Herlick glanced in the mirror and felt a swell of pride. He looked sober, respectful and, with the maroon against his stark white shirt, almost debonair. Like Cary Grant, if he had gone into the funeral business.

Herlick heard the eight cuckoos from the clock that had hung in the downstairs hallway for as long as he could remember. It had been a gift from his great grandfather to his grandmother. Herlick went downstairs and removed one of the weights. A perfect lead pine cone. He thought it unseemly for the cuckoo to cuckoo during a funeral. He put the weight in the pocket of his suit coat. No one seemed to notice that he was only lopsided on funeral days.

Herlick strolled into the Everlasting Life Room. Just a last-minute check on Mrs. Andersen to make sure she was ready to receive. He had left her to herself last night after one a.m. The neck issue had taken him much longer to deal with than he had expected. He had thought a scarf, high-collared dress and heavy-duty makeup would have taken care of things adequately. But, he still wasn't satisfied. He knew most people would have been. Herlick was a perfectionist. It was something that kept him up at night. Reviewing past embalmings and wondering if he could have done a better job.

Finally, Herlick decided to change the lightbulbs in the viewing room to a lower wattage. That seemed to help. However, this morning with the bright July sun highlighting everything like an operating room, he decided to draw the draperies. A little murkiness couldn't hurt. Crossing the room toward the windows he noticed them. Ants. Black and the size of wild rice kernels, but fat and with the requisite amount of legs. They marched with military precision from the cold air return grate across the carpeting to the display module the casket rested upon. Through some miracle of nature they managed to cling to the fabric covering and make their way to the rim of the coffin. Without hesitation they continued across Mrs. Andersen's deflated bosom and disappeared into the satin lining at her left hip.

"Uh-oh," Herlick said to no one in particular.

Auntie Potts thought there was no greater pleasure than the first Lucky Strike of the day. Though now she put off having it until at least nine o'clock. That was part of her cutting-back scheme. Auntie settled into her rocker at the gas station and sipped from her first cup of joe. For her money you just couldn't beat Maxwell House. She put her feet up on the windowsill. The rasp of her lighter sounded loud and she could hear the tobacco in her cigarette catch fire. She drew the smoke deep into her lungs and started to cough, hacking up a glob of phlegm the size of a meatball, which she spat, as good as any man, into the wastepaper basket. Another sip of Maxwell House soothed her throat.

She'd always got up early. A throwback from her days working in an industrial laundry feeding wet sheets into the mangler. She'd never forget when Mrs. Morganstern, who was gossiping about her neighbor's drinking, lost four of her fingers when she left her hand on the sheet just a second too long. Mrs. Morganstern had bled like the pigs her father used to butcher. Two hundred pounds of sheets had to be rewashed which put the floor manager in an even lousier mood than usual. He'd forced them to work through lunch.

The only good thing about that laundry was meeting Max. He was just back from Iwo Jima where he lost all the toes on his left foot and most of one eyebrow. Max limped and looked like he was about to ask a question all the time. He was hired as a mechanic, which was what he did in the army. He fixed the washers and dryers, steamers and toilets, and the ancient sewing machine the little Chinese woman used for mending.

It always seemed funny to Auntie that Max had survived World War II just to get crushed by a car in the repair bay of their gas station ten years after they were married. Life was funny, Auntie thought as she smoked her Lucky. Well, actually it wasn't but you had to act like it was or go completely crazy.

CHAPTER SEVENTEEN

I centered Gert's diary on the cutting board, the same cutting board that had insulated the countertop against the cleaving of chicken breasts and the slicing of bread loaves. The ball-peen hammer felt nice in my hand as I gave it a practice swing. I had used this hammer on my gold-seeking expeditions when I was a kid. It busted up rocks nicely. I had hoped I'd find enough gold to get my own apartment as far away from Delicious as possible. Mavis joined me in my plan. All she wanted was a new purple spider bike with a silver banana seat and tassels that hung from the handgrips. I swung the hammer at the lock. It made a dent. The lock held. The strap would not budge. I gave it another try. A deeper dent. No give. Shit.

Maybe the ball-peen was too delicate. Maybe I needed the twelve-pound hammer my father had used to repair roofing shingles. I went out to the shed and looked where the hammers had always been, hanging from the plywood unit my father constructed. It showed off his hammers in ascending order with the sledgehammer being the last in line. Why mess with the twelve-pounder? Why not skip right to the sledge? If it was capable of sinking a fencepost, surely it could crack the lock on Gert's diary. I didn't dare swing that one in the kitchen. Though it might've been nice to take out Gert's collection of commemorative teacups, I decided to wait until after I read the diary.

I brought the diary out to the backyard where the woodpile had always been. The enormous maple stump my father had towed out of the woodlot with the tractor and used to chop wood on was still there. Not that anyone could have moved it. It was badly scarred from its run-ins with the ax. I laid the diary in the exact center of the stump and gave a mighty heave of the sledgehammer. My trapezius and deltoids protested at being asked to do something everyday life in Northampton did not require. I could hear the whistle the hammer made as it sliced through the air. The sun glinted on the steel head. It connected. The diary went flying. My arms vibrated from the impact. I crossed my fingers and picked up the diary. The lock was mashed flat. I wiggled the strap. Nothing. If anything, the lock seemed fused together.

I needed Plan B.

Plan B involved the ruination of the strap. I thought about the serrated bread knife. It made short work of an English muffin but the strap would probably be too much for it. Then I thought of the hacksaw. Versatile, capable of cutting metal and, if required, wood.

The diary and I went back to the shed. I looked through my father's saw display. It seemed I had a choice. A short six-inch or the fourteen. Then I spied the bandsaw. That's what I needed. Electricity powering the blade. But, I could see from all the junk piled around it that it hadn't been used since my father died. I wondered if it still worked. Was the blade still firmly attached? Fused with rust? Had the electrical cord been chewed to sparking stage by some hungry mouse? Something else occurred to me.

Was I going too far?

It's a habit I have. Going too far. Sticking with something way beyond its usefulness. I stood in the half-lit shed, morning sunlight visible out the window. Even the July sun could not cut through the grimy panes. Evidently, Gert's Olympic cleaning marathons did not extend out here. Even she could probably feel the ghost of my father. I know I could.

"Ain't it too noisy to read out here, Jenny?" He turns off his jigsaw.

"Not really, Dad. Gert's on the warpath again so it's pretty noisy in there."

"You shouldn't call your mother Gert."

"Really? What should I call her?" I close *Valley of the Dolls*. I haven't been able to put it down since I checked it out of the library. I had read all the books in the children's room and graduated to the adult section. Not bad for twelve-and-a-half-year-old. Mrs. Dickson, the librarian who was older than dirt and twice as wrinkled, frowned at me when I presented her with it for check out.

"This book could be considered trash," she told me. "If you are going to read this, take out some Jane Austen or Emily Brontë to offset it."

"Yes, ma'am," I had said. I didn't want to upset Mrs. Dickson. She was my pipeline to other worlds. Reading was the next best thing to leaving Delicious.

Gert wasn't fond of all my trips to the library. She thought the only thing worth reading was the H.B. with concordance or *Good Housekeeping* and *Ladies Home Journal*. She asked me about *Valley of the Dolls* just this morning at breakfast. I told her it was a book about a young girl who went around the world collecting dolls for her sister who had gotten struck down with polio and couldn't get out much anymore because of the iron lung she found herself in.

"Well, Jenny, I know it's hard sometimes to know what to call her." Dad spreads out the checkers he's cut out and counts them.

That was for sure. I had heard him call her the "ball and chain," "bitch" and "ball-breaker" to name a few.

"But, she's your mother."

"I wish she wasn't."

Dad goes to the secondhand fridge he keeps loaded with beer. He pulls the tab off a can of the nectar of the gods, Budweiser, and tosses it into a bucket. It pings off the hundreds of others already in there.

"Your mother isn't a happy woman." He fishes his corncob pipe out of his shirt pocket and fills it with Half and Half tobacco which he keeps in a tin on his workbench. He uses the empty ones for nails, screws and bolts. He lights it with a wooden match. I watch him draw hard on the stem until it gets going.

"No, that's not quite right. Your mother has never been a happy woman. I don't suppose there's anything any of us can do about that. My advice is go about your business and stay out of her way."

"That's not so easy, Dad. It gets dark and I have to go inside eventually." Nights are the worst. Usually he isn't home to see how bad it can get. That's when the enemas happen.

The whole house has to be clean, clean, clean, Gert will scream. She yanks me out of bed and forces me down into the bathroom. Cleanliness is next to godliness. You are a dirty, dirty girl. I will wash Satan out of you, yet. Dorothy knows not to come out of her room. Gert will have the water bottle filled with hot soapy water. Sometimes it feels like I will explode from the tidal wave of lava inside me.

It happens a lot less than when I was younger and smaller. Now I fight more and both of us end up looking like we've been in a brawl.

My father opens a drawer of his workbench and takes out a paintbrush. "You want to paint the red ones, Jenny, and I'll paint the black?"

I looked at the flathead and Phillips screwdrivers. Wrenches.

Ratchets and planes. I swore I could still smell the incense of Half-and-Half tobacco and wood dust.

I prayed for the ability to let it go.

Let the diary go.

Let Delicious go.

Let me go.

Home.

CHAPTER EIGHTEEN

I was on my way to Healey's for afternoon visiting hours when I decided to take a side trip into the cemetery and jerked to a stop just inside the wrought iron gate, parking in the shade. There was a family reunion's worth of Andersens buried under the well-cared-for lawns. My father, a victim of himself in a way, had been the most recently interred and that was twenty-one years ago. I shook my head. That didn't seem possible. I did a quick calculation. Dorothy had been married just over a year and had recently moved into her dream house. I was still living at home, working and going to the community college. Ruthie came home every weekend, dividing her time between the Missing Link and me.

I smiled to myself, remembering how I still believed then that I might win the Ruthie tug of war. Another example of not being able to let go, I guess, thinking of Gert's mashed diary back on the kitchen counter. I looked toward the place I'd last seen what was left of my father.

"Your father is dead," Gert announces to Dorothy who sits in Dad's recliner copying a recipe out of a *Good Housekeeping* magazine. Neither of them looks at me.

"What?" Dorothy stops writing.

"He is not," I say from my spot on the couch. "He's fishing at Trout Sussman's bullhead pond."

"Shows what you know, Miss Smarty-Pants." Gert smirks, her top lip curled. An expression I know well. It usually means she knows something nobody else does.

"Healey's got him. Chief Warwick stopped by around suppertime to tell me. Trout found your father and called the chief who went out there. He was floating in the pond. For quite a few hours..."

I feel tonight's baked chicken and mashed potatoes rising in my throat.

"...figure he was drunk, hit his head and fell into the water. We shouldn't have expected anything else from him. He was a sinful, sinful man who laughed at God once too often." An odd smile crosses Gert's face. "The man drank like a fish and died with the fish. God had the last laugh."

It seems more like Gert is having the last laugh.

"Let that be a lesson to you, missy." Gert's eyes lock onto mine. "You are a bigger sinner than your father. He was putty in the hands of Satan because he could not put down the Devil's poison.

"The Lord God knows what you do and will strike you down just as he struck down your father. You will burn in the fires of Hell, just like your father. You will scream for all eternity as your flesh falls from your bones in burning clumps. You will know agony for all the days of time. You will..."

Dad had asked me, early this morning, if I'd wanted to go fishing with him. But I said no because I'd planned to spend the afternoon with Ruthie. "Are you sure, kiddo?" he had said. "The bullhead will be biting today. I'll make us some ham sandwiches."

"Maybe some other time, Dad," I said. "I'll help you clean the fish later, though."

Ruthie and I had gone out Mountain Road to our special place. We went there a lot. Eager to be alone. Sometimes we didn't make it to the rock before we were ripping off each other's clothes.

This afternoon, Ruthie had told me about her Friday night date with Missing Link.

I was so cross-eyed jealous of that guy and couldn't stand it. They'd gone to the drive-in.

"He wanted to kiss me." Ruthie rubbed her finger over my lips. We were lying side by side on our rock.

"Did you let him?"

"Just a little."

My stomach ground into itself.

"Did he kiss you like this?" I pressed my lips against hers. Hard. She opened her mouth under mine. Warmth flooded my crotch. I kissed her neck and bit her earlobe.

"Ow, don't bite."

"Did he do this?" I slid my hand under her shirt, pushed up her bra and ran my fingertips over her swollen nipple.

"Oh, God. No. He tried, but, I wouldn't let him under my shirt."

"How about this?" I snaked my hand inside her jeans and under the band of her underpants.

"Jenny, I wouldn't let him do that. It's all for you." She held my burrowing hand against her, hips rocking.

While my father was dying, I was dying for Ruthie.

"...Jameson coming over to pray with us and help plan the service. Go change your clothes, Jennifer. Dorothy, maybe you should call Jimmy and tell him what happened and that you might be late getting home. I'm going to go make coffee." Gert stalks into the kitchen.

"I can't believe it." Dorothy gets up and puts the magazine on the coffee table.

I don't seem to be able to move.

"Come on, Jenn. Do what she says. She's upset and you know what that means."

"Just a second." I rush into the bathroom and snatch the enema bag off the shower rod.

It wasn't even rational, Gert hadn't tried to give me one of her clean-out specials since I was twelve or thirteen. I don't know why she'd stopped. Probably it was the black eye I gave her. Maybe my father had figured out what Gert was up to and put an end to it. I was just so grateful they'd stopped I hadn't wanted to think about it more than I had to. But, now that he was dead, I wasn't going to take any chances. Gert was already on her holy roll. I didn't want to get in her way. Tonight I'd be sure to lock my bedroom door.

For good measure, I stuff the thing under my shirt. Later I would bury it in the pasture.

Dorothy is waiting for me. "Come on, Jenn. I'll help you find something to wear." She reaches under my shirt and takes the enema bag.

"I'll get rid of this," she says and leads me upstairs by the hand.

I stood in the cemetery, staring at a huge mound of dirt covered by inadequate strips of lime green plastic grass, the cemetery worker's version of the patterned scarf Herlick wanted last night. I walked to the edge of the grave and looked in. The smell of soil that had never felt the sun plucked at my nose. What a place to end up. Especially Gert. Much as she hated dirt, it seemed the cruelest of jokes to put her into a hole without her Electrolux, or at the very least, its cousin, the Dustbuster.

The family plot, to be owned by Andersens into perpetuity. Bought when my father died. Big enough for six, if no one wiggled. And no one would because Gert, number two in interment, would keep everyone in line. No boundary dodging. Leave the Moriartys and Pratts alone.

"Your peace and quiet is over, Dad," I said to his headstone. "Tomorrow Gert will be by."

A breeze rustled through the Moriartys' lilac bushes. She would be very offended by their gravestone. It was the size of a pyramid and depicted two women supporting a slumping Jesus. All in white marble with fuzzy moss growing on the north side. The Pratts were Methodists and so given to understatement that their grave marker was flat to the ground and could be mowed over.

"You probably don't know it yet, but Gert hanged herself in the barn. Nobody really knows why, and I can only guess. When Dorothy called me, I couldn't believe it. But, I saw Gert's body last night. She's definitely dead."

Another breeze rattled the leaves of Moriartys' lilac bush.

"That breeze feels good. As you used to say, Dad, it's hotter than the hammers of hell today."

Growing up, I heard a lot about those hammers. Gert talked about them so much it was almost as though she could hear them ringing in her ears. For the life of me I could never figure out why a god of punishment was so attractive to her. Well, it wasn't just her. The Fry-Your-Ass was full of people who seemed to be looking forward to being skewered by the devil's pitchfork.

"There's no more imaginative a hell than the one we make for each other on earth, right Dad?" I said.

A stronger breeze blew through.

"Or make for ourselves," I murmured. If misery loves company then my father had better strap in for the long ride to forever. I shivered. Why did I have to come from a family who buried and moldered? Why couldn't we incinerate and scatter?

CHAPTER NINETEEN

Heat vapors rose off Healey's parking lot, shimmering and undulating in the sun. Even with my detour to the family plot, I was still early. Dorothy wasn't here yet. Probably home putting the finishing touches on her face. I parked under a maple and left the windows rolled down.

Healey's was beautifully landscaped, which I hadn't noticed last night when I was on scarf delivery. Ancient-looking rhododendrons were made less forbidding by the profusion of black-eyed Susans and sweet williams that crowded around them. I watched the bees drift from blossom to blossom and a few butterflies fluttered along behind them. I longed to drag one of the wicker lawn chairs from the front porch, put it under the shade trees in the front yard and watch the flowerbed for the rest of the afternoon. I wouldn't even mind if those same bees swarmed and stung me countless times. Today's visiting hours were going to feel much worse.

A rush of air-conditioned air greeted me as I opened the front door. My nipples hardened instantly. Goose bumps popped out like chicken pox. It took a moment for my eyes to adjust to Healey's. Wall sconces threw a low-wattage murk on the flocked wallpaper. Uncomfortable looking chairs that were at least a hundred years old sat around in small groups waiting for the bereaved to make use of them. There was an arrangement of gladiolus and lilies on a round table in the center of the foyer. The air was so sweet my teeth ached and my sinuses closed up. Elevator music emanated from somewhere. I wondered what Bruce Springsteen would think of the musak version of "Born in the USA."

I preferred Herlick's embalming room to this.

"How are you...ah...this afternoon, Jennifer."

Speak of the devil.

"Just fine, Herlick. I know I'm a bit early."

"I believe Mrs. Andersen is available. She is receiving in the Everlasting Life room. That is on the left as you...ah...make your way down the hallway."

The Everlasting Life room? I looked at Herlick's face to see if he was making a joke. The half-light of the foyer made it hard to see my own feet let alone his expression.

"The ladies' lounge, should you require it at some point over the next few hours, is on the right just past the Meek Shall Inherit the Earth room." Herlick tightened the Windsor knot of his maroon tie.

"Thank you." I searched my mind for something else to say. The fatigue I felt from my night on the lawn chair and my marathon runs down memory lane made small talk impossible. I needn't have worried. Herlick seemed to vaporize. Maybe there was a secret panel in the wall behind me. The carpet muffled my progress toward the Everlasting Life room. Whatever happened to names like the serenity room or the peaceful surrender room? I wondered if there was a fast train to hell room.

I stood on the threshold of my mother's last room.

If possible, it was darker here than in the foyer. I could see a lump over in the corner, which I took to be Gert and her boxcar. Except, it seemed to be moving. I blinked and blinked again. No. Something was moving around over there.

"Gosh darn it." The lump spoke. I heard more fumbling and a clank of metal and finally a light went on. The lump was an organ and the movement was a woman wearing a black muumuu patterned with red hibiscus, struggling to get herself onto the organ bench. Herlick might have to get a step stool.

"Hello," I said.

The woman screamed.

I turned around, searching for whatever it was she was screaming at. As far as I could tell, we were alone. Except for you-know-who, who was laid out behind me.

"I didn't mean to startle you. I'm Jennifer Andersen and I'm here for the wake." I walked closer to the woman, offering my hand.

"I'm sorry for screaming. It's just, well, I'm a little jumpy. This is my first suicide." She whispered the word suicide. "And I'm hoping the Good Lord doesn't think I condone that sort of thing." She offered her hand, which was as cold and damp as a piece of haddock. "I'm Mrs. Earle. Who did you say you were again? I have a little trouble hearing."

"Jennifer Andersen. Pleased to meet you." I was just full of understatement lately.

"Andersen. Andersen. Where have I heard that name before? It sounds so familiar." She patted her carrot-colored bouffant.

I wondered if it was a wig and if she'd been involved in a horrible car accident and received a brain injury, which had turned her frontal lobe into succotash. I wondered if I would survive this afternoon. I wondered if she would survive, once it penetrated her consciousness that I was the lesbian daughter of the suicide. Imagine what the Good Lord thought of that.

"Andersen is the name of the suicide." I whispered the word. "And I'm her daughter. The one from Northampton."

Mrs. Earle's eyes widened as she fumbled for the cross hanging around her neck. It was encrusted with rhinestones. "Deliver me, Lord Jesus."

"Oh...ah...I see you two have met." Herlick materialized

behind me. "Mrs. Earle is going to be offering musical accompaniment to this afternoon's gathering."

"How nice."

"Yes. A medley of...ah...hymns and Johnny Cash tunes. Apparently your mother was quite a fan."

Mrs. Earle opened her briefcase and removed a three-inch stack of music. It appeared she had an extensive repertoire.

"Mr. Healey? Would you mind turning on a few more lights? Even with the lamp on the organ, I'm not sure I'll be able to see my sheet music."

"Oh...ah...is it dark in here?"

"Even I think it's dark, Herlick, and I'm usually happy lurking in the shadows," I said. Mrs. Earle clamped her lips together and gazed toward the ceiling.

"Well, of course. Just a moment." Herlick disappeared.

I wandered toward Gert. Even though I had seen her last night, I still wasn't prepared for the sight of her all gussied up in her high-necked dress with ruffles down the bodice and lace around her chin. The scarf was tied like a gift bow. Her makeup job seemed to have been done in primary colors and her hair was ratted out like a drag queen doing Dolly Parton. It seemed I had accidentally stepped into Madame Trousseau's wax mortuary. A couple of wall sconces sprang to life and one floor lamp. Now it was dim instead of dark.

"I don't...ah...think anyone can tell. Do you?" Herlick glanced around the floor and at the cold air return across the room. I wondered if he had dropped something.

"Tell what?"

"That she met death by her own hand."

"But, everyone knows Gert hanged herself, Herlick. Why are we pretending it didn't happen? Everyone will probably be disappointed they can't see evidence of it."

Herlick squinted at me. "You might have a point, Jennifer. It's been...ah...my experience that people are strange about death. Everyone pretends it isn't going to happen to him or her. They relish knowing everything about how it happened, so they can avoid making the same mistakes."

"Well, this mistake will be easy to avoid. Just stay out of the barn if you're carrying a rope with a hangman's knot." I watched him continue to scan the carpeting. "Did you lose something, Herlick?"

He glanced up at me. His eyes seemed unnaturally bright. "Yes...ah...but, that's all right. I won't miss it." He smiled or grimaced, depending on your viewpoint, and vanished.

The strains of "Amazing Grace" filled the Everlasting Life room. That's when I noticed the wall mural. I hadn't before because of Herlick's aversion to light. Suddenly, it was all I could see. It was a triptych. The first part showed Jesus, complete with crown of thorns, dragging a cross along the west wall past the emergency exit sign. In the middle section he was hanging on the cross with a Roman soldier's spear sticking in his ribs, and a thermostat protruding from his belly button. The final segment depicted Jesus outside his tomb, a beatific smile on his face, gazing upward toward his heavenly father who reclined on a cumulus cloud with an auxiliary light fixture nearly obscuring his flowing white curls.

Mrs. Earle swung smoothly into "I Walk the Line."

My foot started tapping in spite of myself.

CHAPTER TWENTY

Auntie Potts taped the Closed Early, Sorry for any Inconvenience sign to the front door of her gas station. She had just enough time to change and get over to the funeral home for two o'clock. It was probably overkill for her to attend both the wake and funeral, seeing how much she hated Gertrude Andersen. But, she had to look out for Jenny. Her daddy would want someone to watch over her and Auntie had decided she was going to be that someone.

Bob was a long time dead, but Auntie still felt a loyalty to her old friend. She couldn't do much about the way he had died. It had seemed suspicious to her at the time. Bob had been fishing and drinking for practically his whole life and often at the same time. It just didn't wash that he'd fallen and knocked himself out. But, she supposed, anything could happen once. And she had never figured out who would've wanted him dead. Gertrude hated him but surely not that much.

Best to let sleeping dogs lie. She could make sure Jenny got back to her real life without too much harm coming to her. Delicious could be a dangerous place. It looked good from the outside but underneath it was a regular nest of snakes.

Auntie had spent some time in the historical room at the library. She'd grown up in Equally Delicious, the next town to the west and the only reason she'd come to Delicious was that she and Max could get their gas station and the house across the street really cheap. They were both sick of working at the laundry, and when her Daddy died, she took the money from the sale of Tatro's Junkyard Emporium and put it toward the property in Delicious. Her mother moved in with her and Max. Auntie was worried about her marriage going to hell in a handbasket because her mother had always seemed a shadow who kowtowed to her husband and moped around, saying "I told you so" whenever anything went wrong. But her mother turned into a different woman with Daddy gone.

She stopped crocheting toilet paper and toaster covers, joined a square dancing group in Westfield and began playing bingo four evenings a week. Auntie was shocked at the change in her mother and felt ashamed that she'd always believed her father when he said her mother was a stick-in-the-mud who never wanted to go anywhere. Max and Auntie barely remembered what her mother looked like with all the gallivanting she was doing.

Auntie and her mother had had a standing date on Saturday morning. They went over to the library and got their week's worth of reading material. One day the door to the historical room was open so they had wandered through it. That's when Auntie found out more than she ever wanted to know about Delicious.

Delicious was incorporated the same year the Colonies thumbed their noses at the King of England. Boston was a thriving city at that time, but Western Massachusetts was a wilderness. People who were upset with all the temptations offered city dwellers and wanted a more pious existence were the ones who settled Delicious. As Delicious grew and more farmers and trappers and merchants arrived, so arrived some of the problems that prompted the original settlers to leave the big city. The most serious difficulty being the consumption of alcohol or the Devil's Spirits, as a clergyman from the early 1800s, a certain Samuel Tryon, had proclaimed. He urged the residents to form the League of Sobriety, which had many members in the leaders and churchgoers about town.

Delicious, eventually, dried up. No longer could you go into the tavern and have a beer or whiskey or wine with your meal. Folks who wanted a bit of the spirits had to make their own and keep quiet about it or end up in the town jail.

Auntie always suspected some of the private distillers sold their moonshine to the members of the league who gave lip service to the prohibition while drinking like fish at home. People were people and religious people were sometimes worse than those who weren't. Of course, that wasn't mentioned in the historical room. What was mentioned was that crosses were often seen burning on Gemorrah Mountain. The league was given the credit. Auntie didn't think they sounded much different from the Ku Klux Klan.

Eventually the tavern owner left town, along with quite a few others who were weary of being told what to do by a board of selectmen who, curiously enough, were deacons in Reverend Tryon's Federated Church. The people who left settled Equally Delicious. The tavern was turned into a Grange hall. It was still impossible to buy a six-pack in Delicious.

Auntie had to stop at the top of the front stairs to Healey's and catch her breath. Maybe she should cut back to fifteen cigarettes a day. That would make Doc Delerzon happy and keep her out of Healey's for a bit longer. Not that Auntie was particularly frightened of dying. She figured she'd see Max again and maybe her dog Lulu. Hopefully she wouldn't have to pump gas anymore. There'd be pizza three times a day, fountains of bubbling Pepsi and all the Lucky Strikes she could smoke and since she was dead, none of it would kill her.

"Well, don't you look nice." Dorothy's voice rang throughout the Everlasting Life room.

I jerked around and beheld my sister decked out in a gray pantsuit made of some shiny fabric. There was a red and hunter green paisley scarf knotted around her neck, very similar to the one Gert was wearing. Her pearl earrings glinted in the available light.

"Thank you, Dorothy. So do you." I smoothed my navy blue linen trousers.

Dorothy went to stand closer to the coffin. It occurred to me that she hadn't seen Gert since she'd found her in the barn.

"Oh, my God," Dorothy said under her breath.

I moved closer. "What? Is something wrong?" Besides the obvious, I thought to myself.

"She just looks so..." Dorothy's voice drifted off. She took a Kleenex out of her tan wicker pocketbook.

"Dead?" I muttered under my breath.

"How did she get that scarf?"

"Herlick called last night. He needed a little extra coverage, so I dropped it by."

"The Lord works in mysterious ways." Dorothy blew her nose.

"Oh?" I remembered that was one of Gert's favorite homilies when I was growing up. She dragged it out whenever I didn't like something.

"Mother and I got these scarves when we were down in Florida a few winters ago. Jimmy wanted to go down for some antique car rally at Daytona Beach; so, I said let's take Mother and have a little family vacation. We did a lot of shopping while Jimmy was looking at cars. We got these at a darling little shop owned by this black lady, who was a Christian. We could tell by all the Bible verses she had embroidered and hung all over her shop." Dorothy dabbed at her eyes, carefully avoiding her mascara.

The only mystery in that, as far as I could see, was why Dorothy and Jimmy would want to take Gert anywhere.

"This morning while I was setting my hair I prayed to Jesus. 'Jesus,' I said, 'I need a sign from you that Mother's all right.' The scarf is it. It's her way of saying, 'Don't worry, Dorothy.'" She blew her nose and put the moist wad back into her purse.

Mrs. Earle segued into a Sousa-like version of "Onward Christian Soldiers."

"Good afternoon, ah...Dorothy."

"Hello, Herlick. I must say you've done a wonderful job. Mother looks as though she was having a little nap."

"Yes, well, that is my hope." Herlick scanned the carpeting. "Will ah...James be joining us for the afternoon?"

"He's parking the car."

"Of course. I have put these chairs here for the three of you." Herlick gestured toward three upholstered chairs set up at Gert's feet. "Mrs. Andersen's visitors will want to pay their respects and then speak with her family...ah...you. Should you become fatigued, you can sit and rest yet still be part of the proceedings."

I was starting to feel more and more uncomfortable at the thought of the proceedings. My stomach was churning with a vengeance I remembered from my drinking days. The I-better-find-a-place-to-puke-or-I'll-ruin-my-shoes feeling.

Who would be coming?

A lot of people I knew growing up and would no longer recognize. There were probably some new people who had moved to town after I'd left. I knew Auntie would come and the Lewkowskis. Estelle should be arriving soon. And, of course, Pastor Jameson, whom I wanted to boost into Gert's coffin and slam the lid shut on.

Who was I kidding? The one possible attendee who made me feel sick was Ruthie. But why would she bother to come? She'd barely known Gert. She didn't live in Delicious. I was probably worrying for nothing.

My lungs feel like a bellows, sucking air in and out as I run up the stairs of the parking garage at Baystate Mall in Springfield.

I am late. Ruthie is expecting me on the rooftop parking deck at two o'clock. The parking garage is closed, filled with holiday shoppers on this day after Thanksgiving. I had to park at the bus station a few blocks away and run.

My watch says two fifteen.

I slam through the door and scan the parking lot. Cold wind pulls at my scarf.

"Over here." Ruthie waves at me from the far corner.

The car is warm as I slide into the front seat. I lean over to kiss her. She pulls back.

"Jenn, someone might see."

"Who? We're in Springfield. No one from Delicious is likely to be here." My voice sounds annoyed. I am annoyed. I hate starting out this way, when we haven't seen each other in a few weeks. Ruthie is away at nursing school in Albany. She doesn't get home very often. I go to Greenfield Community College and work almost full time at Merlin's Donuts. So, I haven't any time to get out to see her.

We sit and stare out the windshield. I watch fat gray clouds scuttle through the gray sky. November. The month depression is made of.

"How's school?" I ask.

"Hard. I hate organic chemistry."

Back to the windshield. Finally, I can't stand it anymore.

"Why did you want to meet here, Ruthie? I feel like we're in a spy movie or doing a drug deal."

"I have something to tell you, Jenn, and...well...you're not going to like it." Ruthie's voice fades away.

My stomach grips my spine.

"So, tell me."

"He wants to marry me." Her voice is small.

"Missing Link wants to marry you?"

"David."

Uh-oh. Now he is David.

"David wants to get married in June. During apple blossom time."

Of course, I think. What else? That's when I notice Ruthie fingering something in her palm.

"What's that, Ruthie?"

With her thumb she turns a ring around so the stone faces up. A diamond. Big as a wisdom tooth. Even though I know the answer, I ask the question.

"What did you say?"

"What could I say, Jenn? I've been dating him since I was sixteen. Everyone expects it. Him. My father." She looks at me. Tears glitter in her eyes.

"I suppose the truth never occurred to you, huh, Ruthie?"

"Herlick, you may have to set up another chair. My partner, Estelle, is coming this afternoon and she will need a place to sit."

Dorothy looked at me like she didn't know who I was.

"Oh, ah...of course." Herlick vanished.

"Jennifer, I'm not sure that's really appropriate." Dorothy patted her hair.

"What's not appropriate, babycakes?" Jimmy gallumped next to Dorothy and put his arm around her. It'd been a long time since I'd seen a leisure suit.

"Jennifer's partner? Is that what you called her?" Dorothy blinked her eyes as if she had a sty.

"Sometimes, though, I also use her name. Which, in case you can't remember, is Estelle," I say.

"Anyway, she's coming and Jennifer wants her to sit with us." Dorothy nodded toward Herlick who was moving a fourth upholstered chair into place. "Jennifer is being selfish, as usual, and just thinking of herself."

"Actually, I was thinking of Estelle. I know you'd be happy if she sat out in the parking lot, but, that's not going to happen."

"Just think for a minute, little sister-in-law. How's that going to look?" Jimmy jammed his hands into his pockets and began jiggling change.

"Just think for a minute, Goofball brother-in-law. Gert hanged herself. How's that look? I think my lesbian partner pales in comparison to the rope burns around Gert's neck. Don't you?"

Dorothy burst into tears, which sounded unnaturally loud because Mrs. Earle had stopped playing and was staring at us with her mouth hanging open.

"Can I see you for a minute, sister-in-law?" Jimmy jerked his head toward the door and walked out, legs as stiff as pool cues.

Dorothy fumbled in her purse for the Kleenex glob and settled into one of the upholstered chairs. Mrs. Earle began an adagio version of "Onward Christian Soldiers." Dorothy offered her a weak, little wave.

I met up with Jimmy in the foyer next to the flower arrangement.

"Something I can do for you, Jimmy?"

"Yes. I don't want you upsetting the little woman."

"You mean Dorothy?"

"Well, I sure don't mean your mother." Jimmy took a deep breath and closed his eyes.

I was pleased to have that effect on him.

"Dorothy is upset. This thing with your mother has taken a lot out of her. I think it would be nice if you could see your way clear to keep your girlfriend—"

"Estelle."

"Uh...Estelle out of here."

"I don't think so, Jimmy. But, I can promise that we won't kiss or have cunnilingus on the carpet."

Jimmy grabbed my upper arm and squeezed. "Listen, you little bitch, I don't care what the hell you do in that den of iniquity you live in but, you will not be doing it here. This is a Christian town." He dug his fingers into my deltoid.

"Take your hand off me, you homophobic asshole, or you'll be taking your balls home in a doggy bag." I flicked my finger at his knobby Adam's apple.

The front door swung open. Auntie Potts stood in the doorway.

"Am I early?"

"No," I said, yanking my arm free. "I'd say you're right on time."

CHAPTER TWENTY-ONE

Herlick nearly stumbled down the back stairs to his embalming room. He pulled back the starched cuff of his shirt and glanced at his Timex. Ten minutes before two o'clock. He estimated he could take the next five, perhaps seven minutes, for himself. He crossed the embalming room and entered his own office; the desk chair squealed as he settled into it. He slid open his file drawer. Under 'V', dangling in a hanging file, was a flask of Stolichnaya. The flask belonged to his father. When he'd retired to Boynton Beach, Florida, Harrison had gifted it to his son. It was silver and ornately engraved with a horned monster, tongue lolling out of its mouth. Harrison was a big man with a barrel chest so no one ever noticed the flask in the interior pocket of his suit jacket. Herlick knew there was no concealing it on his person, so he had taken to keeping it in his desk.

Herlick unscrewed the top and took a swig. He wished he had the time to fill a tumbler with ice and the potato juice (his father had called it that) He loved to listen to the ice crackle as the alcohol washed over it. The second swig made Herlick's stomach relax and he felt he could take a deep breath for the first time since the ants had showed up. He hoped they were happy with the bowl of sugar he left for them in the basement. The boric acid he'd mixed with it would kill them eventually.

Herlick had adopted his father's drinking method. It had stood him in good stead since he'd inherited the family business, and he saw no need to change. Harrison's method had three points. *Wait until noon.* Harrison felt drinking before the noon hour would only invite disaster and the loss of control. *Have no more than a shot an hour.* At that pace it was impossible to get drunk. A drunken mortician would be a poor mortician. *Always drink vodka.* It didn't smell so it didn't invite speculation from the public. It was clear, and therefore less stressful on the body than cloudier beverages.

Harrison had never steered him wrong. Herlick knew how fortunate he was to be able to say that. His father had also told him that death brings out the worst in people and it really wasn't fair to judge them too harshly while they were bereaved. Still, those crackpots upstairs deserved to be judged. The Andersens were all crazy. By the sounds of things, over the intercom monitoring system Herlick had installed a few years ago, James Fifield was arguing with his sister-in-law, Jennifer. Herlick permitted himself a chuckle. He wouldn't care to bet on the outcome. Jennifer Andersen was a bit of a legend around Delicious. Like werewolves or Jesse James. Her reputation was blown all out of proportion.

Herlick took another swig before he thought about it enough to stop himself. He capped the flask tightly and filed it. Yep, he'd never forget that wedding. Pastor Jameson's daughter Ruthie and that Bishop kid. Herlick had attended with his father and mother. Not that they were particularly friendly with the pastor. The Healeys were Catholic, but they did a lot of business at the church and Harrison had wanted to be respectful.

To this day he could still hear the God-awful scream that

erupted from the back of the church and then Jennifer Andersen ran down the aisle and tackled the pastor. The two falling into the baptismal font where they struggled for quite a few minutes before anyone from the congregation realized she was trying to drown him. The two deacons who pulled her off and yanked the pastor out of the water. By that time she was crying and swearing.

Deacon Phillips soon realized that Pastor Jameson wasn't breathing and threw him down on the floor to perform mouth-to-mouth resuscitation. The police chief, who was a wedding guest and dressed in his all-purpose navy blue suit, got up from his seat at the back of the church and hurried toward the pastor. As he passed the volunteer fire chief, he tapped him on the shoulder and sent him for the ambulance.

Before the police chief could get to him, Pastor Jameson vomited baptismal font water all over the carpet, took a great, shuddering breath and yelled out, 'I now pronounce you man and wife.' He then passed out.

The organist seemed unsure if she should play the recessional, starting and stopping several times before giving up entirely. The white aisle cloth got trampled under the feet of the volunteer ambulance crew who wheeled Pastor Jameson out to the waiting ambulance. A crying Ruthie and her pale-faced husband followed behind in a Ford Torino decorated with shaving cream and tin cans. Jennifer was taken into police custody until it became clear whether she would have to be charged with attempted murder along with drunk and disorderly.

After the pastor was taken out and Jennifer was removed to a holding cell, the wedding celebrants sat in the pews wondering what to do with themselves. The hum of conversation grew in the room. People speculated on what had caused Jennifer Andersen to go berserk. Was it jealousy? Maybe she'd wanted to marry what's-his-name Bishop. Was it drunkenness? After all, look what had happened to her poor father.

Finally Gert Andersen had stood up and said why didn't they go down to the fellowship hall and celebrate the pastor's daughter's marriage. There were finger sandwiches, coffee and wedding cake that somebody might as well eat. Everybody got up and followed Gert downstairs. Most felt sorry for her and were a little afraid of her as well. Gert Andersen had more bad luck than anybody should and it made folks uncomfortable.

Herlick figured he was one of the few people in the church that day who knew what made Jennifer behave as she had. He had the habit of walking around town late at night. Most folks would be asleep in their beds, houses dark but for a nightlight here and there. Herlick was enjoying a stroll in the moonlight one night when he noticed a pickup parked behind the groundskeeper's shed at the public school. He'd gone close enough to see Jennifer and Ruthie kissing and hugging in the cab of the truck. The moon was bright enough to see their closed eyes and swollen lips.

Herlick had never said anything to anyone.

The front door buzzer buzzed. Herlick stood up, sprayed breath mint into his mouth and adjusted his tie.

Mrs. Andersen's guests were here.

CHAPTER TWENTY-TWO

"Why won't you work?" Ruthie hissed under her breath as she ran the nozzle of her pump hair spray under hot water. "If there was ever a time I needed to look perfectly coifed it's today."

She pressed the dispenser up and down. The sweet scent of TheWay's Hurricane Hold Hairspray filled the bathroom.

"Thank God," she murmured as she sprayed the air around her head and swirled her head through the mist. At the last TheWay weekend, Ginger Thompson, a Cadillac, had shown Ruthie and the other TheWay wives this technique.

TheWay business was wonderful. She loved how they had named the different levels of business success for luxury automobiles. David and Ruthie had started out with their Learner's Permits and had worked up to Cruise Control pretty quickly. Ruthie quivered with anticipation at reaching the upper echelon, which was Rolls Royce. That meant they had to drive the Buick, Cadillac and Lamborgini lap of TheWay's speedway of success before they reached the glittering, high gloss shine of the Rolls Royce level.

Then there was the shopping. All she had to do was order from TheWay's Can't Live Without It catalogue, everything from corn chips to laundry soap to underwear. Ruthie loved shopping and now David never complained about what she bought because it increased their personal "trunk space." She still went to the mall occasionally because there was nothing like the smell of sizing in the clothes, the clatter of the plastic hangers and the peppy music from the overhead speakers, the rush of acquisition. It felt almost sexual when she watched the saleswoman wrap her purchases in tissue paper and place them carefully in heavy paper shopping bags with the cloth handles. It almost felt like Ruthie was being touched and not her purchases.

She took a hair pick out of her toiletry bag and picked the hair at the crown of her head. Aerosol spray cans were preferable to pumps. Too much hairspray weighed down her fine hair. She would have to write a letter to TheWay's product development department with her concern. People said aerosol sprays were bad for the environment but she couldn't really see how something so small could be to blame. All that global warming propaganda put out by the environmental groups. Tree-huggers David called them.

There, she thought as she held a hand mirror behind her, allowing her an unobstructed view of the back of her head. My hair is perfect.

Last weekend, while David and the other husbands were meeting to discuss strategies for increasing "trunk space" and "mileage," the ladies were meeting to discuss the new line of cosmetics and to pick up a few helpful hints for makeup application in order to achieve a more natural appearance. It had been a truly awesome weekend. She and David had driven from Rochester to their home in Albany listening to a cassette of Rolls Royces, Merwin and Polly Lou Simpson, telling their story in the business. It gave her goose bumps to hear how Merwin had worked his way up from delivering propane and Polly from sorting eggs at an egg farm.

Ruthie and David practiced their Rolls Royce story together a lot.

David's story was an inspiration to her. He was determined to be as successful in TheWay business as he was with his Chrysler dealerships. He had started selling TheWay's Way to Clean household cleaning supplies in college and had worked at it steadily since then. When they had gotten married and started working together things had gone faster. They slowed up a bit when the twins were born. Or rather, she did. Luke and John were both fussy babies. Ruthie just didn't have the energy, but David kept right on building their business like the "pit boss" he was.

Where was her new tube of Simply Sand Dune? It was part of the summer line of cosmetics TheWay was promoting.

"I could've sworn I put it in here in the toiletry bag when I packed."

They had just gotten home from their weekend in Rochester when Daddy called wanting her to come to the funeral. David had pouted about that. He hated Delicious. It was too small he said. Ruthie knew he really meant that everyone remembered everything. Even after over twenty years of marriage David shivered whenever he remembered their wedding and practically had a stroke when he heard the name Andersen. That's why she had told him nothing about why she was really going. If he'd known Jennifer was in town he'd have forbidden her to go.

And she had no choice. So, she told David to stay home and make sure the boys got to their lacrosse practice and music lessons. It was only a doctor's appointment Daddy wanted her to accompany him on. Nothing to worry about. He was so grateful that before bed he had painted her toenails with TheWay's Mauve Machinations. Then they played his favorite game of Rolls Royce level TheWay business tycoon punishes a hitchhiker for low gas mileage; which involved David blindfolded and tied to their four-poster bed, and Ruthie wearing three-inch heels and a corset she had been unable to buy from their TheWay Can't Live Without It catalogue.

"There you are." Ruthie found the lipstick behind her packet of Fresh Face Makeup Remover pads.

When she pulled into Daddy's driveway this morning he hobbled out to the minivan to bring in her luggage. He wasn't much help because his hip replacement surgery had left him unstable on the right side. He was struggling with her garment bag when he told her that when he'd seen Jennifer she'd seemed very repressed and angry. Just like she'd been growing up. How she'd barely spoken two words to him and avoided prayer by excusing herself early to go do "heaven knows what people like that do."

Ruthie's hands started to shake. She'd never known Jennifer to be repressed, just the opposite in fact. Angry was certainly possible, considering how she felt about Daddy, but Jennifer must have restrained herself if she barely spoke to him. Then Daddy mentioned Jennifer's hair being as short as a man's and her clothes being entirely inappropriate for mourning. She'd dropped her keys twice before managing to lock the car and twice more on her way into the parsonage.

Ruthie blotted her lipstick and took her mauve silk blouse off the hanger. Daddy probably wouldn't approve of mauve for a wake but it really brightened up her taupe skirt and blazer. Just as she was buttoning the blouse she realized she had forgotten to put on her pantyhose. She was definitely discombobulated. All because of Jennifer. Not that she would admit it to anyone. It was important to act like that little episode in her life had never happened. She told herself all the time that Jennifer had taken advantage of her because of her mother's passing.

Ruthie had been sad after her mother's death. Daddy was busy with the congregation and had no time for her. When she tried to talk with him about how lonely she was and how much she missed Mommy he had told her to pray for deliverance from her selfishness. Didn't she know that her mother had been released from the pain and suffering of her ovarian cancer and was certainly in the kingdom of heaven? Didn't she know how important it was to show the congregation a brave face so they would know the Grace of the Holy Spirit and not turn away from the Lamb of God in their darkest hour? Didn't she know that as the minister's daughter she had a sacred obligation to fortify herself with the Word of God and be grateful that the Lord thought enough of her to test her faith with grief and loneliness? Would she rather locusts and boils as Job had been tested with?

Jennifer had made her laugh. Ruthie loved how blasphemous she was. Loved how she said the most shocking things and then laughed like she didn't care who heard her. But, they weren't really friends until the seventh grade when her friend Mavis left Delicious public school to go to the Catholic school in Equally Delicious. Daddy had always forbade her to associate with Catholic kids more than was absolutely necessary.

She and Jennifer had started hanging around together between classes, at recess and during lunch. Ruthie convinced her to join the Youth for Christ Prayer Group at the Federated church that Mrs. Andersen had been trying to get Jennifer to join for years. Not that she behaved like a willing participant, arguing with Mr. Douglas, the group leader, at every possible opportunity.

Ruthie opened a package of TheWay Run-Proof sheer pantyhose with the newly designed ventilated crotch panel and sat on the edge of the tub to put them on.

The summer before their freshmen year in high school Jennifer had upped the ante when she told Ruthie that she loved her 'like girls usually loved boys.' Ruthie had been stunned. She hadn't known that was even possible. As time passed and Ruthie got used to the idea she grew to like the feeling that she was getting away with something. It was exciting and dangerous. Up until then her life was anything but exciting and had never been dangerous. They had almost gotten caught so many times it wasn't even funny. Like that time behind the grammar school.

Ruthie could still see the glow-in-the-dark clock hands of the old Timex Jennifer's father looped over the volume knob of the radio in his truck. It was after ten p.m. and dark, or should have been except the moon was full and bright as a spotlight. Jennifer had borrowed her father's truck and they'd gone to a movie and were on their way home. They'd been holding hands under their coats during the movie and they kissed a few times in the parking lot but there were too many people around and Ruthie couldn't relax.

Jennifer pulled into the school parking lot behind a shed and started kissing her, biting her ear lobes and neck. Ruthie had tried to tell her to stop, that someone might see. After a few minutes Ruthie didn't care who saw. Nothing could stop Jennifer from pushing up Ruthie's shirt, unbuckling her bra and kissing her way down Ruthie's belly. Ruthie still blushed all these years later when she remembered unbuttoning her own Levi cords and pushing them down and off. Jennifer licked and sucked her clitoris until Ruthie's orgasm exploded. Her legs were spread open, one leg across the back of the seat and one against the dashboard. She remembered screaming and pulling Jennifer's mouth against her vagina, never wanting it to end.

Sex with Jennifer was addictive. She made Ruthie feel things that she'd never felt before or since. Made her lose control of herself. Ruthie had done things that caused her to blush when she thought about them after all these years. Which wasn't very often, thank God, because she was so busy with David and the boys and the house and yard and the TheWay business that she didn't have time to think.

Ruthie remembered when Daddy had decided she should start dating David. Initially, Ruthie felt panic at never seeing Jennifer again. But, Daddy was insistent. David's family had just moved to town and joined the church. She learned later that their fathers arranged their first date. David took her to a basketball game at the high school and then out for hot fudge sundaes at Friendly's. He was nice but he talked a lot about himself. Ruthie didn't understand the things that made him laugh. Ruthie was relieved that David seemed satisfied with a kiss on the cheek.

Jennifer insisted on still seeing her. Ruthie enjoyed having a double life. It was thrilling to have a secret nobody would suspect her of having.

Soon Ruthie was seeing David every Saturday night. They went to dances and out for cheeseburgers. They went to the movies and out for ice cream. David started expecting more than a kiss on the cheek. Ruthie stayed in control with him. She left her body and observed David kissing her. Observed him rubbing her breasts and trying to unbutton her blouse. Observed him reaching under her skirt and pulling her underwear aside to plunge his finger into her vagina. Observed him opening his fly and begging her to rub it until he filled her hand with semen.

She was never a part of it. It was safe. It was normal. Something she could tell other people about if she wanted to.

Ruthie spent Friday nights with Jennifer.

It was perfect until graduation.

"Did Jennifer really think it would go on forever?" Ruthie said to herself as she gyrated in front of the mirror on the back of the bathroom door, alternately pulling on the right and left leg trying to get its crotch to line up with hers.

CHAPTER TWENTY-THREE

I hate receiving lines. The entire population of Delicious stood in line to gawk at Gert, shake Jimmy's hand, kiss Dorothy's cheek and grimace at me. Just who is doing the receiving? I didn't want anything from them. Most of them seemed afraid that what I had was contagious. The "so sorry to hear about your mother" and "does anyone know why" and "God-fearing woman" washed over me like boiling water. I don't know how I managed not to bite some of them. And it was only a little after two o'clock.

I excused myself and went in search of a quiet place to be alone. But, where? A funeral home is not the place to open unlabeled doors. I settled on the Ladies' Lounge. The cloying smell of airfreshener slapped me in the face as I pushed open the door. A nightmare mingling of PlugIn Citrus Grove and the tooth-aching sweetness of a large, vaginal lily assaulted my nose. The room I had entered was like a living room in a hotel suite. Except the hotel would have hired a decorator who would surely not have chosen pale pink flocked wallpaper and maroon carpeting. The end tables were glossy woodgrain something or other that could be sprayed with Windex and wiped with paper towel. The furniture was overstuffed and looked comfortable. I tried the loveseat. It was as unforgiving as a park bench. Several lamps were dimly lit. Six decorative boxes of Kleenex were placed about the room as though they were valuable Hummels.

I pushed through the next door and was faced with three stalls. Pink. Pink toilets. Pink floor tile. Two pink pedestal sinks. I crossed the room to the left stall, not that I had to pee. Even though it had been hours. Since my arrival in Delicious my bodily functions had almost shut down. The small amount of cinnamon roll I'd had for breakfast squatted in my stomach like a lawn ornament. The stall would offer some privacy, a scarce commodity in Delicious.

It felt weird to sit on the toilet seat with my pants on. I leaned the side of my head against the tile wall. It was cool against my forehead. Organ music hummed into my skull. "What a Friend We Have in Jesus." The uninvited words vibrated through my brain. Over and over. Finally, Mrs. Earle segued into "A Boy Named Sue."

I must have been nearly asleep when the door swung open. I sat up. Almost before I realized that I was doing it, I picked up my feet and held them out in front of me. Hoping whoever it was wouldn't choose my stall.

The door opener's high heels tappy-tapped to the sink, hesitated and turned to the stall two away from mine. I heard the rustle of clothing. Whisper of skirt being raised, pantyhose down. Exhale of breath. The delicate, almost musical tinkle of urine hitting toilet bowl water. The unfurling of toilet paper. A barely audible dabbing. The rush of flushing water. Outfit reassembling. Tappy-tapped back to the sink. Slurp of liquid soap, faucets turned on and then adjusted for temperature and splash. The ratchet of dispensing paper towel.

A purse snapped open. Something unzipped. I recognized the rattle of plastic cosmetic containers as the correct implement was searched for and searched for until a "darn it" was exclaimed under Tappy-tap's breath. Purse snapped shut.

Just when I thought I could lower my feet, the ladies' room door pushed open and someone humming "Folsom Prison Blues" entered.

There was a pause as Tappy-tap and the hummer sized each other up.

"Ruthie Jameson is that you?"

I recognized Auntie Potts' voice. Tappy-tap was Ruthie? I squinted through the crack between the stall door and wall.

"Oh, I know it isn't Jameson anymore. I just can't think of your married name."

At that moment I almost shouted "Missing Link." It would've been funny and I'm sure she, of all people, would've expected it from me. But by the looks of her, a limited view to be sure, she looked like she'd been possessed by a Stepford Wife.

"Bishop," Ruthie said.

"That's right. I don't know if you remember me. I'm Auntie Potts."

"Of course, I remember. How are you doing?"

"Just fine for an old lady." There was polite laughter on Ruthie's part, gruff hack on Auntie's.

"When did you get into town?"

"This morning. Daddy asked me to come."

Antichrist asked her to come?

"Really? Were you close with Gertrude?" Auntie seemed as surprised as I was.

"Well, not really. Of course, I went to school with Jennifer..."

Went to school with Jennifer? Ruthie's understatement didn't surprise me in the least.

"I remember you two being great pals." Auntie cleared her throat. "Always saw you together riding your bikes or in Jenny's Daddy's truck."

"Well, yes. But we grew apart when I went off to nursing school in Albany. You know how it is."

"Yep. I sure do know how it can be. Kind of sad when such good friends lose touch."

"Have you seen Jennifer around?"

I squinted through the crack. She was turned away from me. Auntie's expression was perplexed. Like she wondered how much to say.

"Yep. She stopped by to see me yesterday when she got into town. She was at the wake earlier. Heard she was expecting her friend to join her. Maybe she's waiting for her outside somewhere."

"Oh? Her friend is coming?" Ruthie stressed the word friend. Highlighted it. Bold relief. Italics.

"That's what she said. Expected her about two o'clock."

I glanced at my watch. It was almost three. Where was Estelle? Lost in Delicious? An involuntary shudder ran up my spine.

"Maybe I'll go look for her. I'd like to offer my condolences. I know she had a difficult relationship with her mother. Daddy was saying this morning that conflicted relationships could lead to unresolved feelings of grief and desperation. He was very concerned that Jennifer might do something regrettable."

Ruthie was still a ventriloquist's dummy for the Antichrist.

"Well, I don't think the pastor needs to worry about that. She's a grown woman. She can take care of herself just fine."

"I'm sure you're correct. It was nice to see you and have a moment to chat." Ruthie tappy-tapped to the door and swung it open.

"Same here. I'll see you around." Auntie waggled her fingers at Ruthie.

The door was barely closed before I heard Auntie mutter, "Good riddance." She proceeded to use the stall Ruthie recently vacated.

Antichrist was concerned I would have unresolved grief. How touching. He was probably afraid I'd try to kill him again. For old times' sake.

I waited until I heard Auntie leave before I stood up and smoothed my trousers. Time to go look for Estelle's mint condition Chevy Nova and the woman who drove it.

CHAPTER TWENTY-FOUR

I got as far as Healey's front porch before I realized I didn't know where to look for Estelle. She was probably running late. I crossed the front lawn and stopped at the curb. There was nothing coming from the direction I expected her except the mirage of water made by the sun against asphalt. The cicadas ground their tune into the thick air.

A thunderstorm would be nice, a monumental upheaval in barometric pressure. How I longed for a looming black sky and gusting winds turning the leaves inside out. My wish to smell rain made my nostrils quiver in some evolutionary carryover. I scanned the sky for gathering clouds.

I hadn't felt this out of sorts in years. Since my twenties when I was a nerve ending crackling with plenty of nervous energy and nothing to expend the energy on.

I run an upright vacuum with a headlight back and forth across the miles of carpeting in the lobby of the Worcester Marriott and Conference Center. This gorgeous woman emerges from the revolving door. Blonde hair. Ray-bans. Expensive leather jacket. Louis Vuitton luggage piled on a luggage trolley and pushed by Manuel Ruiz, my bellhop buddy and roommate. He'd been thrown out of his house when he was sixteen after his father caught him kissing his lab partner, Ramon. Manuel is a queen but he butches it up for his shift at the hotel. He waggles his eyebrows at me as he follows Ms. Expensive Leather jacket to the front desk.

While she checks in, I edge toward him, vacuuming in his direction. He whispers that she is driving a black Camaro with leather seats and a pink triangle in the back window.

"Either she's a member of the family or she borrowed somebody's car."

I beg Manuel to let me take her luggage up. Mostly I need a diversion since the roar of the Hoover gives me too much time to think. The joint we'd shared over morning coffee had long since worn off and it was hours before I got off work. Since he needed a cigarette break he didn't mind.

Ms. Expensive Leather Jacket moves so quickly toward the bank of elevators that I can almost see the air currents left behind in her wake. I catch up with her as the doors whisper open. The Marriott's elevators are big enough for ballroom dancing so there is plenty of room for the two of us and her mountain of luggage. We are whisked up to the fourteenth floor.

"The fourteenth floor is really the thirteenth floor," Ms. Expensive Leather Jacket murmurs in my ear as she struggles to put the key in the lock of door number 1407.

"That's right. I guess you're not superstitious," I say, marveling at the size of her pupils. The irises are so marginalized it is impossible to tell the color of her eyes.

"Actually, I am. But, I like pushing it. I have a black cat. Every New Year's Day I break a mirror. I walk under ladders. I drink and drive."

I nod. She shares almost the same worldview as I do. I wonder what drug she'd taken to turn her eyes all pupil. Finally the door swings open and I follow her into her suite.

"Would you like your luggage in the bedroom?" I say, already moving in that direction because nobody ever wants luggage in the living room.

"Sure. Thanks." Ms. Expensive Leather Jacket follows me into the bedroom and throws herself on the king-sized bed. She watches me unload each piece of Louis Vuitton and pile it neatly next to the armoire that conceals a television.

"Can I get you anything else?" I say, wondering why I had asked Manuel to let me bring her stuff up. She was way out of my league and besides that, I couldn't think of any way to move this from lackey to a drink later at The Girl's Club.

"Why did you want to bring up my things? That cute guy was supposed to do it. But you did instead." She flips off her loafers, which hit the carpeting with a muffled thud.

What the hell, I wondered. *Should I tell the truth?* I lived on what the hell, so why should now be any different.

"Manuel saw the pink triangle on your car window and since I have one on my truck, he thought that maybe we belonged to the same sorority."

She looked me up and down, taking in my navy blue polyester uniform pants, bagged at the ass and knees, my wrinkled white blouse and my name tag which hung above my left boob.

I watch as thoughts cross Ms. Expensive Leather Jacket's face and it doesn't look like "what a cute dyke" is one of them.

That's when I realize that I have to make some changes. Stop planning my life around the next joint. The next beer. The next no-name fuck. Get away from the city and back to the country where it is quiet enough to figure out what I want to do with my life.

Ms. Expensive Leather Jacket rolls off the bed and walks over to me. "It's my sister's car." She gives me a five-dollar tip.

I give the five to Manuel and my two-week notice to the housekeeping manager that afternoon.

A tooting horn snapped me back to Healey's front lawn. Estelle pulled up beside me and rolled down the passenger window. "Hey, babe. You're a sight for sore eyes."

I burst into tears.

CHAPTER TWENTY-FIVE

It wasn't about the splotch of purple on Estelle's white blouse. Though that was what made me cry. Not polite tears either or the catch-in-the-throat variety. More like an animal caught in a trap. Eyes and nose swollen and running. Saliva pooling in the mouth and overflowing the chin. Bend over from the waist; sink down to the ground, unsupportable kind of crying. All because of that splotch. The color of raspberry ice cream. Inkspot. Punctuation to some snack.

Estelle opened her car door and rushed around to me, a pathetic ashamed-to-be-me, version of me. She squatted down so she could put her hands on my head and kiss my eyes, swollen as plums. She pulled me to her. The smell of her neck made me cry harder. Her hands rubbing my back made me cry harder. Murmured nonsense words made me cry harder.

I knew I could never let go. I was so relieved she'd arrived even though it meant she'd see the crazy, nowhere place I came from. A town full of religious zealots, alcoholics and the idiosyncratic. I knew I would have to tell her everything. Even those things I barely remembered.

Her hair smelled like the shampoo we used at home. Our bathroom flashed before my eyes. The big bathtub that Estelle often filled with bubble bath and sat in looking like dessert.

If Gert could die anyone could.

Even Estelle.

How was it possible to know that and not die myself?

Somehow she got me up and into her Nova. The mint condition Nova she was so proud of you'd think she'd put it together herself on some Detroit assembly line. Estelle gave me a mountain of rough Dunkin' Donut napkins. And waited.

I blotched and blew and wiped.

Still she waited.

When I could breathe without the air getting caught in my throat she turned the key in the ignition. The engine caught. Pistons moved smoothly in the Nova's four-cylinder engine.

I watched her depress the clutch. Saw the band of muscle rise in her calf. Whisper of gearshift into first. Synchronized tango of the clutch and accelerator. Her skirt rose a bit on her thighs. Quick glance in her side mirror. Nothing coming except a dog crossing from the town green toward the general store. Estelle pulled out onto Main Street.

"So babe, why don't you show me around Delicious. I've never been here before."

Ruthie wasn't in any rush to go back to the wake, even though she knew she should. Being a minister's daughter was a part she could play in her sleep except she hated it. It was all she would ever be when she was in Delicious.

That was the nicest thing about being married and living in Albany. Only her closest girlfriends knew that her father was a minister. There she was David's wife and Luke's and John's mother. She didn't stand out because every woman she knew was somebody's wife or mother. Ruthie sat in one of the overstuffed chairs in a corner of the foyer. Thank goodness Mr. Healey kept the place dark. She would be able to blend in quite nicely and she had the perfect vantage point to see who came and went. Maybe she'd get a look at Jennifer before Jennifer got a look at her. Ruthie knew she needed to get the upper hand immediately. It pleased her to think she was poised, for once, to get one up on Jennifer.

In Albany she almost always knew what was going to happen before it did. Ruthie spent a lot of time trying to think of every possible outcome to every situation or issue and plan a response beforehand. That assured her being prepared for any eventuality. For example, when David had the car commercials for his Chrysler dealerships made, Ruthie possessed the foresight to bring two extra pinpoint dress shirts because she knew David always perspired when he was nervous and he was always anxious during filming. Especially the last time because he had insisted on using the elephant and trained dogs, and though he hated to admit it, he didn't really like animals. He found them dirty. Ruthie had also packed two extra pairs of shoes. The dogs were housebroken but the elephant wasn't. What a fiasco that had turned into. She for one was certainly grateful for the can of Lysol spray she kept in her purse.

Ruthie noticed Mrs. Potts leave the ladies' room and walk back toward the wake.

Goodness, what a crowd there was. People Ruthie vaguely recognized paraded back and forth. Before she'd gone into the little girl's room she'd stood in a line that wrapped around the Everlasting Life room. Finally she'd reached Dorothy and Jimmy to pay her respects. Dorothy looked just awful, though she was wearing a nice scarf knotted in a most interesting manner. Maybe before she went back to Albany the day after tomorrow she'd find an opportunity to talk with Dorothy and Jimmy and see if they were interested in TheWay. Hopefully their minds hadn't been poisoned by that smear campaign about TheWay being a pyramid scheme that had been going around a few years back.

Daddy had said Dorothy discovered Mrs. Andersen. Which

in Ruthie's mind was the most perplexing part of the whole incident. They had always seemed like such a close mother and daughter. She could remember Jennifer saying the two of them finished each other's sentences. What mother would want her child to find her hanging from the crossbeam in the barn? Tears pricked Ruthie's eyes as she imagined Luke or John finding her in such a state.

Ruthie heard the inhale of the Ladies' Room door opening. She looked over and saw Jennifer smoothing the pleats of her navy blue linen trousers.

God, she looked good. A little heavier than when Ruthie had last seen her. She wore a pair of the ugliest sandals imaginable and had a terrible haircut but, otherwise she looked, well, almost normal.

Ruthie watched Jennifer take off her glasses and blow on the lenses.

Ruthie wondered why Jennifer had never gotten contact lenses. She had beautiful blue eyes that would've been shown to greater advantage if they weren't hidden behind glasses. Ruthie squinted and decided that Jennifer wasn't wearing eye makeup either. Imagine a woman her age not wearing a little mascara. Maybe it was a rule in the gay community. Perhaps she would get the opportunity to slip Jennifer TheWay Summer Sensations Makeup Catalogue. A little subtle enhancement couldn't hurt.

Jennifer put her glasses back on and opened the front door. It closed silently behind her. That was strange. Ruthie hoped she wasn't leaving early. That would mean coming back for tonight's visiting hours so she could accidentally run into Jennifer.

CHAPTER TWENTY-SIX

Auntie Potts put extra ice into her Red Sox commemorative beer mug and filled it with Pepsi. The bubbles fizzed against her cheeks as she tipped her head back and guzzled half of it. After a moment a burp erupted out of her stomach like a rocket and echoed off her kitchen cabinets. Yep, there was nothing quite so satisfying as a Pepsi. Except a Pepsi with a bowl of Wise salt and vinegar potato chips sitting next to it.

Auntie took her snack into the living room and turned on the five o'clock news out of Springfield. They had a different newscaster. At least he looked different than the one usually sitting there. It was hard to tell because they all looked alike.

Auntie thought about the afternoon at Healey's. When she'd arrived she'd walked in on Jenny and her brother-in-law having one of those whispering kind of fights people have when they don't want to be overheard. Jennifer had left him standing there rubbing his throat and gave Auntie a rib-crushing hug. Which let Auntie know right then that Jenny was feeling bad. The only other time they'd ever hugged each other was when Jenny's Daddy had drowned.

Auntie would never forget that day a couple weeks after Bob's funeral. Jenny had driven her daddy's truck into the gas station and screeched to a stop nearly hitting the unleaded pump. She'd flung open the door and lurched out barely making it to the trash barrel Auntie kept between the pumps before she'd puked her guts up. Auntie had put down her morning crossword puzzle and rushed out to Jenny, who'd dropped to her knees and hung onto the rim of the trash barrel like she'd be sucked off the face of the earth if she didn't hang onto something.

"Goodness, Jenny. Come on now. Get up and come inside." Auntie dragged her up and supported her until Jenny steadied. They walked together inside Auntie's store where Jenny collapsed in Auntie's rocking chair.

"She's throwing everything out," Jenny whispered.

Auntie leaned close to hear.

"Dad's not even cold in the ground and she's getting rid of all his clothes. His shoes. She said she's going to burn it all in the brush pile."

Auntie knew Gertrude was capable of it but hoped, this time around, she'd be more like Rufus, Max's long-dead dog, and bark not bite.

"She said she won't even donate it to the Christian Relief Fund because even heathens in Africa don't need a sinner's clothes on their backs." Jenny's lips began to tremble and her eyes filled with tears.

"He was the only one in that house who loved me. Maybe if I'd gone fishing with him he'd still be alive." Jenny fell against Auntie and cried until Auntie's shirt was soaked.

Auntie had never felt so useless in her life.

An ice cube cracking in her mug brought Auntie back to the recliner in her living room. She crunched a potato chip. According to Doc Delerzon she wasn't supposed to have chips. He said they were loaded with hydro-something fats, which clogged the arteries quicker than steak and gravy. But after the afternoon she'd had watching people act so sorry about Gertrude when they spoke to Dorothy and then talk about Gertrude outside in the parking lot, to say nothing of all the gossiping about Jenny and her lady friend, well, it just brought out the chip-eater in her.

And then there was poor Dorothy. Always so well put together but looking kind of rough around the edges as the afternoon wore on. Auntie still couldn't get her mind around Gertrude letting Dorothy find her. That was the kind of thing you never forgot. Like when she found Max crushed by that Buick. She could see it just as clear as if it were happening now.

Auntie sipped her Pepsi.

Yep. That was even over the top for Gertrude.

"Here, babe, let me." Estelle removed Gert's diary from my hand. "You really crushed the hell out of this."

We were sitting on the back porch sipping ice tea and trying to regroup before the golumpki dinner at Mrs. Lewkowski's. I couldn't imagine forking mounds of hot cabbage stuffed with rice and ground meat into my mouth on such a humid evening.

"I was a little nerved up."

She laughed and began examining the diary from every angle.

"Does your mother have a boning knife?"

I got up and went into the kitchen to get Estelle her knife. The blade was long and narrow. Curving toward the tip. It gleamed in the sunlight that slanted through Gert's kitchen window. Though I had no doubt it could separate flesh from bone I wasn't sure it could separate Gert's diary from its lock.

"Thanks." Estelle began to methodically remove the stitching that held the flap with the lock to the front and back covers of the diary.

Now why hadn't I thought of that?

"You should have been a brain surgeon," I said, transfixed by the flashing blade. Cutting each stitch. Each sliced thread brought me closer to the contents of Gert's diary. Hopefully it chronicled more than a daily weather report and the litany of daily activity.

"What do you hope to find in here?" Estelle's voice was quiet as she concentrated.

"Some answers."

"To what questions?"

"Why the rope? Why did she plan it so Dorothy would find her? Was she the heartless bitch she always seemed to be?"

Estelle took her eyes off the stitching and glanced up at me.

"Are you prepared for answers to the questions you aren't asking?"

"What do you mean?"

"Well, babe, think of your own journals. Are you always the person in them that you present to the world? Maybe your mother will not be the person you've always thought she was." Estelle went back to unstitching the diary.

"Maybe. Mostly I'm afraid that she's exactly who I've always known her to be," I said, watching Estelle wield the knife.

CHAPTER TWENTY-SEVEN

July 8 1998

Dear God,

I know it means that I will burn in Hell. But, I plan to do it anyway. There's been a lot of things in my life like that because I am a sinner and there is nothing that can save me from that.

I know that is why you have given me this sickness to teach me to be a better Christian. This is my punishment and I have tried to accept it. But I am not strong enough to get helpless and be a burden to Dorothy. So I am going to kill myself.

I went to the library and looked up on the Internet to see how to tie a hangman's knot. It's amazing what the Internet will show you how to do.

I got myself a good stout rope. I will tie it to a crossbeam in the barn and jump off the rung of the ladder. The barn seems like a good place in case something goes wrong I don't want there to be a mess in the house.

Friday night is the night. I invited Pastor Jameson over at eight o'clock on Saturday morning to work on the program for August's Sunday services when he'll be on vacation retreat in Pennsylvania. I promised there'd be coffee and my cinnamon Bundt coffeecake with Sour cream icing. He always says he'd go to the ends of the earth for a piece of my coffeecake.

This way he'll be the one to find me and the note I left for Dorothy that will explain everything.

I hope someday I will be forgiven for this but I don't see how.

Your Faithful Servant
Gertrude

My chest felt as though it were full of quick set cement. My ribs couldn't expand because all the oxygen had been sucked out of the universe. The lowering sun cut through the branches of a poplar tree filling the back porch with bright light of operating room intensity that shines in your eyes just before you succumb to anesthesia and the surgeon slices you open.

I looked at Estelle.

She looked like someone who had just seen something horrible and couldn't think of any way to describe it.

"Mavis, honey, can you go get the extra fans from the guest room closet? This kitchen is hotter than Hades." Mrs. Lewkowski blotted her upper lip with the edge of her apron.

"Jeez, Ma, I don't think this is going to help much." Mavis struggled into the kitchen lugging a box fan in one hand and an oscillating fan in the other. "Maybe we should eat out at the picnic table."

"That doesn't seem special enough for Jenny and her...what do you think she's called?" Mrs. Lewkowski opened the oven and peeled back the tinfoil covering her roasting pan. Steam billowed out, fogging her glasses. Maybe Mavis was right. It would be cooler outside.

"I can't remember her name. I'm not sure Jenn ever told me when I saw her this morning."

"No, dear, not her name. What's the term for the woman Jenny lives with. Like a wife only they aren't married."

"Well, Ma, my friend, Kathy, uses girlfriend. But, they're just dating. My neighbors Peter and John call each other their S.O.s."

"S.O.?"

"Significant other."

"Oh." Mrs. Lewkowski lowered the oven temperature. "Do you think if we put the red and white checked table cloth on the picnic table it'll be all right for company?"

"Ma, since when is Jenn company?" Mavis went to the linen closet in the hall and got the tablecloth and five red napkins.

"Oh, I know you're right. I'm just nervous is all. I've got a horrible feeling in the pit of my stomach. Like something bad is going to happen."

"Hasn't something bad already happened?"

"Well, yes. I just don't think we're at the end of it is all. Something else is on the way." Mrs. Lewkowski opened the silverware drawer and counted out five forks, knives and spoons and put them on the enameled Nauset Lighthouse serving tray. She put the rye bread in a basket and covered it with a clean dishtowel.

"Mavis, honey, get the butter out would you? Oh, and that HeartSmart business your poor father is supposed to use." Mrs. Lewkowski crossed to the salt and pepper shaker display cabinet Earl had made for her on their twenty-fifth wedding anniversary. She contemplated a moment and selected the miniature conch shells emblazoned with Key West.

Mrs. Lewkowski always prided herself on setting a nice table.

CHAPTER TWENTY-EIGHT

"Why don't you just tell him?" Estelle swirled the ice cubes in her glass. "Tell him what your mother wrote in her diary and then ask him why—"

"Why Dorothy was the one who found Gert," I said, interrupting her. Something I'm always doing though I know it drives her nuts.

Estelle nodded. "What's the minister's name again?"

"I call him the Antichrist though I'm sure he uses Pastor Jameson on his business cards."

"That's catchy, babe. Was he at the wake?"

"Not to my knowledge. I saw him, very briefly, at Dorothy's house last night. Maybe he's saving himself for the big show tomorrow morning."

"Saving himself may be the point." Estelle leaned closer to me.

"What do you mean?"

"Maybe he found your mother—"

"And didn't tell anyone?"

"Yes." Estelle nodded warming up to the topic. "He found her and didn't want to get involved or something and—"

"Skulked away like the dirty dog he is," I said.

"Exactly. Your mother left a note—"

"She said she would. For Dorothy."

"Right. Maybe he—"

"Took it," I said

Estelle nodded. Her eyes gleamed like they do when she's trying to figure out a really complex murder mystery.

"But, why?" we both said in unison.

A very good question.

Was he worried he'd be blamed? No one could imagine a man as old and decrepit as he was carrying a bag of groceries let alone killing a woman and hauling her body out to the barn and making it look like she'd hanged herself. Plus he was a minister. That went a long way with some people.

Maybe Gert left a note for him and he didn't want anyone to know it. So he took his note and Dorothy's note and left. But, Mrs. Lewkowski didn't mention seeing his car in Gert's driveway last Saturday morning. Maybe she was busy and missed him. Maybe he never showed. If that was the case, where was Dorothy's note?

"I think I should show this to Dorothy." I crunched an ice cube in my teeth.

"I agree. She must feel perfectly awful and this may help a bit."

"Do you think I should show her tonight at visiting hours?"

"No, babe, I don't. Especially after the little disagreement you told me about having with them. I think you should go see her now."

"Now? We're supposed to go across the street in—" I glanced at my watch. "Fifteen minutes."

"Why don't you go see your sister and I'll go across the street and meet the Lew…"

"Kowskis."

"Lewkowskis."

"Won't you feel awkward going over there without me?"

"I've felt awkward since I arrived. Besides, I love golumpkis and I love you. That will give us a place to start."

Dorothy shivered in front of the air conditioner's fan. She had set it to high cool before she stripped down to her underclothes. She had every intention of lying down for a few minutes while Jimmy made supper. Salami grinders with provolone cheese, coleslaw, Bermuda onion and horseradish deli mustard wrapped in tinfoil and melted together for fifteen minutes in a 350-degree oven. The thought of it made her stomach lurch.

Anyway she was going to lie down but when she tried it felt like her skin would crawl off her bones. Nothing helped until she got up and organized her lingerie drawer. She positively had to get a new black bra. The underwire was threatening to poke through the tricot, which was a disaster in the making; especially if it happened at church or choir practice. Dorothy didn't have much use for black in the summer months but fall would come and it was important to be prepared.

Tears pricked Dorothy's eyes as she thought of all the times she and Mother had gone shopping at the Holyoke Mall. This would've been one of those times she would have called Mother up and told her she needed a new bra and invited her to Lord & Taylor. After shopping, Mother had always liked going to Friendly's in the food court for lunch. Dorothy could almost see Mother flipping through the menu, her reading glasses low on her nose as she decided on the Big Beef Cheeseburger. She always decided on the Big Beef Cheeseburger.

Dorothy imagined they would've made a date to go this coming Saturday. Dorothy would've picked her up. They would've chatted about the songs the choir was considering for the Christmas pageant. Whether Mother should get new café curtains for the kitchen. If Dorothy and Jimmy should go to the Berkshires or the White Mountains for Columbus Day weekend. All the day-to-day stuff Dorothy always talked to Mother about.

Dorothy sat on Jimmy's side of the bed and picked up his pillow and buried her face in the percale. She had bought these sheets at Filenes's January white sale this past winter. Mother had got herself a new chenille bedspread.

Dorothy inhaled the lingering scent of Jimmy's Brut cologne. She hoped he wouldn't be offended but she didn't think she'd be able to eat much more than a piece of toast for supper.

He'd probably eat his grinder as well as hers. Jimmy had done nothing but eat since he'd seen Mother hanging in the barn. Eat and spend time in the bathroom. Jimmy hadn't really said very much but Dorothy felt like he had trouble looking at her since Mother had done what she'd done. Though he certainly had read Jennifer the riot act when she threatened to bring her whatever-she-was to the wake. Dorothy had not seen Jennifer come back to the visiting hours after Jimmy took her out to speak with her. He wouldn't tell Dorothy what he had said to Jennifer but she could imagine. Jimmy didn't get mad very often but when he did, well, look out.

Jennifer probably just snuck away which was just so like her. Though Dorothy had seen her car when she and Jimmy had left Healey's and drove home to have supper and regroup. Well, it wasn't any of Dorothy's business. She hadn't seen Jennifer for years. After all, it wasn't like they meant anything to each other.

Jimmy swore if he didn't have hemorrhoids before this whole thing with Gert, he sure as hell was going to have them after. Maybe his bowels would calm down after tomorrow's funeral. But, that meant he had tonight's visiting hours to get through. A cramp grabbed his guts and twisted. This was worse than that time he went to the Federated Church's wild game supper and ate some bad bear.

CHAPTER TWENTY-NINE

Since my car was still parked on the street in front of the funeral home, I took Estelle's car to Dorothy's. It made her nervous when anyone other than herself drove the Nova. Not that Es would admit it. Her dilated pupils and quickened breath gave her away every time. I managed to make it to my sister's without incident.

I wasn't looking forward to a visit with Dorothy. If I'd had more time to think about it I wouldn't be doing it. My little altercation with Jimmy earlier made me uncomfortable at seeing him again so soon. And on his own turf. It was always strange seeing Dorothy because I made her so nervous. It was almost like she thought I'd jump her bones because she was a woman. Never mind that she was my sister. I wondered how she would take Gert's last diary entry. Would it ease her mind? Make things worse? I took a deep breath and knocked on the screen door. The smell of something burning wafted out to greet me. I knocked again. Louder.

"Hello?" I questioned the empty kitchen.

Where were they?

I clutched Gert's diary tighter, opened the screen door and stood on the braided rug just inside the door.

"Hello? Anybody home?"

Nothing.

I noticed Jimmy's light blue leisure suit jacket folded over the back of a kitchen chair. Dorothy's wicker purse sat on the counter with the scarf she'd worn to the wake tied around the handle. The table was set for two. A small dish of ripe olives and baby gherkins crowded a jar of deli mustard with extra horseradish in the center of the table.

"Dorothy? It's Jennifer."

Whatever was in the oven smelled like it was burning. I opened the oven and saw four tinfoil-wrapped torpedoes oozing cheese onto the electrical coil. I lowered the temperature and hoped it wouldn't ruin Jimmy's grinders. My brother-in-law must have a galvanized stomach.

Where were they?

Dead?

"Don't be silly," I murmured to myself. Ever since Gert hanged herself all I'd been able to think about was death, the melting of glaciers, wildfires, lightning strikes and swarms of locust.

I decided to investigate. Hopefully I wouldn't come across them having sex in the living room.

Ruthie hated iceberg lettuce but that was all she could find in Daddy's refrigerator. Romaine, red leaf and a little radicchio were necessary for a decent salad. On top of it, Daddy only had French salad dressing, that bright orange concoction that wilted lettuce instantaneously. She couldn't even make her own because Daddy had no balsamic, just white vinegar and the only thing she knew to do with that was clean her Braun coffeemaker.

Daddy had been in a terrible mood since she'd arrived. He'd been grumpy and uninterested when she'd tried to tell him about the boys' lacrosse tournament in the summer league. He'd stared off into space when she mentioned the upcoming Labor Day TheWay weekend in Atlanta where she and David would receive a plaque for selling the most TheWay Garden of Eatin' Fruit and Vegetable Dehydration Systems.

Ruthie opened the freezer and scanned the contents. Daddy had it neatly stacked with Stouffer's macaroni and cheese, stuffed peppers and creamed chipped beef. There were a few boxes of Gorton's crunchy fish fillets and several bags of Ore-Ida crinkle cut fries.

None of this was on her TheWay Waist Watchers plan. Maybe Daddy had some tuna.

Gosh, it was hot in this kitchen, she thought while scanning the pantry shelves. She smiled when she saw the cans of Dinty Moore beef stew. Daddy had always loved that stuff. As long as she could remember there had been at least three cans in the kitchen at all times. There were countless nights she remembered waking up in the middle of the night and coming downstairs to find her father eating a bowl of Dinty Moore and planning his next sermon.

Just last week she'd been doing the family shopping when she became convinced her father was in the store. It wasn't even rational because she knew Daddy was in Delicious. She had spoken with him that morning. But she just couldn't shake the feeling. It eventually made sense when, at the end of aisle five, she found a product promotion for the new meatier Dinty Moore. A retired man was handing out samples from a bubbling crock-pot full of the stew. Just the smell of it made her think of her father.

Ruthie reached for a can of Chicken of the Sea.

Daddy had never rearranged the kitchen after she left home so she was able to move around with ease, never having to look twice for anything. And miracle of miracles, Daddy had celery and low-fat mayonnaise.

Goodness, where was he? She hadn't seen him since she

got home from the wake and found him sitting in his study staring out of the window at the hay fields that stretched behind the parsonage and the church. She had stood in the threshold watching him for quite awhile before he even realized she was there.

"Daddy?" she asked him. "Are you all right?"

"Yes," he said. "Just planning my sermon for the funeral tomorrow. Is the wake over so quickly?"

"For now. I expected you to come over, Daddy. I waited for you." It wasn't entirely true. She was really waiting to speak to Jennifer. But, there was no reason he had to know that.

"A man of God is called upon to witness occurrences ordinary men cannot fathom. Isn't it enough that I buried my wife and now to find Gertr—" Daddy's voice had an edge to it before she watched him make an effort to control it.

"God, umm...God I meant to say, has confronted me with a...ah, has brought a Bible verse to mind and I wanted to contemplate and pray about the services tomorrow."

There was no Bible lying open on his desk and his yellow legal pad had a few doodles on it.

"How about I make you a glass of iced tea. It's stuffy in here."

"Thank you, Ruth."

When she returned with the tea, Daddy was flipping through the New Testament and scribbling on the pad.

Ruthie cut out the core of the head of the iceberg and ran it under the cold water tap. Goodness, what she wouldn't give for her salad spinner. Pools of lettuce water accumulating at the bottom of a salad absolutely drove her nuts. Thankfully Daddy had some beautiful tomatoes lined up on his windowsill. Probably a grateful parishioner had dropped them by. They would be delicious in the salad. And it was going to prove to be very difficult to avoid having a slice of that lovely looking coffeecake with sour cream icing for dessert. It was so carefully wrapped, another gift no doubt, and left on the kitchen table looking absolutely sinful.

No doubt Daddy would attend the wake tonight. It wouldn't look strange if she went with him because she was the minister's daughter and it would be expected. Her stomach fluttered as she thought about speaking with Jennifer and offering her condolences. She would have to think about what to say.

She arranged the lettuce, tomato and tuna salad on two dinner plates. Presentation was everything.

CHAPTER THIRTY

Estelle crossed the street to the Lewkowskis feeling as shaky as a poplar leaf in a high wind. She had yet to meet anyone in this strange little town. Of course, all little towns were strange no matter where they were located. She knew that from growing up in one in Kansas. For a long time she'd believed there was something about small towns that attracted unusual people who married other unusual people and gave birth to more unusual people making small towns the unusual places they were. But, when she went into social work it became apparent that unusual people lived everywhere, they were just more noticeable in a small town.

Nana had always said all people were strange, to somebody else, no matter where they lived. City, country or suburbs didn't matter. The human race was a weird bunch and should be caged in a zoo instead of the monkeys. "Imagine honey," Nana would say, "that someone is watching us from above and laughing until they wet their pants."

Estelle hoped Jennifer was all right down at Dorothy's.

That diary was a time bomb.

Maybe it would ease Dorothy's mind. Jennifer's too. But, it was more likely that it would unsettle everything. Diaries weren't meant to be read by the diarist's relatives. Their mother sounded so sad in her diary entry, resigned to her suicide and unable to see any other way. It was interesting how hopeless Jennifer's mother seemed in spite of her strong religious belief. And imagine the minister finding the body and pretending he hadn't. Estelle knew ministers were just people struggling to do their best just like everyone else and if they didn't act like such hypocrites it might be easier to forgive them when they screwed up. And screw up they did with appalling regularity.

The Lewkowskis' picnic table was shaded by a large, spreading maple tree and set with a tablecloth, plates and cutlery. Thank God they'd be eating outside where a stray breeze could blow over them if it happened by.

Suddenly a grandmotherly-type woman launched herself out of the screen door and bustled across the lawn carrying a tray with a pitcher of lemonade and several glasses filled with ice cubes.

"Hello," Estelle called and waved. Here goes nothing, she thought. Jennifer said the Lewkowskis had saved her life when she was growing up. She was determined to make a good impression.

Why is it when you don't want to make any noise, all you can do is make more noise than you've ever made in your life?

The stench of burning cheese followed me out of the kitchen and into the hall. The wood floors creaked under my Birkenstocks. All I could hear was the ticking of the grandfather clock and my breathing.

"Dorothy?" Now why was I whispering? I wanted to be heard.

"Dorothy? It's me. Jennifer." Better. But I sounded apprehensive. Not good. Like blood to my family of sharks.

I continued into the hall and around the corner leaning through the living room archway. The television was on. A big wide-bodied model with the word mute emblazoned across the bottom of the screen. Something murky sweated in a glass on the end table next to a recliner. A defiled Springfield afternoon edition lay on the braided rug. I expected to see my brother-in-law out on the deck pissing over the railing but there was no sign of him.

"Dorothy? Are you here? It's me, Jennifer," I called, making my way toward the bedrooms in the back of the house. My voice echoed in the darkened hall, dark because the doors to all the rooms off the hall were closed.

If memory served there were three bedrooms and a bathroom. Which door was which?

"I've come to show you something." I raised my voice even louder.

My sweat glands shifted into overdrive, soaking the collar and armpits of my blouse. I was going to look like hell by the time evening visiting hours rolled around. Where could they be with the local news on the TV, dinner in the oven and the table set for two? Baby gherkins and all.

Just as I had my hand raised to knock on door number one, it flew open to reveal a red-eyed Dorothy in her bra and half-slip. She screamed so loud I dropped Gert's diary on my foot. The door behind me, the bathroom door apparently by the amount of air freshener that billowed out, jerked open to reveal Goofball standing there in a pair of boxer shorts littered with little crucifixes.

"What the hell—" He slammed the door. "Is she doing here?"

"Jennifer? What are you doing here?" Dorothy held her hands over her breasts.

"I wanted to show you what I found in Gert's diary."

"Dorothy!" Jimmy shouted through the door. "She's seen me in my underwear."

I burst out laughing. I couldn't help myself. It was probably my relief at finding them not dead, maimed or fornicating. And seeing him in his shorts. The trouble was I couldn't stop. Not when Dorothy escorted me into the kitchen. Not when my trousered brother-in-law offered me a glass of iced tea. Not when Dorothy opened Gert's diary and read the last entry.

It was only when the tears started to flood her eyes and her bottom lip began to quiver that I was able to get a grip. She looked at me.

"Where did you find this?"

"In Gert's desk."

"I didn't know Mother kept a diary." Dorothy's eyes went back to the page. I watched them track the words back and forth as she read it once again.

"Me neither. Last night when Herlick called for a scarf I went upstairs to look for one and found all these medical reports about Gert having Lou Gehrig's disease. So, I got more and more curious and went through her desk. That's when I found the diary."

"She never told me she was sick."

"Lou Gehrig's disease is pretty bad isn't it? I mean, isn't it fatal?" Jimmy bit into what looked like a salami grinder. It oozed and dripped all over his fingers.

"Yes. There was information in the file explaining that it's the deterioration of the sheath around the muscle, which renders the muscle progressively non-functional. First you lose the use of your extremities and it works its way toward the torso until it affects the ability to swallow and breathe. Eventually you suffocate."

"Jesus," Jimmy muttered as he reached for a pickle.

Dorothy seemed transfixed by the jar of deli mustard.

"The mind is unaffected. A mixed blessing if you ask me. As you might imagine, depression is often a significant issue."

"Well, if that's what she had, it kind of makes sense what she did. Not that I agree with it, mind you. Our Lord is the only one who should take a life. This just makes it more understandable." Jimmy took another bite.

"She must have felt so alone." Dorothy glanced at Jimmy. "Wipe your mouth, honey."

Gert had probably spent most of her life alone. Even back when my father was alive and Dorothy and I still lived at home. She was one of those people most people wanted to stay away from. Even her friends from church. They never just dropped by for coffee. Dorothy was probably her only friend. And maybe the Antichrist. Though I wasn't so sure of that anymore.

"Mother had seemed kind of down lately and every time I asked what was wrong she always said nothing or her arthritis was acting up."

"The medical reports indicate she was diagnosed in January of this year. Apparently she went out to the Albany Medical Center for tests." I took a sip of iced tea.

"Didn't your mother go away just after Christmas last year? She said she was going on a Bible retreat or something." Jimmy went to the fridge and got a bottle of horseradish, which he slathered on the remainder of his grinder.

"Mother would never have wanted to be a burden on anyone. Or end up in a nursing home." Dorothy reached for a napkin and blew her nose. "I feel just terrible. Mother must have felt deserted by everyone. Even God."

"Here, honey." Jimmy handed her his neatly folded handkerchief. "Napkins are too rough."

Dorothy smiled at him. "Thanks, sweetie."

"Hey, anybody want one of these grinders?"

"No thank you." I'd rather drink a Drano cocktail.

Dorothy blew her nose.

"There's one other thing that Gert's last entry seems to indicate." I tapped the diary.

Dorothy glanced back down.

"It looks like Gert's intention was for Pastor Jameson to find her body. Not for you to find her." I put my hand over Dorothy's.

Dorothy's hand jumped and quivered under mine like a fish on a hook.

"Let me read that thing." Jimmy reached over and grabbed it, smearing the cover with mayo and horseradish.

I waited.

Dorothy got her pocketbook off the counter and opened

her compact. Her eyes narrowed as she scrutinized her puffy, raccoon eyes.

"Holy Christ! According to this she left a note for you, honeybunch. I never saw any sign of that when I cut your mother down." He popped another baby gherkin into his mouth.

"Which means he must have been there first and picked up his note and Dorothy's note and left. Without calling the police or letting anybody know. The bastard left Dorothy to find her," I said.

"Jennifer! What a thing to say. Pastor would never do anything like that. He's a man of God." Dorothy clutched the handkerchief like she was trying to kill it.

"Don't be naïve, Dorothy. Men of God are always stealing from the church building fund, paying for prostitutes to give them blow jobs or fucking little boys."

"Jennifer, you know I don't like that kind of talk. It's...it's..."

"Honeybunch, I think she might be right." Jimmy took a bite of his grinder.

I couldn't believe my ears.

"Jimmy, how can you believe her?" Dorothy waved in my direction. "She's always been a troublemaker. She's never had a good word to say about the pastor...about Mother—"

"Now, love dumpling—" Jimmy waved his second grinder at Dorothy.

"About me or you. She calls you Goofball, for goodness sake, and here you are, believing her over a man you've known since you were a boy. Pastor Jameson married us and—"

I just love being talked about as though I'm not in the room.

"Baby love, I know your sister isn't to be trusted. But, look here." Jimmy pointed at the diary with the remainder of his grinder.

"How do we even know Mother wrote it. Maybe Jennifer forged it or something."

Forged it?

"Okay, sweetheart, I know you're upset. But, you're not making any sense. This sure looks like your mother's handwriting to me. Listen now to what she says. 'This way he'll be the one to find me and the note to Dorothy that will explain everything."

Jimmy unwrapped the third grinder and spooned it full of horseradish.

"The question is why." I got the diary away from Jimmy's vicinity just as a blob of fire-breathing coleslaw hit the table.

Jimmy nodded, unable to speak with the huge wad of food in his mouth.

"It just doesn't make any sense." Dorothy jerked to her feet and ran out of the kitchen.

"Shit," Jimmy mumbled.

I couldn't have agreed more.

CHAPTER THIRTY-ONE

That evening the two Joannes came to Gert's second showing. It gave me the willies to watch my real life mixing in with Delicious. Estelle stood next to me in the receiving line. We looked like respectable people in spite of our proclivities and then the Joannes, prototypes for the butch and femme lesbian, showed up. It created an unsettling cocktail in my brain. Almost like I was coming down with the flu. I watched their approach from my spot between Estelle and Dorothy. Jo was wearing a summer-weight seersucker trouser and vest combo. Inappropriate in Delicious even if a man had been wearing it. Anne wore her lilac colored Donna Reed number, usually seen only during Northampton's Pride festivities.

The Joannes were my good friends. I'd known them for years. Jo was my mechanic down at Earline's Gay-rage, specializing in older model Toyotas. And Anne baked bread at the Crafts Avenue Bakery where I bought raisin bread, challah and sticky buns. They invited Estelle and me over for their twice-a-year solstice parties. I loved them yet found myself wishing they hadn't come. They were just so queer. I hated that it bothered me.

Besides, with the two of them and Es and I, Delicious's Lesbian Critical Mass was about to be reached. Soon the earth would split open and suck us all down like a bathtub drain.

Gert's mourners, all their heads moving in unison, followed the Joannes' progress toward me as Jo and Anne crossed the room. My sister looked at me in horror. Goofball put his arm around Dorothy and pulled her against him as though there were a marauding bull loose in the Everlasting Life Room. Too bad the Antichrist hadn't shown yet. The expression I imagined seeing on his face would make this trip to Delicious worth it.

"Hi, Jennifer." Jo hugged me to her, crushing the air out of my lungs. She moved to Estelle.

"Jo. Anne. What are you guys doing here?" I said.

"We wanted to be supportive in your time of crisis." Anne kissed me on both cheeks.

"Exactly. That's why we borrowed a bus," Jo said.

"A bus?" Estelle smiled at the both of them. She always liked shaking things up. I usually do too. Except when I'm the one being shaken.

"It was Jo's idea." Anne dabbed at the lipstick deposits she'd left on my face with a lace hanky. "She thought you were probably dying out here for lack of lesbian energy."

"I wondered what it was that was killing me." I scanned the room. All eyes were riveted our way. Mouths hung open. Some lips were pursed. Though we whispered in the quiet room it seemed as though we were shouting.

"So, Jo rented a bus, not a big one but one of those cute little yellow school buses. She has an in with Pat Marcovini who owns the bus company. Anyway we filled it with all your friends. Darlene and Cindy. Babs. Vic and Janice. Di. Paula and Deb. Claudia and Lynnie. Mary. Becky. They're all out there."

"Holy shit," I said.

"Totally. The problem is we're having trouble finding a place to park. Some bohunk in a cop suit is telling us we can't park in front of the funeral home because of some zoning regulation. Darlene is driving the bus around the common while we check it out." Jo jammed her hands in her pockets.

"Ah...perhaps I could be of some assistance." Herlick popped out of nowhere.

Estelle and the two Joannes stared at him.

"Yes, Herlick, my friends need parking for a small bus."

His eyebrows rose to his Brylcreemed hairline. "Auntie... ah...Potts offered her parking lot across the street for overflow. I'm sure there would be room for a bus there."

"Oh-ke-doke." Jo sauntered out of the room.

Annie squeezed herself between Estelle and me, hooking an arm around each of our waists. "Who are all these people?"

"Just the people who live here," I said, facing the crowd.

They all looked like they'd been cast in stone.

Auntie Potts sat in her office in the back of the gas station figuring out the quarterly taxes. She was in danger of going over her fifteen Lucky a day limit. Who could blame her? She hated paying taxes. No, that wasn't quite right. Paying them was all right. It was just that she almost never agreed with what the politicians spent money on. Usually raises and health plans for themselves while letting the little people go hang. She winced at the unfortunate turn of phrase. It was impossible to think of much else.

Funny how with Gertrude's passing she'd been thinking so much of Bob. She wished he was still alive to see how nicely Jenny had turned out. Or, maybe he wouldn't think so because of the gay thing. That was hard to know. She glanced at Max's Timex. A bit past eight o'clock. Time to get a move on if she expected to get to Healey's. She'd seen too much of Gertrude by far but she wanted to check on Jenny. And it'd be nice to meet her lady friend.

What was that beeping? She squinted through the crack in her office door and out the front window just in time to see a school bus backing around the side of the building. Jesus, now what?

"Jenn, are you all right, sweetie?" Anne squeezed my arm.

I nodded. Was I all right? Probably. Just scared shitless. It felt like I was standing in a demilitarized zone. But, the war was inside me. These women were my friends. My family. More my family than my family had ever been. I loved them. I knew they loved me. But…but what?

Anxiety must have given me bionic hearing. I heard Healey's front door open. Felt the energy shift.

"The Andersen viewing is in the Everlasting Life Room down the hall," Herlick intoned.

"Thanks a lot, man," Jo said.

"The Everlasting Life Room? Are you shittin' me?" Claudia asked.

At least I think it was Claudia.

"Sssshhhh. Maybe we should keep our voices down," Cindy said.

"Yeah. We are in enemy territory," Babs said.

"Remember girls, we aren't in Kansas anymore," Mary said.

"Where are my ruby slippers when I need them?" Vicki wondered.

"And we aren't in Oz either," Lynnie said.

"We seem to be in East Bumfuck," Claudia said.

"Who knew East Bumfuck was named Delicious," Becky said.

"I'm so nervous I could swallow my own tongue," Darlene said.

"Sssshhh. Here's the Everlasting Life Room. Let's get it together," Cindy said.

I scanned the room. All eyes were riveted on the doorway.

"I wonder if the Second Coming of Christ would get this kind of attention," I whispered to Estelle.

She put her arm around me. "Don't worry, babe. It'll be fine," Estelle whispered back.

"I know."

"This is an opportunity to present these folks with a different point of view," Estelle said.

"It's just a little unsettling," I said.

"Imagine how they feel?" Estelle smiled.

Babs poked her head around the corner. Her eyes widened. She looked from right to left, located the coffin, paused on Mrs. Earle playing "Folsom Prison Blues" and finally settled on the triptych. She'd gotten a crew cut since I'd last seen her. The magenta tips looked very festive. Her head disappeared.

"Girls, let's make the sisterhood proud," Babs stage-whispered in a voice loud enough to carry across the common.

Jimmy's guts were in an uproar. He guessed he should never have eaten his salami and cheese torpedos for supper. That horseradish must have pushed his stomach right over the edge. He should've done what Dorothy suggested and had toast. Something bland. He reached into his pocket for the antacids.

He winced. This busload of dykes driving into Delicious, parading through Healey's was twisting his guts into knots. Maybe next time Dorothy would listen when he told her not to do something. It was a mistake telling Jennifer about Gert's death. It would've been enough to deal with the hanging. But now everyone in town was here to see Jennifer's friends, if you could even call them that, paying their respects. If people like them even knew what respect was. Women wearing men's clothes. Strange haircuts. Weird shoes. It was unnatural.

The only thing worse would be if that hypocrite Jameson showed up acting all sympathetic. Just like he had last night. Eating Dorothy's key lime pie all the while knowing what he'd done.

Jimmy pulled Dorothy close. He had to protect his little sugar plum.

Dorothy felt faint. The room was hot and all she could smell were Jimmy's wintergreen antacids. The walls seemed to be inhaling and exhaling like lungs. The past couple of days had been too much. First, Mother killing herself and then finding out that she'd been sick. At least that explained why she'd done what she'd done.

Almost worse was finding out that Pastor Jameson knew what had happened and didn't do anything about it. Just kept it to himself. She hardly knew what to think. Maybe he was senile or having those mini strokes old people had.

And now, this. Jennifer and her friend, Estelle, would've been bad enough but at least they looked almost normal. These newest arrivals, one of them wearing a man's seersucker suit... well, it just wasn't right. This wasn't God's intention when he made Adam and Eve. Men were men and women were women and they should look that way.

Vicki walked through the doorway first, resplendent in a red blazer. She had one for every occasion. Every season. She had impeccable manners except when crossed. I once witnessed her take on a blanket of queens at a Provincetown beach who had refused to turn down their Andrew Lloyd Webber.

"Hey, honey. How're you doing?" She leaned forward to kiss my cheek.

"Fine, Vic. I'll be glad when all this is over." I squeezed her hand.

"Hey, there." Vicki kissed Estelle. "You girls are looking a little green around the gills." Vic glanced at Gert and brought her eyes back to mine.

"It's that whole fish out of water thing," Estelle said.

"Oh, I can see that," Vic said. "You know what they say. It's not where you come from. It's where you end up."

Vicki moved down to Dorothy, offering her hand and miracle of miracles, Dorothy took it. Maybe this wouldn't go too badly after all.

"Sorry for your loss." Janice was right behind Vicki. They'd been together for years. Jan was from Brooklyn. When she was nervous, and who wouldn't be, it came out in her accent.

"Thanks for coming," I said, surprised that I was starting to feel that way.

"You girls doing okay?" Janice looked around the room and winked.

"Just fine," Estelle said. "But, it'll be nice to get back home."

"I'm thinking the same thing and I haven't even been here an hour." Jan smiled and moved down toward Dorothy who was chatting with Vicki. I heard something about hymns. Maybe Vicki's Baptist upbringing was coming in handy.

Ruthie sat in the third row, in the back. She was spellbound. She'd never been this close to so many gay women before. Some of them had quite a fashion sense and others, well…suffice to say, they looked a trifle mannish. Maybe she'd add a little p.s. to her letter to TheWay. After she offered them her suggestions about the Hurricane Hold hairspray, she'd approach the topic of the gays. It was an untapped market and goodness knows most of these women could make use of TheWay's Re Do You makeup catalogue.

Goodness where was Daddy? He had told her to run on ahead and he'd be right behind her. What was taking him so long?

"Sorry about your mother," Mary said and shook my hand.

"Thanks for coming. I know you don't bring out the Glen plaid for just any occasion," I said.

"I couldn't wear black, appropriate though it may be. Too humid for black wool," Mary said.

"It is too humid to breathe," I said.

"How are you both doing?" Mary asked, kissing Estelle's cheek.

"We're holding up. How's Northampton without us?" Estelle asked.

"It misses you," Mary said as she moved around Vicki and Janice who were still in conversation with my sister and brother-in-law.

Auntie Potts thought it was real nice of Jenny's friends to drive all the way from Northampton. They seemed like a friendly bunch of girls. They'd even offered to pay for parking. Whoever heard of such a thing?

She hung back, letting Jenny's friends go first. She felt weary all of a sudden and she didn't think it had anything to do with quarterly taxes. Maybe she was just tired of people. Her neighbors in particular. Look at them back away and cram themselves into the corners. Jenny's friends just didn't seem that dangerous. Sure, they dressed a little funny. Especially for Delicious. Some of them had very short hair and quite a bit of jewelry. And they lived in the big city. But, people were people. Pumping gas for folks had taught her that.

"You look like hell," Claudia said, hugging me so hard I heard my vertebrae crack.

"Claudia, really." Linny finished breaking my spine when she hugged me.

"You know what I mean, right?" Claudia looked at both of us.

Estelle nodded. "We do look like hell. There is some kind of weird energetic field around here…" Her voice faded away.

It was hard to put Delicious into words. It wasn't quite so bad in the open air. But, inside? All bets were off.

"When do you leave?" Linnie asked.

"Tomorrow. After the funeral," I said, hoping it were true. I'd gotten out of Delicious once. I'd be able to do it again. Wouldn't I?

"I'll bring you some of my vegetable soup tomorrow night," Linnie said. "You need fortification."

Claudia and Linnie moved around Vicki and Janice who were still talking to Dorothy. Those two should get battle pay.

"Excuse me. Excuse me."

My ears twitched at the sound of the Antichrist's voice. I knew the bastard was bound to show up sooner or later.

"Let me through."

"Can I...ah...help you, Pastor Jameson?" Herlick asked from his place near the doorway.

"I want to get through these people..."

"Daddy. Daddy, let me help you..." Ruthie seemed to leap up and tried to cross the room which wasn't possible with the rows of chairs and people standing around.

"I'm perfectly capable..." The Antichrist shrugged off Herlick's hand and pushed past Babs, Becky, Paula and Deb, Di, Cindy and Darlene who had been waiting in line. They shuffled aside but there wasn't enough room to get out of anyone's way.

"Who are all of these...these out-of-towners?"

"Daddy, wait for me."

"I got a bone to pick with you," Jimmy growled, stepping in front of the Antichrist and abandoning Dorothy to the lesbians.

Mrs. Earle stopped playing "Ring of Fire" and turned to stare. Any murmuring that had been going on around the room ceased.

"You owe us an explanation." Jimmy stopped in front of the Antichrist and folded his arms across his chest.

"Jimmy...don't...." Dorothy's voice faded away.

"Good evening, James. Whatever is the matter?" The Antichrist's smooth, sermon-voice slicked over the carpet. He stopped and peered up at my brother-in-law.

I took pleasure in noting the Antichrist looked a lot older than he had last night at Dorothy's.

"You know what's the matter." Jimmy stepped closer. His ears were red, his voice flat.

"You're upset. We're all—"

"You bet your ass I'm upset," Jimmy said.

"Now, Jimmy, don't swear," Dorothy said, her voice sounding breathy as though she couldn't get enough air.

Why not swear? I was just about to put my two cents in when I felt Estelle's hand on my shoulder.

"Babe, don't say anything. It'll mean more coming from one of his own," Estelle whispered.

"It is just your grief talking, son. Now, James, let me pass." The Antichrist attempted to step around Jimmy who shifted to block his path.

"Daddy!" Ruthie sounded nearly hysterical.

"You owe my wife an apology, you old goat, and you'd better make it a good one or I swear—"

"Apology? You're not making any sense, James. Now, let us pray and take sustenance in His words. 'Our Father who art in heaven, hallowed be thy na—'"

"You just don't get it, you damned hypocrite! Gert kept diaries!" Jimmy shouted and punched the Antichrist in the nose.

Blood spouted out of his face like somebody had turned on a garden hose. For the second time that day I started laughing and might have never stopped if Dorothy hadn't fainted.

CHAPTER THIRTY-TWO

Gert never told me much of anything I wanted to know. The only statements I can see that I've benefited from were "use hydrogen peroxide to get Eve's sinful blood out of your underwear" and "cook eggs on low or they'll be tough." Both Gert-isms have stood me in good stead these many years. The crotches of all my underwear are free from any menstrual residue. My overeasies have impressed many overnight guests. Except for Estelle who wouldn't have anything to do with chickens since her marriage to the Kansas corn farmer.

Gert told me plenty of other things I'd like to forget.

"Just what are you up to with Pastor Jameson's daughter?" Gert's hiss slithers out of a shadowy corner of the kitchen.

I am late. It is well after my eleven p.m. curfew. I used my father's truck because he's out of town with his friend Horsie for a weekend of bass fishing. I know I am running late but I don't care. Ruthie's worth it. Some of my bravado slips away when I hear Gert's voice.

"Nothing. We went to see a movie and it ran a little longer than we thought it would." I struggle to make my voice sound nonchalant.

"Hah! You must think I was born yesterday," Gert sneers. I can hear her lip curl.

When I drove up to the house I thought she'd gone to bed. The house was dark except for the porch light and a small lamp on Gert's desk in the living room. My father's technique of turning off the truck's headlights and coasting into the driveway came in handy.

How could I have forgotten Gert never sleeps?

"We saw *Annie Hall*. Then stopped at Friendly's for a hot fudge sundae."

I don't tell her we went parking at the cemetery and performed 69 for the Revolutionary War soldier who died during the battle of Lexington. Even though I'd washed at the flower-watering spigot I worry Gert will smell Ruthie on my face.

In the light of the quarter moon Gert's stove, counters and porcelain sink gleam. I can hear the hum from the kitchen clock and imagine the gold-toned sweep of the second hand making its steady progress, touching each Roman numeral with minimal affection. The fridge lurches on, drowning out what the kitchen clock has to say. Seth Thomas, always a scene-stealer, gongs twelve times.

Spillover from Gert's desk lamp throws light through the living room arch across the kitchen table and its red and white checked oil cloth, the lazy Susan, depository of a bottle of Tabasco which my father shakes over everything, the napkin holder, salt and pepper shakers shaped like the tablets Moses brought down the mountain. *Thou Shall Have No Other Gods Before Me* through *Honor Thy Father and Mother* on salt, *Thou Shalt Not Kill* through *Thou Shall Not Covet* on pepper. Gert's door prize at the Western Massachusetts Evangelical Outreach Breakfast and Bible Study held in Pittsfield. Made by a woman in Dalton who owned The Holy Spirit's Ceramic Studio and donated, every year, a set of commandment S&P shakers, a Calvary tea service, a Palm Sunday serving tray, two Tower of Babel candlesticks and a Moses parting the Red Sea spoon rest.

As my eyes adjust to the light, the shadow of Gert fills in. Chenille bathrobe. Hair set in rollers for church tomorrow. Hands folded across the H.B. I think about telling Gert the truth. Reckless as a trip down Mountain Road blindfolded. She is suspicious. Better to give her some tidbit to chew on.

"I had a couple beers. Ruthie didn't. Just me." No use getting her in trouble.

"I knew it." Gert strides over and grabs my face in her right hand. She squeezes so tight my lips purse as if for a kiss. Her fingers press into my jawbones. She sniffs my breath.

I flinch at her proximity. Try to pull away which makes her squeeze all the tighter.

"I would think you could see what beer has done to your father. And yet you insist on going his way." She squeezed tighter. "You ignore the word of God and court the devil." I feel my teeth cut the inside of my mouth. "No doubt he is drunk this very minute." Gert pushes me away from her and I stumble back a few steps.

"You are a dirty sinner. Go take a shower. I don't want your dirty skin touching the clean sheets I put on your bed." Gert heads toward the stairs.

"Oh, and plan on going to church in the morning. The only way you're getting out of it is if you're dead. Your father won't be here in the morning to rescue you either. And another thing, you better not be drinking and driving. Anything happens to the pastor's girl you better hope it happens to you too."

I sit in the shower. Warm water beating on my head. Water sluicing down my face. Rivulets run off my chin and nose. Down my breasts and belly, gathering in the pool made by my crossed legs. I unfold one of Gert's bobby pins. Open it to a forty-five degree angle. Chew off the wax tips thoughtfully placed by the manufacturer to keep Gert from scratching her scalp, when I would gladly dig a trench to her brain. Holding the bobby pin in my right hand, I examine the skin in the crook of my left elbow. So pale. Blue veins trace beneath. How deep?

The bobby pin is sharp against my skin. Not like a razor. A ragged sharp that tears rather than slices. My first cut is two inches long. I cut back over it. Again. Again. Until the skin is gone and the flesh oozes. It doesn't bleed much. What blood there is comes out red. I think it should be black and thick. Like roofing tar. It doesn't hurt. I am not surprised. I am numb. Made of wood. Or Styrofoam.

I wonder if I cut myself enough that sooner or later I will feel it. Eventually it will reach the one last nerve that Gert has not worn away and I will be able to cry in pain. But that won't be tonight. I wash the wound before I get out of the shower. And my bobby pin too. Who named it Bobby? Why not Joe? Why not Jennifer?

I turn off the shower and step onto the bath mat. I wipe off the foggy full-length mirror on the back of the bathroom door. All I can see is an angry slash. I save the bobby pin for another night and go to bed with my skin still damp.

Estelle and I dragged ourselves into Gert's house after the seven to nine p.m. shift at Healey's. Estelle was speechless. Maybe would be for the rest of her life. Delicious could act, on the unsuspecting brain, like a neurological event. A glitch that made half the body unresponsive, speech an impossibility.

It was my fault. I hadn't warned her enough. Hadn't used language blunt enough. Not enough adjectives or the right kinds of nouns. Never said how far Delicious could push. Cutting had been one of my coping mechanisms growing up. Thankfully, no longer necessary. My liberation, years of therapy and Estelle had insured that. Now, I coped with black tea and the occasional vat of hot buttered popcorn.

I put on the teakettle. It may have been seventy-five degrees with air thick as carpeting, but hot tea was in order. Estelle stumbled to the kitchen table and sat down. She stared.

"Are those what I think they are?" Estelle murmured.

"Only if you think they're the Ten Commandments."

"Jesus. How did I miss them before?"

"Actually, it was Moses. And you missed them because we were preoccupied with Gert's diary and dinner across the street." I put two tea bags into the teapot.

"Are you hungry, Es?"

"After all those golumpkis?"

I took two cups and an unopened package of Pecan Sandies from the cupboard. There wasn't any popcorn.

"Not that they weren't delicious...they were the best I've ever had. It's just that there were so many of them. And the pickled beets. And the rye bread. I thought I was going to explode."

The water began to boil.

"Then Mrs. Lewkowski brought out that blueberry pie, I've never seen a crust so perfect, I almost died..."

I poured the steaming water into the pot. Gert's Spic and Span-ed linoleum was cool on my feet as I took the tea tray to the table. Estelle ripped open the cookies and crunched one in her mouth.

"That was the best pie I'd ever eaten. Which is really saying something because Nana's pie could make a girl swoon. How I managed to eat that slab of pie she cut for me is really beyond my comprehension." Estelle popped the rest of the cookie in her mouth.

"...really the nicest people. Your friend Mavis is very sweet and is engaged to a handsome—she showed me a picture, guy who owns a bunch of greenhouses. Did you know she's a landscape architect? They hope to expand his business to include landscape design. So, I told her about our problem with that mountain ash. She thinks it might be fire blight or something like that." She reached for another cookie.

"It's the weirdest thing, babe, but I've craved nothing but carbohydrates since I drove into this town."

I poured us each a cup. The air was so humid the steam was unable to rise and hung over the table like a fog bank.

"Good thing there's no pizza place because I'd be snarfing

down a party-sized pepperoni right now." The cookie crunching seemed loud in the room.

"You know, Es, you don't have to come to the funeral tomorrow if you don't want to. I'd understand. Tonight's wake was enough for anyone. Especially after the two Joannes showed up. To say nothing of my brother-in-law decking the Antichrist." I blew across my cup.

"Don't forget the Caravan of Queers. That's what Di called the entourage. It was nice of them to come."

"Nice, but uncomfortable. It reminded me of the early days of the Northampton Pride parade when all those born-agains would show up and chant at us about burning in hell. It brought up my lesbian separatist hackles."

"You know, Jenn. It is good for these people to see that there are all kinds of people in the world. They experienced everything from a hypocritical minister to a busload of lesbians and all in one evening, in their own little town. I am sorry the strain of it all made your sister pass out. Oh, and let's not forget about the diary. It must have been more than she could tolerate."

"I thought Jimmy would die when Jo offered to help him carry Dorothy out to his truck." I laughed, remembering the look on my brother-in-law's face.

Estelle giggled. "I can still hear her say, 'Hey, man, can I help you get the little lady out to the truck?'"

We both laughed.

"I think he surprised himself by clocking the Antichrist. I know he surprised me. I'll never call him goofball again."

"So, that old guy who offered to pray for Dorothy was the minister you tried to kill all those years ago?"

"Yes, that was my buddy the Antichrist. Pastor Jameson to those who don't know him so well." I sipped. The tea was perfect.

"Your brother-in-law punching him in the nose was the best thing that could've happened. Though, having met Jimmy I'm surprised he accepted your version of events."

"It's all there in Gert's handwriting. Besides, he's looking for someone to blame. I still don't understand why the Antichrist did what he did. There's something more going on here."

"I agree. If this were a mystery novel we'd only be two-thirds along. And it would be impossible to put the book down."

I finished my tea. "Anyway, you really don't have to go tomorrow. You've already won the good girlfriend award."

"Are you kidding? And miss something?" Estelle broke a Sandie in half. "And what about that mortician? He looked like a cast member from *The Munsters*. I expected 'Thing' to pop up at any time."

"Wait until you see the Fry-Your-Ass Federated."

"The what?"

"The Delicious Trinity Federated Church. Where Baptists sit on the right of the aisle and Congregationalists sit on the left."

"I don't think I should miss it. Besides I don't want to stay in this house alone. It's creepier here than at Healey's." Estelle knocked back her tea like it was a shot of bourbon.

CHAPTER THIRTY-THREE

The edges of the old cardboard suitcases were frayed. Indistinct. Blending into the gray painted wood floor of Gert's attic. Estelle was sleeping downstairs on the makeshift bed we'd constructed from the couch and chair cushions. Sleeping was something I should have been doing but there was no way I'd be able to sleep tonight. I waited until Estelle was drugged by her carbohydrate bonanza, and went in search of Gert's other diaries. I was sure Estelle had been right when she said that there had to be others.

I opened all five suitcases. There they were. Packed so carefully. Each wrapped, like a gift from the great beyond, in white tissue paper. All labeled. A complete set from 1945 through the fifties. Nothing from the sixties and a few from each of the seventies, eighties and nineties.

I was overwhelmed.

Where to begin? Should I employ the random open-a-book-and-point method? Gert's favored technique where the H.B. was concerned. No morning passed, no breakfast complete without the suitcase-sized King James being brought to the table and plunked down amidst the plates of French toast or fried eggs. Gert would raise her eyes to the heavens or maybe it was the oracle of the overhead light fixture and beseech the Lamb of God, the Savior of the Unredeemed, the Big Kahuna to bless us with His Guidance for the day.

I was able to open 1945 after performing the boning knife surgery taught to me by Estelle. The breath caught in my throat when I saw Gert's writing. It looked juvenile and innocent.

January 1st

Daddy gave me this here diary for Christmas. I also got a flannel nightgown and a book of morning devotionals. Grown-up gifts for a grown-up daughter Daddy said. I know I am sixteen on my last birthday but don't feel so grownup. Maybe I will eventually. I don't have much to say except these are my New Year's resolutions.

1.) Memorize a Bible verse every day.

2.) Help Mother in the kitchen without being asked.

3.) Continue on the honor roll at school.

4.) Write every day in this diary. I can't think of anymore now except trying to be good but that's not really a resolution.

Gerty

Gerty? I felt a shiver up my spine. It was hard trying to imagine my mother at sixteen. It seemed like she'd been born as Gert. Gert of the furrowed eyebrows and curled lip. But, here she was. Receiver of flannel and morning devotionals. Honor roll student. Doer of kitchen chores. Diary keeper.

I rewrapped 1945 and put it back. I wanted to read more. At least I thought I did. After reading January first I felt like something was holding me back. Maybe it was the privacy aspect of diary keeping. After all, these were Gert's private thoughts. Though this one had been innocuous enough, I felt pretty sure that future entries might not be. I was very well acquainted with her public thoughts and those were terrifying. I didn't know if I had the fortitude to find out what she was really thinking.

Maybe she was nice underneath it all. A sweet woman who was so sensitive she had to armor herself with bitterness and anger to get by in the world. Hah! I sat under the glare of a 100-watt bulb and listened to moths throwing themselves against the screen like kamikaze fighter pilots.

Gert was dead. If she hadn't wanted this stuff found she would've burned it all before she had her date with the crossbeam in the barn. I snatched 1979 from the suitcase, the year of my emancipation when I watched Delicious recede in my rearview mirror for the last time. I flipped to June seventeenth. The day after Ruthie's wedding. The day I was sprung from jail. The day I received my walking papers.

Gert's handwriting had changed into that odd combination of cursive and printing I recognized from the 1998 edition. She had pressed down so hard on the page it was lumpy. I ran my fingertips over it as though I were blind. Trying to find my way.

June 17, 1979
Dear God,
Pastor Jameson was as good as his word and didn't press charges. He isn't always. Sometimes he forgets that a deal is a deal. Jennifer came home and I had everything ready for her to leave. I told her to get out. She's always wanted to go so she was glad and I was too. It'll be easier for everybody with her gone. Jennifer doesn't belong in Delicious. It's the kind of place that will chew you up and spit you out if you don't belong. After she drove off I polished the silverware and cleaned the oven. Dorothy invited me for supper. Her chicken croquettes were a bit salty but she tries hard.
Your faithful servant,
Gertrude Spencer Andersen

What deal had she made with the Antichrist?

June 21, 1979
Dear God,

Pastor Jameson came for his visit today. He wanted what he always wants. Please forgive me, but I hate him. I know You will damn me to Hell. I expect I'll see him in Hell with me. Hopefully he goes first so I can get some peace on this earth. But he won't. That's how life is. Sometimes I wished he wanted money. That's when he laughs and says it's easier for a camel to get through the eye of a needle than it is for a rich man to get into the kingdom of heaven. I hope Jennifer is all right. She won't call and I can hardly expect her to. If it hadn't been a Sunday when she left I could have got to the bank and given her more money. No use crying over spilt milk. She'll be better off away from here. First day of summer. I got to get the lawnmower tuned up, it billows smoke something awful.

Your faithful servant,
Gertrude Spencer Andersen

August 4, 1979
Dear God,

Today is Jennifer's birthday. She is 21 years old. I remember when she was born. It took most of a whole day. I knew You were punishing me, God. Her whole life was my punishment. She was different from the get-go. I didn't know how different until Dorothy was born. Jennifer wasn't much of a girl like her sister. Always interested in boy-type things. Bob made it worse taking her with him everywhere. He didn't care what she was like. I tried to keep her in line though I knew it would never work. I know she is the way she is because of me. There's something wrong with the Spencers. Uncle Ralph and his fancy Boston life brought shame to the family. I brought a different kind to the family and continue to. I put up twelve jars of dill pickles. Pastor Jameson is away on retreat for the month of August so I don't have to worry about him.

Gertrude Spencer Andersen

My head was swimming. Reality slipping away. Everything I had thought was true didn't seem to be. Who was Uncle Ralph?

Was he queer? Did she think I caught it because she brought her twisted chromosomes to the hereditary cesspool? Could Gert have hated the Antichrist? Hell? Him? With her?

What was their deal about? Sex? Who would want to have sex with either of them? Could that have been the deal Gert made? He wouldn't press charges if she'd have sex with him? That must have been it. Get me out of town and fuck Gert for payment.

Tears gathered in my eyes.

For my mother.

CHAPTER THIRTY-FOUR

Estelle heard Jennifer clunk down the stairs with a suitcase, tiptoe through the living room and kitchen and let herself out. She heard the familiar purr as the Nova started and alto whine as Jennifer backed out of the driveway and headed off toward town. That girl was just going to drop from exhaustion.

Estelle got up to pee, not bothering to turn on a light. The little ducks that swam across the miniature ponds dotting the café and shower curtains really bugged her. Estelle knew it was irrational, but that cutesy stuff drove her nuts. People rarely matched their décor. Jennifer's mother didn't seem cute at all. Based on what Estelle had seen at Healey's. Of course, the absence of animation would make anyone look severe. Look at what happened to Nana. When she was alive she bore a startling resemblance to a folksier version of Endora on *Bewitched*. After the undertakers got through with her she looked like Granny Clampett from *The Beverly Hillbillies*, with a bouffant.

Estelle had been relieved when Nana came to her in a dream the very night of her funeral. She looked just like her old self except for the navy blue pantsuit Aunt Maureen had insisted Nana wear.

"Can you believe this drab thing I've got to go through Eternity with?" Nana had said. "Why didn't they go with my red one?"

"You know how proper Aunt Maureen can be. Funerals demand black or navy blue," Estelle said.

"You be sure to tell her I would've preferred the red. I can petition for new clothes but it promises to take awhile. No one's in much of a hurry in Eternity." Nana waved goodbye.

Nana visited often but had been conspicuously absent since Estelle's arrival in Delicious.

"What a creepy little town," Estelle said aloud as she flushed.

It was about four thirty a.m., too early to be up but she could tell sleeping was impossible at the moment. She walked through the darkened house. Faded squares of moonlight slanted through the windows and patterned the floor. She felt like she did when she'd visited historical battlefields like Manassas or Lexington and Concord. If she could just listen hard enough she'd be able to hear the battle's roar and the soldiers scream. Those places barely held their ghosts from spilling over into the conscious world. This house was like that.

Last night at dinner with the Lewkowskis they had talked a lot about Jennifer as a kid. She was always outside, as far away from her mother as she could get. Jennifer was invited over, to play, for dinner and sleepovers, as often as it was allowed. But, it never would've been enough. Mavis told Estelle how one night when Jennifer had been sleeping over, an unholy screeching had woken them up. They crept over to Mavis's bedroom window and peeked over the sill to see Jennifer's father cowering on the lawn while her mother beat him with the family Bible.

Mrs. Lewkowski said Jennifer's father was hardly ever home and if he was he was drinking. Mr. Lewkowski said he would, on occasion, run into Bob Andersen down at the VFW in Southwick. They were both veterans of the Korean War. They'd have a couple beers together and watch the game. But, Bob had never said one word about what went on at his house even though everyone knew something was going on. Especially during the warmer weather when the windows were open. Mr. Lewkowski felt it wouldn't be right for him to say anything either though he would mention how Jenny had been over for supper or something. Then Bob's eyes would get teary, though it could've been the lighting, and Bob would thank him for watching over his daughter. That was exactly how he put it too. Watching over his daughter. It was enough to make the very short hairs on Mr. Lewkowski's neck stand on end.

Mrs. Lewkowski told Estelle about the circumstances of Jennifer leaving Delicious. Being Catholics they had not been invited to Ruthie's wedding so they'd missed all the excitement firsthand but Mrs. Lewkowski's friend from the board at the public library, Esther Peabody, had been there and seen it all. Everyone in town had been surprised when Pastor Jameson had declined to press charges and forgave her, publicly, from the pulpit once he'd regained the voice he'd lost from being intubated. By that time Jennifer was long gone, without ever saying goodbye. Mrs. Lewkowski felt just like one of her own daughters had vanished without a trace.

Estelle went upstairs and found the attic door open and the light still on. God, it had to be a thousand degrees up here. There among the Christmas decorations and cardboard boxes were several open suitcases scattered across the dusty floor. Pieces of crunched up tissue paper had been tossed aside. Diaries were stacked up here and there.

Jennifer's mother's diaries.

Estelle could almost hear Nana's voice; "Curiosity killed the cat."

Why didn't Jennifer's mother have the good sense to dispose of them before she hanged herself? There must have been something she wanted someone to find out about. Dorothy didn't seem like the type to snoop around. Could Jennifer's mother have guessed Jennifer would show up for the funeral?

She certainly would've known Jennifer was the type to rummage around where she shouldn't. And leaving her most recent diary in the desk downstairs when that desk would have to be gone through to finalize the estate. It was just the place for those important papers that sum up our lives to be kept. And that last entry. A tip-off to how she planned her body to be discovered. It's almost like Jennifer's mother knew that things weren't going to go according to her plan. That minister had to be at the bottom of this.

Estelle turned off the light, closed the door and made her way back downstairs. She filled a glass with iced water and had a good long drink. Those golumbkis seemed to be stuck, like a family of rats, in her small intestine. She took her glass and went out the back door to the chaise lounge she'd seen on the lawn earlier today. Make that yesterday. Time seemed to be standing still.

The stars were beginning to fade as dawn drew nearer. If Estelle had to guess she'd guess that Jennifer went to see Auntie Potts. They'd met last night after the wake. The woman looked older than dirt. If anyone knew the truth it would be her.

Estelle stretched her legs out and wiggled her toes. The back lawn was very peaceful with the mourning doves cooing in the underbrush. Imagine the gardens you could grow here. She thought of the flowers in the gardens at home and missed their cheerful faces even though she could see their cousins around her here and there. This place was a postcard promoting the benefits of country life. She put her glass down on the lawn and closed her eyes inviting sleep to come to her.

"Let me tell you," Nana said from her spot on the old tire swing that hung from the silver maple. The old rope creaked in the breeze coming up with the sun. "That woman is a strange one."

"Nana what are you doing here now? You usually visit when I'm asleep." Estelle's eyes snapped open as she sat up straighter in the chaise lounge.

"Waking and sleeping—there's really not much difference." Nana swung her feet.

Estelle noticed she was wearing different shoes. Gone were

the navy blue pumps with the sensible one-inch heels, replaced by a pair of flip-flops with a big plastic flower across the top.

"What woman is strange?"

"Jennifer's mother. Crazy as a bedbug. She's running all over the place looking for God. Jesus in particular. She had to be sedated. I don't know what makes her think he's here."

"But, Nana, most people think God is in heaven." Estelle watched the sun glitter through Nana's white hair.

"Now, Estelle honey, I never said I was in heaven."

Estelle thought about it. "I guess you're right. You've always said eternity."

"Exactly. There is a big difference."

Estelle reached for her glass and sipped her iced water. Her hands were shaking. This was the weirdest visitation she'd ever experienced. It seemed so real.

"Explain it to me, Nana."

"Heaven is something invented by people to keep them from being afraid when they die. Eternity is what God is." Nana got off the swing and joined Estelle on the chaise lounge. "Jennifer's mother is in Eternity looking for God when God *is* Eternity. It's like looking for the ocean when you're swimming in it."

"Oh," Estelle said.

"It's a mind blower isn't it, honey." Nana patted Estelle's foot. "I like this color pink on your toenails."

"Thanks Nana. Will Jennifer's mother be all right?"

"Oh, probably. After a while. Folks like her have quite a period of adjustment. Sometimes they have to take a workshop in Existential Philosophy or Abstract Painting. I was a little befuddled until I took up Topiary Sculpture."

"I'm worried about Jennifer and those diaries, Nana."

"I imagine you are, honey."

"Any suggestions?"

"Just remember, sweetheart. The truth is relative."

"To what?"

"To who is doing the telling." Nana's gray eyes were bright.

"Are you sure, Nana? Isn't truth a constant and people's perception of it the variable?"

"That's what people think while they're alive. When you're

dead you'll see that truth is like that ocean we were talking about. Shifting. High tide and low tide. Never the same from one moment to the next."

"That's unsettling."

"I know, honey. It's a lot to get your mind around. Tell Jennifer what I said. Maybe it'll help."

"Okay, Nana." Estelle couldn't imagine what that conversation would be like.

"Well, sweetheart, I've got to go. I'm playing in a badminton tournament and I have to stretch my hamstrings before we start."

At least Eternity didn't sound boring. "Bye, Nana. See you later."

"You betcha'." Nana blew Estelle a kiss and was gone.

Estelle blinked hard. Awake or asleep, she decided she'd wait for Jennifer right where she was even though things didn't seem as peaceful as they had a little while ago.

CHAPTER THIRTY-FIVE

Auntie Potts woke with a start. Had there been a noise or something? And she was dreaming so good too. Something about a cookout. There were hundreds of big, fat bratwursts spitting and popping on a Weber grill the size of a kid's wading pool. There it was again. Someone was banging on her front door. Jeez Louise, what time was it? Auntie squinted at her alarm clock. Four thirty a.m? Could that be right? She blinked hard and shook her head. Yep. Four thirty. Auntie fumbled for her bathrobe.

Who the hell would be waking her up so damn early? She squinted through her curtains toward her gas station across the street. There was no glow. At least the place wasn't on fire. Hopefully it wasn't the cops reporting a break-in like two summers ago when the Lessardi brothers got pissant drunk and ran out of cigarettes. They broke her plate-glass window looking for their Camels. Auntie hadn't pressed charges, just made them fix it and scrape and paint the gas station a pink color that stood out so nice.

More banging on the door.

"All right! I'm coming!" she yelled out her open window before heading downstairs.

Auntie flicked on the porch light. There was Jenny Andersen holding a big, old suitcase. Had she had a fight with that nice woman Estelle and come to stay the night?

"Good morning, Jenny. What brings you by so early?" Auntie held the door open.

"I know it's early, Auntie. I'm sorry. I, well, it's kind of hard to explain." Jenny plunked the suitcase down on the floor.

Auntie gave Jenny the once-over. Goodness sakes, the girl looked like hell. Eyes all bloodshot like she'd been crying, wearing a ratty T-shirt and a pair of gym shorts. Barefoot. Hair sticking out all over her head like a cartoon character who'd been electrocuted.

"How about I make a pot of coffee. If we got to be up this early we might as well have some." Auntie headed toward the kitchen waving Jenny along behind her.

Coffee should be made proper or it shouldn't be made at all. That's why it was important to start out with cold water. Auntie let the water run while she filled up the basket with four scoops of the Maxwell House. She didn't hold with paper filters. What was the matter with a few coffee grounds anyway and, besides, she swore they diluted the coffee until all you had was a cup of brown water. At least that part of things she could control. What she couldn't control and what really drove her nuts was how they'd whittled a pound of coffee down to 11.5 ounces and for the same amount of money. Just who did they think they were kidding?

After the water was good and cold she filled up the percolator to just below its spout. She put the basket on its leg and put it inside the pot and snapped the lid on, making sure the glass bulb was tight. Auntie lit the stove and put the pot on the burner. Seven minutes after it came to the boil she and Jenny would have themselves a couple cups of the nectar of the gods. She got two mugs and the sugar bowl out of the cabinet and the carton of heavy cream out of the fridge and put them on the table.

Doc Delerzon was after her to use that light half & half. He told her there was too much fat in the heavy cream she was so fond of. Auntie had thought about it long and hard and decided there wasn't much point in living if she couldn't have her coffee the way she liked it. No amount of light half & half was going to keep her from dying. Besides, it was going to take all her willpower to give up the Lucky Strikes.

Auntie watched the clock. At the conclusion of the seventh minute she removed the coffee from the heat, filled the mugs and poured the leftovers into her thermos. Actually it was Max's old thermos but he had no use for it. She added cream to her cup and waited for Jenny to start talking.

"Did you know Gert kept diaries?" Jenny bent over and opened the suitcase. It was jammed with the little books. "These are just a few of them."

Looked like Gertrude kept a lot of diaries.

"Nope. I had no idea." Auntie took her first sip. Now all she needed was a cigarette. She'd try to wait. It wasn't even five a.m. and she had to ration them out.

"I found them in the attic and I started reading..."

Gosh darn it, wasn't life funny. If you told her a couple days ago that she'd be sitting here having coffee with Jenny she never would've believed it. She reminded her so much of Bob. It was almost like he was sitting across the table having coffee. Though to be honest she rarely saw him drink anything other than Budweiser. Poor son-of-a-gun. Auntie sure hoped Jenny was happier than Bob had ever been. His drowning had never set right. She had no trouble believing he was drunk, but he was always drunk so he'd have been used to it. Besides, why would he have parked his truck so close to the pond that when he fell he'd hit his head on the front bumper?

Auntie had even gone so far as to talk to Trout Sussman about it. He thought it was strange too because most times Bob had been there fishing he'd park under the trees where the dirt road ended about a hundred feet back from the pond. He'd take his cooler and pole and walk to the water and sit under a weeping willow on the south side of the pond. Trout also said that once Bob was so drunk he drove the front wheels into the pond and then had a hell of a time getting them out of the mud. Maybe it was just that some things, when they happened, were just too hard to take. So we looked for reasons when, sometimes, there just weren't any. Except bad luck.

"...Some kind of deal with Pastor Jameson all those years ago. To say nothing about what he did Saturday morning to Dorothy..."

Nothing Pastor did surprised Auntie. He was one of those preachers who thought he was better than everybody else was because he was a pastor. Look at what he did to his poor wife. There she was sick with that ovarian cancer and him not wanting her to have any more treatment because it meant she'd have to stay in Boston and he'd have to manage the house and Ruthie, who couldn't have been more than eight at the time, and his congregation. Mrs. Jameson had told Auntie on one of the last good days when she'd walked around the town green for exercise and had to stop for a breather at the gas station, that the prayers the pastor was treating her with didn't seem to be working.

"...Looking at their wedding picture last night and finding all that stuff about Lou Gehrig's. Anyway Dad always joked about Grandpa Spencer and his deer rifle making him marry Gert because she was pregnant. According to the diary she was pregnant, but not by my father."

Jeez Louise.

"Listen to this. 'Robert Andersen caught me throwing up behind the bushes at the town barn where we wait for the school bus to take us to the regional high school. I told him I had the grippe. He looked like he didn't believe me.'"

The hell with it, Auntie thought as she got up and took a fresh pack of Lucky Strikes out of the carton she kept in the fridge. This was going to be a day when there wasn't enough nicotine in all the world.

CHAPTER THIRTY-SIX

I watched Auntie light her cigarette from a kitchen match she got from a tin dispenser screwed to the wall near the stove. The rasp of the match head and hiss as the flame consumed oxygen were as loud as a church bell. Sulfur overpowered the smell of coffee for a moment.

"Your daddy wasn't Dorothy's daddy."

"What?" I couldn't have heard what I just heard.

"That grippe your mother wrote about was morning sickness." Smoke curled out of Auntie's mouth like her insides were on fire.

"Have some coffee, Jenny. Sometimes it's a help to do something normal when you're hearing things you can't believe."

The coffee was hot silk against my mouth and throat.

"I never understood why Bob married her except that he felt bad for her."

I didn't know where I was anymore. Auntie's kitchen surrounded me but none of it seemed real. Like maybe if I turned around real quick I'd see the lights and camera behind me and I'd know that I was filming a movie.

"I'm probably not telling this story very well. That's the thing about secrets. They always come out and usually when you aren't expecting it." Auntie poured herself some more coffee.

"Start at the beginning. Please." I held onto the coffee mug.

"Your mother's family, the Spencers, were real religious. Her father was a deacon in the Federated Church. There was no smoking or drinking in his home. He didn't believe in dancing or card playing. Old Man Spencer was wound tighter than a watch spring. Anyway, back in the late forties the church was looking for a new minister. The old one had a heart attack while he was taking his morning constitutional around the town green. That's when Pastor Jameson came to town."

"The Antichrist," I whispered.

"The what?" Auntie ground her cigarette out in the ashtray.

"Antichrist."

"Well, that's closer to the truth than you probably know." Auntie lit herself another cigarette.

"Old Man Spencer thought Jameson was the best thing since Wonder Bread. Religious as all get out, on the surface anyway. And in those days he was good looking though you wouldn't know it to see him now."

I watched the fingers that held her Lucky Strike tremble.

"He wasn't married either. His sermons were all fire and brimstone. Max and I went to church when he first moved into town. But, he was a little too hell and damnation for our blood. Anyway, he'd get people whipped up into a frenzy. Soon all them married women around town were bringing by pies and casseroles and fighting over who was going to clean the parsonage and do his laundry."

My skin began to crawl.

"After Max got himself crushed by that car Pastor Jameson started sniffing around here." Auntie stared off into space like she was seeing it all again. "I told him where the bear shit in the buckwheat and that put a stop to it. Anyway, Bob used to stop by when Max was alive and hang around the garage after school. He liked to tinker with cars. After Max died he continued to come and help me out. We got to be friends and stayed friends over the years. That's how come I know so much about your mother and father."

"Who was my father?" I asked.

"Now, don't rush me, Jenny. Let me get this out in my own way." Auntie took a last drag and crushed her second cigarette out next to the first.

I felt my heart rate pick up. Sweat popped out across my upper lip.

"After about two weeks of Gertrude puking behind the bushes, Bob finally put two and two together and asked if she was pregnant. Gertrude burst into tears and got so hysterical he took her into the woods near the town barn where the kids waited for the school bus to take them to the regional high school. There was an old road back there that led to nowhere about a mile in. That's where they dumped all the old town equipment that wasn't worth fixing anymore. Anyway, they missed the bus. While they waited for the bus to come back at the end of school, Gertrude told your father the story." Auntie lit another Lucky.

"Pastor Jameson had planned to take Gertrude and her sister Gladys to a Bible study at Calvary Baptist Church in Westfield. He'd been in seminary with the minister there. It was sort of a reward for memorizing Psalms. Anyway, the Wednesday night they were supposed to go, Gladys sprained her ankle when she tripped over the laundry basket hanging up the wash. Gertrude was very disappointed because she knew her father would never let her go alone, without a chaperone. Old Man Spencer surprised her when he sent her off with his blessing. On their way back to Delicious, Pastor pulled off Mountain Road onto an old logging road..."

It had to be the same road Ruthie and I used to go to. I shivered to think of it.

"...And had his way with her."

"Jesus," I murmured. It was hard to believe and easy to believe.

"Your mother was scared her father would find out she was pregnant. Scared the pastor would find out and want to marry her when she hated his guts. She didn't know what to do."

"And Dad married her because he felt sorry for her."

"That's what he always said." Auntie sipped her coffee.

"Then she had a miscarriage and Dad stayed married to her anyway?"

"Not quite, Jenny."

"What do you mean, not quite."

"There was no miscarriage. You were that baby."

No miscarriage. That meant that…

"Oh my God! The Antichrist is my father?" I jerked to my feet.

"Jenny. Now calm down…"

"Calm down! Calm down? How can I…"

"I know it wasn't what you were expecting to hear. But…"

"But what? This is worse than having a brain tumor," I screeched, amazed that my voice sounded like metal grinding metal. "Auntie, do you know how much I hate him? Have hated him my whole life. Gert always said I was Satan's spawn. The thing is it isn't far from the truth!"

I flung myself across the kitchen and out the back door to the porch.

I thought I was going to puke. Saliva pooled in my mouth and several gulping breaths quieted my rebellious stomach. I could vomit for the next twenty years and never purge the Antichrist from my system.

"How're you doing, kid?" Auntie joined me on the back porch.

"I don't know yet."

"Bob Anderson raised you like his own daughter. You seemed so much like him sometimes growing up that I'd forget. Even now there's something about your expressions that remind me of him. He did right by you. Pastor Jameson was no more than a sperm donor." Auntie rested her hand on my shoulder.

"I know you're right. Except…that means…" I stopped talking. How much did Auntie know about Ruthie and me? I turned away and puked into Auntie's lilac bush.

"Come on now, Jenny. You come on in the house and lie down a minute."

I allowed her to lead me into the house like the catatonic mental patient I felt I was becoming. The reality I'd grown up believing, was so sure of, wasn't reality at all. Now something else was true but felt as surreal as a dripping clock painting. I couldn't decide which was worse. My paternity or my years-long affair with my own sister. Half sister, really, but that was hardly enough for a margin of error.

Auntie helped me lie down on a daybed in her living room. I closed my eyes.

"So, that story Dad told about his shotgun wedding wasn't true."

"Oh, it was in a way. Except Old Man Spencer was pointing his deer rifle at the wrong man."

"Do you know why the Antichrist didn't press charges when I tried to drown him? Gert's diary indicates that the two of them made a deal."

"Only a guess. The Antichrist," she chuckled under her breath, "stayed away from Gertrude as long as Bob was alive. But, afterwards...well, I think he saw an opportunity and took it."

"Do you think the Antichrist killed Dad?" I opened my eyes and looked at Auntie. She didn't seem surprised by my question. Could that old hypocrite have wanted access to Gert that badly?

"Now, it's funny you should bring that up. I was just thinking about that this morning." Auntie settled herself on a hassock next to the daybed. "It never set right with me, Bob dying the way he did. Don't take this wrong, Jenny, but he was used to being drunk. He lived his life drunk. I always wondered about him being drunk enough to kill himself doing something he had done so many times before, if you know what I mean. I'm probably not saying it right."

"I know what you mean. He could cut out checkers on his jigsaw after drinking all day."

"But, Jenny, anything can happen once. Like Max getting crushed by that car. Sometimes the truth is terrible."

"Does the Antichrist know I'm his daughter?"

"I'm sure he don't. That was one thing Gertrude and Bob agreed on." Auntie rubbed my knee and disappeared toward the kitchen.

I listened to her do dishes and go upstairs and have a shower. I got up and put the diaries back in the suitcase and snapped the lid shut. I didn't know what I expected the truth to be but it sure wasn't this.

When Auntie came back downstairs dressed for a funeral I told her about Gert's last diary entry.

"I'll be damned." Auntie poured herself a half cup and held the thermos in my direction.

"No thanks." I shook my head. "I better get back. Estelle will be wondering where I am. Thank you for letting me in and talking. And thanks for the coffee."

"You're welcome, Jenny. You going to be all right?"

I took a deep breath. My lungs worked.

"I'll be better when all this is over," I said, even while I wondered if anything was ever really over.

"Estelle?" I shouted opening the door. Jesus, where was she? I ran into the living room expecting to see her curled on our makeshift bed asleep. Not there and not in the bathroom either. I looked out the kitchen window and there she was, sitting in the chaise lounge I'd spent the night before on, sipping tea and staring at the tire swing with an unusual intensity. I rushed out the back door.

"Estelle!"

"Hey, babe." She smiled and swung her legs to the side so I could sit down.

"Nana was just here. She said your mother's having a terrible time in Eternity."

"I'm not surprised. She had a terrible time on earth," I said, reaching for Estelle's cup and taking a sip.

"Did you know I slept out here last night?" I said, putting her legs in my lap.

"I'm not surprised. Your mother's house has ghosts."

I nodded. I knew about those ghosts.

"So, did you take the diaries to Auntie's?"

I didn't bother asking how she knew I'd found my mother's diaries or how she'd known I'd been at Auntie's. Estelle was one of those people who knew things without being told.

"Yes. I figured if anyone knew the truth, it'd be her. I'll have to send her a gift certificate for a carton of cigarettes or five pounds of coffee. I woke her up." I rubbed my eyes. They felt like they were made of hot sand.

"What did she say?"

"The long and short of it is the Antichrist is my father..."

"Your father?"

"Which, unbelievably, isn't the worst thing..." I sipped more tea, hoping whatever was growing in my throat would wash away.

"There's something worse than having a rapist for a father..."

"He raped your mother?"

"That's what she told Bob Andersen who told Auntie."

"What's worse than that?" Estelle asked.

I didn't really know how to articulate the notion...well, it was more than a notion, it was fact. Sweaty, grappling adolescent fact.

"Wait a minute," Estelle said. "Wasn't your high school sweetheart the pastor's daughter?"

I nodded, relieved that I didn't have to say it aloud. Now if I could just quiet it down inside my own head.

"Wow." Estelle whistled under her own breath.

"Icky isn't it?"

"Icky is the least of it." Estelle sat up and scooted around until we were sitting side by side.

"It's amazing the secrets we keep isn't it?" Estelle murmured.

"What's amazing is that people bother with them at all. Truth always finds its way out, no matter how deep you think you've buried it."

"I know. I remember Nana saying once that secrets take hostages." Estelle folded my hand in hers.

"I guess I now know why Gert never loved me. How could she?"

Estelle kissed my palm.

"In a way, babe, this has nothing to do with you. You were the innocent here. Just a baby trying to get herself born. It's on the adults in our lives to love us and care for us when we're young, no matter the circumstances. And when they don't it's because of them and their own shortcomings, not about the innocent child. Unfortunately, the innocent child lives with the effects of whatever shit storm they were raised in."

"And the therapy bills," I said.

"And the therapy bills." Estelle traced my lifeline with her fingertip.

"People make their own way, are on their own path and for the most part, do the best they can. Your dad, Bob Andersen, is an example of that, not perfect but he tried. Your mother was a victim and she could never escape from that. And the pastor is an example of someone who has very little redeeming value. It's best to ignore them as much as possible."

"I'd say the Antichrist has made ignoring him just about impossible," I said.

We both stared off into space. Estelle toward the tire swing and me toward the barn.

"She was more trapped than I was," I said.

"What do you mean?"

"It's dangerous growing up in a small town like Delicious when you're different. I knew I was queer from before I even had words for it. I knew I'd never belong and so I never expected to. Gert must have thought that if she did everything right, went to church and was a good girl that she'd always belong. She must have woken up many a morning wondering what she had ever done to deserve such an unhappy life." I kissed Estelle's shoulder.

"Anyway, I escaped. Granted, I almost committed murder to do it...but, Gert, she never got away. I think her life might've been different if she had. She never had a chance."

We sat together, thigh to thigh.

"I remember looking up homosexuality in the Encyclopedia

Britannica at the Delicious Public Library. I was probably twelve or thirteen," I said.

"Hmmm?" Estelle squinted at me.

"That's when I found out I was a sexual deviant. I had to consult Webster's to find out what deviant meant though somehow I knew it wasn't good."

Estelle chuckled.

"What?" I asked.

"Goodness, babe, I wonder what Mr. Webster and the Encyclopedia Britannica would say about this latest development?" She burst out laughing.

I started laughing too. Like my heart would break.

CHAPTER THIRTY-SEVEN

Herlick liberally sprinkled his torso and genitals with a generic brand of medicated powder. He loved that medicinal odor. The morning news was predicting standard issue weather for July in New England, a seventh day of heat and humidity with possible thunderstorms. Prickly heat could take off like wildfire if proper precautions weren't taken. He sprayed his underarms with a double application of Right Guard. Cotton underwear was essential, as well as a liberal sprinkle of anti-fungal powder in his shoes. This insured a calm and collected demeanor throughout a funeral and interment.

Herlick dressed except for his tie and jacket. Those he carried downstairs to the kitchen and draped over a kitchen chair. He was hungry this morning and contemplated bacon and scrambled eggs. But, that might be too heavy for the weather.

A bowl of cornflakes and a banana would do. He flicked on the coffeemaker. It began to gurgle and soon the smell of coffee filled the kitchen. If only there were no funeral today Herlick might consider taking a drive into the Berkshires and looking through some antique stores and stopping by to see his friend from funeral director's school, Nathan LaValley, who operated a funeral home in Lenox.

While the coffee was dripping he decided to see how Mrs. Andersen had fared the night. He was never so relieved as he was last night when he locked the door on the last of her mourners. The busload of queers had nearly worn away his professional demeanor. He had a disconcerting moment when he wondered if he was going to laugh out loud. Fortunately, by biting the inside of his cheeks, he'd managed to retain decorum.

He turned on the overhead lights in the Everlasting Life Room and lifted the sheet he was in the habit of laying over the deceased when no visitors were expected. A little trick he learned from his father. "You never know what will fall from above, my boy," Harrison had told Herlick when he was still in high school. He had also learned not to seal the casket too soon. Family members often woke up the morning of the funeral with a desire to see their loved one, one last time. Thank goodness, there were no ants meandering on or about Mrs. Andersen. The boric acid must have done its job. He would enjoy telling Nathan that story. Perhaps today's proceedings would end early enough and he could drive out there. Nathan's vodka martini was without compare. Herlick would just have to see how things went. He lowered the lid of the coffin and wheeled Mrs. Andersen out of the viewing room and down the hall to the service door. He'd have his breakfast and then load her in.

The cuckoo clock cuckooed seven times just as Herlick was finishing his second cup of coffee. He stacked his dishes in the sink, took the keys for the hearse and went back to Mrs. Andersen. No one had called and, since the funeral was at nine o'clock, he thought it safe to seal her inside. Once that was done he maneuvered out the utility door and down the ramp to the hearse. He unlocked the rear door and was just ready to slide her inside when he noticed the tire. Left rear all-season radial as flat as a pancake.

Herlick looked at his watch. seven twenty. One hour and forty minutes to get Mrs. Andersen and her flowers to the Federated Church. Plenty of time. It brought to mind another tidbit from his father. "Always start early, son. You never know what's going to happen." Fortunately he had a portable, hand-operated, hydraulic jack. So he should have more than enough time. Though the thought of an undersized temporary donut-tire on a hearse made Herlick very uncomfortable.

Ruthie lay naked on her childhood twin bed in the breeze manufactured by the oscillating fan. The air was humid and smelled like rain. Goodness, what she wouldn't give for central air like they had in Albany. The absence of it made getting ready almost impossible. She would perspire in the shower. Her hair would be frizzy no matter how much Hurricane Hold she used. TheWay's Marathon Magic antiperspirant and deodorant would be hard pressed to be effective much beyond midafternoon. Well, she would just have to make do. Fortunately, her daffodil yellow, sleeveless linen dress was cool though not quite appropriate for funeral wear. The black costume jewelry should tone it down a bit.

Ruthie got up and made the bed. Just moving that little bit caused sweat to gather under her breasts. Today promised to be tedious and now, with Daddy's injured nose, she wouldn't be able to leave later this afternoon as she had hoped.

The doctor at the emergency room at Baystate Hospital in Springfield said it wasn't broken, just severely bruised. There wasn't much to be done except ibuprofen and ice packs. By the time Ruthie had brought him home last night, he was getting two black eyes and was talking like he had a terrible head cold.

Whatever had come over Dorothy's husband Jimmy to punch Daddy in the nose? Jimmy was a deacon after all. Perhaps it was stress. Daddy said Jimmy had cut down Mrs. Andersen's body. That would be enough to make anyone edgy. Though

Jimmy's comment, "She kept a diary, asshole. It's all there," made absolutely no sense. Herlick finally pulled him off Daddy and escorted Jimmy outside while two of those lesbians carried Dorothy, who was still woozy from fainting, to the truck.

Daddy had lain on the floor, his nose streaming blood, in shock and murmuring "diary" over and over while she'd held a wad of Kleenex under his nose. Herlick appeared with an ice pack wrapped in a kitchen towel and helped her get Daddy up and into a chair in the foyer while she ran to get her van and bring it to the utility entrance so she could load him in for the trip to the hospital.

What a fiasco.

CHAPTER THIRTY-EIGHT

The Federated Church smelled like mildew. A twelve-foot cross was suspended from the wall behind the pulpit. Unrelenting morning sunlight poured through the stained glass windows and made a colorful pattern on the worn oak floor.

"How old is this place?" Estelle whispered as we walked down the center aisle.

"Probably close to two hundred," I whispered as we approached the pew Herlick indicated we were to sit in. My mother's casket was front and center, covered in a spray of white gladiolas and pink carnations. Dorothy and Jimmy were already seated. I nodded to Auntie Potts sitting two pews behind my sister and brother-in-law. We slid into the pew behind them. They turned around and nodded to us. I noticed the knuckles on Jimmy's right hand were bandaged. I couldn't get over him clocking the Antichrist the way he had. I thought he would toe the party line but he hadn't. Jimmy really loved my sister and while I wished she had been the one to throw the punch, this was the next best thing. Dorothy's face was a mask. The dark circles under her eyes were painful to look at.

Mrs. Earle, wearing a sedate navy blue muumuu, entered from a side door and went to the organ. She boosted herself onto the bench and began to play a hymn that sounded vaguely familiar but that I couldn't really place. The fact that I couldn't remember it relaxed the tightness in my chest. Apparently, forgetting was possible. I wasn't sure about forgiveness.

The side door opened again revealing the Antichrist, resplendent in black robes and two black eyes. His nose looked like a rotting eggplant. Mrs. Earle glanced toward him after he finally tottered his way to the pulpit. She began to play "Amazing Grace." What else? The congregation stood and began to sing. We were midway through the second stanza when the organ took a deep breath and wheezed to a shuddering stop. I could see Mrs. Earle tapping her patent leathered toes against the pedals. The organ inhaled and intoned a couple of minor notes before it stuttered to a stop. She threw a switch. Pushed a couple buttons. Nothing she did helped. The organ had died.

Estelle nudged me and whispered, "I wonder what this means?"

Good question.

The congregation struggled on, warbling through the remaining stanzas, but with none of the vigor they'd had before the organ bit the dust. Maybe it was my imagination but I could feel the wave of discomfort ripple through the congregation behind me. I watched the Antichrist in his pulpit, chicken neck sticking out of his ministerial collar, Adam's apple bobbing up and down as he tried to sing and think of a way to work the expired organ into the funeral sermon. He'd have to; it was kind of hard to ignore.

Estelle looked at me and raised her left eyebrow. That meant she had something to say but was going to wait until we were alone. Probably her interpretation on this latest symbolism presented to us by the universe. Estelle would never believe the organ had simply worn out.

"We have come here today to say farewell to our sister, Gertrude Andersen..."

If I were my mother my blood would be boiling, listening to that blackmailing, hypocritical asshole giving my eulogy.

"A tireless servant to our Lord and Savior, Jesus Christ, a devoted wife, mother and friend, a good woman, who struggled with her faith as we all struggle with our faith. 'For God so loved the world that he gave his only begotten...'"

The organ inhaled and sighed. Mrs. Earle shrieked and fell backward off the bench. Dorothy burst into tears. I suddenly had to pee, urgently. All that coffee at Auntie's and tea with Estelle had finally caught up with me.

"I'm going to the bathroom. I'll be right back," I whispered to Estelle.

"Are you okay?"

I nodded and rushed out of the sanctuary.

I pushed open the door marked Mary's and hurried into one of the stalls. Not two seconds later the door opened filling the bathroom with the cloying perfume I recognized from yesterday's wake.

"Jennifer?"

Yep. I was right. Ruthie.

Just what I needed.

"Yes?"

"Are you okay? You rushed out and I thought you might need some help."

If there were anybody I would want help from, it would not be Ruthie.

"I'm just fine," I said as I squinted through the gap in the door. Maybe if I took long enough she'd take her yellow self and leave.

"I was hoping I'd get a chance to speak with you before you went back to..."

"Northampton." I didn't think I'd ever peed so much in my life.

"Northampton. You know, catch up with each other..."

I flushed the toilet, drowning her out. I tucked my blouse into my trousers and opened the stall door.

"Oh, Jennifer. I was just so stunned to hear about your mother." Ruthie rushed me and enveloped me in her arms.

"Thank you," I said, trying to pull back.

"I know you two didn't get along but this is the time to take comfort in...in..."

"In what?" I dug my chin into her collarbone. She let go.

"In the love of God."

I glanced at Ruthie. She looked like she'd been fabricated.

"Do you really believe that?" I squirted some soap onto my hands and ran them under cold water. Mary's bathroom had no hot water.

"Of course. His love can heal anything." Ruthie opened her purse and took out a tube of lipstick.

How had I ever managed to love her?

The organ suddenly started to moan a tortured version of "A Closer Walk With Thee." I smiled to myself, maybe Gert was finally pushing back. It was just too damn bad she'd had to die to do it.

"Remember, Ruthie, when we used to make fun of all that crap? Of course, we were kids at the time." I twirled the crank on the paper towel dispenser.

"You remember in Paul's letter to the Ephesians, there is a time to put away childish things." Ruthie leaned close to the mirror and looked deep into her own eyes.

I wondered what she saw in there. Time had been relatively kind to Ruthie. I wondered what the truth of our shared paternity would do to that perfect hair and makeup.

"So, how've you been?" I dried my hands.

I also wondered about signs. I'd been indoctrinated years ago in Estelle's viewpoint on the turning of events. What did it mean to meet my first lover and half sister, though I didn't know that at the time, in a public bathroom in the church I almost murdered our father in, though I didn't know that at the time, on the morning of my mother's funeral? As Estelle would say, on the highway of life this is either a scenic outlook or road construction for the next hundred miles.

"I'm doing awesome. You remember David..."

"How could I forget that one eyebrow?"

Ruthie didn't even blink. I wondered when she had been re-engineered in plastic. Maybe living heterosexually when you weren't did it to you.

"We're involved in this really awesome business opportunity. I'm sure you've heard of TheWay…"

TheWay? Did she say TheWay?

"…It's not the pyramid scheme everyone said it is, that's been proven by the Federal Trade Commission, it is just a bunch of good folks buying everything from tennis shoes to toilet paper from themselves…"

I felt my mind glaze over.

"…Insuring financial freedom, which David and I will soon enjoy. He'll be able to give up his Chrysler dealerships."

Did she say Chrysler dealerships?

"He'll be able to spend his afternoons at the boys' lacrosse games." Ruthie blotted her lips on a tissue. "We are having a lot of fun and it's brought us as close together as when we were newlyweds."

It required Herculean effort not to comment on Ruthie's wedding.

"That's great, Ruthie. It's been nice chatting but I've got to get back to the funeral."

"Wait." She gripped my arm. If she wanted she could've pierced my flesh with her fingernails.

"They don't mind gay people."

"Who doesn't mind gay people?"

"TheWay folks. When you think about it people from your, ummm, people with your lifestyle are an untapped market." She pulled a brochure from her purse.

I took it. But then I take brochures from Jehovah's Witnesses too. Probably why my recycling bin is so full.

"Thanks." I pulled my arm away.

"Don't go, Jennifer. I need to say something else."

Never had returning to a funeral looked so good.

"You and I just have to let go of our past relationship, Jennifer. For me, it was just a silly interlude in my development and, while, I remember it fondly, when I think of it, which is almost never…"

I squinted at Ruthie making her image fuzzy. Indistinct, she was easier to take and barely discernable as that young woman I had known so long ago.

"And I know Jesus has forgiven me for my sin…"

Sin? What would Jesus think of this latest development in Ruthie's and my relationship?

"That's why I've been able to let it go. Let go, let God. Right?"

"Did you know Gert kept diaries?"

"What?" Ruthie looked surprised at my change in topic.

"Diaries. My mother kept diaries, interesting reading, not that I've read them all yet. Auntie Potts filled me in on the salient points."

"Actually, Dorothy's husband mentioned that last night…"

"Right. Right. Just before he socked your daddy in the nose. I hope it's broken, a childish viewpoint I know, but what can you expect, hanging onto childish habits the way I have."

"Why I didn't mean…you're not childish…it's just a more mature love between men and women. More natural." Ruthie edged toward the door.

Mature my ass.

"Those diaries have kind of turned my life around. In the space of a couple hours reality took a nosedive."

"What do you mean?" Ruthie asked.

"Apparently Gert was pregnant when she got married."

"Oh, Jennifer, that's not ideal perhaps but it certainly isn't shocking." Ruthie smiled a woman of the world smile.

"Except the father, my father since I was the firstborn, wasn't Bob Andersen." I leaned against the sink.

"No? Really?" Ruthie took a step toward me.

"Turned out that Pastor Jameson and Gert had a little tumble in the backseat. Parked along that old wood road off Mountain Road. You remember where you and I used to go."

"That can't be…" Ruthie's voice faded away.

"True? Oh, it's true, not the entire truth but a part of it. Auntie Potts is like the Oracle of Delphi. She knows everything."

"But, that means…" Ruthie collapsed into the folding metal chair in the corner.

"We're sisters. Well, half-sisters anyway."

The door opened. Estelle stood there.

"Hi. I just came to make sure you were okay." Estelle looked at me and then at Ruthie.

"Estelle, have you met Ruthie? Pastor Jameson's daughter. She and I went to school together, right Ruthie? Oh, and we had an affair for four years or so. Nauseating now, I know, but..." I shrugged.

"Pleased to meet you." Estelle extended her hand.

That's when Ruthie's manners failed her and she slid to the floor in a dead faint.

CHAPTER THIRTY-NINE

Humidity eventually breaks. Like a gothic novel, dark clouds billowed out from behind Gemorrah Mountain and settled over Gert's interment. Half the sky remained blue until those clouds moved in, turning everything an odd shade of green. Herlick walked to the hearse and rolled up the window on the driver's side.

"Yea, though I walk through the valley of the shadow of death..." The Antichrist's voice rose to be heard over the gathering wind, whipping his robe around his legs. His comb-over waved around his head like a sea anemone. The crowd began to fidget. There were a lot of uh-oh's. Someone wondered if hell was going to break loose.

Estelle looked at me and smiled. She loves weather. So do I. We often greet storms at our house by standing under the shelter of the back porch. But after the incident with the organ I was just a little worried. Gert's powers were ramping up, having moved on from mechanical anomalies to natural disasters.

"Nana tells me your mother is making a difficult adjustment," Estelle whispered in my ear.

"Oh?"

"Apparently Eternity wasn't quite what she had expected."

The crowd became more and more agitated as the sky lowered, thunder rumbled and lightning flickered. The pastor seemed immune to the gathering storm even though the pages of his Bible fluttered like a deck of cards.

"...Fear no evil, for thou art with me. Thy rod and thy staff, they comfort me..."

Dorothy stood transfixed by Gert's coffin, watching as the burnished steel handles of the casket grew darker and darker as light absented itself from the sky. It felt like something somewhere was holding its breath.

"Let us pray. Lord we beseech you to welcome your wayward servant, Gertrude, into the kingdom of..."

A gust of wind caught the carpet of Astroturf surrounding the grave and threw it into the air. A crack of thunder exploded and a flash of lightning struck the Moriarty's lilac bush next to the Andersen family plot, igniting it like a Fourth of July sparkler. Hail the size of peanut M&Ms rained from the sky. Branches of the burning bush dropped onto the Astroturf. The smell of burning plastic filled the air.

Herlick raced toward the hearse. The roar of its eight-cylinder engine was loud as he started it up and threw the vehicle in reverse, away from the blazing inferno as one piece of Astroturf caught another. In his haste he backed into the front bumper of the Antichrist's Mercury Grand Marquis. The car alarm began to shriek. Fire spread across the Astroturf and began to lick at the edges of Gert's coffin, suspended over the grave by a brass frame and some knotted rope.

"What was it she didn't like?" I shouted over the storm.

"Pretty much everything. Nana said she had to be sedated."

"Leave it to her to have to be sedated in Heaven."

"Not Heaven, babe, Eternity. Nana was quite clear on that distinction."

"Apparently she's woken up."

"No shit." Estelle started laughing. "This is unbelievable."

"I wonder if she'll kill him," I shouted.

"Who?"

"The Antichrist."

"Maybe. Your mother is dealing with a lot of unresolved anger."

I could feel the mourners behind me backing away from the spectacle. Could hear the leather soles of their good shoes crushing the hail that had accumulated.

"Give her the grace of your love, dear Lord, and help us to understand and forgive..."

Hail gave way to torrential rain. It put the fire out and left the lilac bush looking like a desiccated stick. Most of the dirt that the cemetery workers would've used to fill in the grave washed downhill toward the Civil War dead. The rushing water made the grave walls unstable until the left side gave way and Gert toppled in. She ended up lying on her side with her feet slightly elevated.

"Come on, babe. We're out of here." Estelle grabbed my hand and jerked me toward the Nova.

Thunder crashed and the ground vibrated. The hair stood up on my arm. I pulled Dorothy and Jimmy away just as a bolt of lightning crackled out of the sky and hit the casket. I watched it bounce and knock the Antichrist off his feet.

We ran for it.

CHAPTER FORTY

Mrs. Lewkowski sat in Mavis's car and considered the possibility of skipping the after-funeral gathering. Her dress was sopping wet and her hair, well, if it wasn't for the perm she'd gotten a couple weeks ago there would just be no hope for anything other than a trip to the hairdresser's. But that wasn't why she didn't want to go to the reception or whatever it was called. Everyone who was at the graveside services would look like a drowned rat. The plain fact was she didn't feel up to it. She felt washed out like after a nasty bout of flu.

It had been years since she'd been in the Federated Church. Not since Sparky, her fellow library committee member and volunteer fire chief's funeral. It had been a peaceful affair. A few hymns and a nice homily delivered by the Pastor. Mrs. What's-her-name kept control of the organ through the whole service. Today was, dare she say it, a fiasco. Too bad Earl hadn't come. Now she'd have to tell him about it and he'd think she was exaggerating.

Mavis put it best when she said Gertrude Andersen's funeral was like an episode of the *I Love Lucy* show. Except that this hadn't been funny and seemed...well, almost sinister. If only it could have been turned off like the television, but, it had just dragged on and on. Not that she was surprised. Gertrude had been hard to deal with alive; it just made sense that she'd be a handful dead.

"Mavis, honey. I'm ashamed to admit that all I feel like doing is going home." Mrs. Lewkowski glanced at her daughter who was looking in the rearview mirror trying to fluff up her hair.

"Me too, Ma. I'm exhausted and it isn't even noon yet."

"Do you think Jenny'll think poorly of us?"

"No, I don't. Knowing her, she doesn't want to go either. I saw her drive in the opposite direction when she left the cemetery."

"Oh good. Let's go home. I've got some nice ham salad for sandwiches. Then I'm going to make some chocolate chip cookies. You can take some home to Connecticut tomorrow."

"You're on." Mavis started her car and pulled out of the cemetery.

Herlick watched as the last vehicle drove away. Thankfully the rain had ended. Frankly, he was grateful the spectacle—there was no more accurate word—was over.

The ants that invaded Mrs. Andersen's casket yesterday had been a harbinger of today's disaster. He should have paid more attention—though who could have predicted the multitude of problems that erupted? Unprecedented as far as Herlick knew. He would most certainly be committing this to paper. It would be named The Andersen Saga because it began with Bob's funeral and would, hopefully, end with Gertrude. The Saga would join the extensive files kept by Harrison and now, Herlick. During his spare time he was converting everything to computer. The document's working title was "The Funerals I Can't Forget."

Barney, Tom and Raymond Aldridge, the brothers who maintained the cemetery, wandered over to survey the damage.

"Jesus H. Christ on a raft, I ain't never seen nothing like that," Raymond said. He was the only Aldridge Herlick had ever heard speak. Barney and Tom grunted or rolled their eyes and occasionally used hand gestures.

"Neither...ah...have I." Herlick wondered how they were going to get the casket out of the grave and back in the right way.

"Barney, why don't you go start up the bucket loader and bring it over here. We'll tie some rope around it, lift her up and set her back down nice and easy."

Barney nodded and loped off. Tom hacked and spit and jerked his head to the left.

"You do that, Tom."

Tom took off for the gardening shed.

"Tom's goin' to get the rope."

Herlick nodded. He supposed he could leave. The Aldridges were perfectly capable of handling the situation. Though the way things had been going it might be prudent to wait until Mrs. Andersen was resting comfortably before he took off.

"Guess we're gonna have to cut down that damn lilac bush. It's burnt to a crisp. Wonder if the family'll want us to plant another one." Raymond lit up a Marlboro.

"And where the hell are we gonna get more Astro-grass before Friday when we got another funeral coming in? Them bozos on the cemetery committee ain't gonna like spendin' the money neither. The perpetual cares are down, you know."

"Let me ask...ah...around. Perhaps one of our neighboring funeral homes will have some we can borrow." Herlick listened to the whine of the approaching bucket loader.

This would be over very soon. Herlick glanced at his waterproof Timex. Eleven forty. He would definitely have time to go home and change into something more comfortable and drive out to see his friend in Lenox. Herlick would bring a couple steaks and convince Nathan to make a pitcher of vodka martinis. They could sit out on the back deck and watch as the day came to an end.

Auntie Potts struggled out of her brassiere. It was so wet it stuck to her body like it'd been laminated. She'd gotten her arms out of it all right but hadn't been able to turn the darn thing around so she could unhook it. On top of that her arthritis was acting up so she couldn't get a good grip. Finally she got the kitchen shears from the butcher block and cut through the tricot between the cups.

"Thank God," Auntie said aloud. She'd probably regret it later but now all she could feel was the relief of being out of her wet clothes. She put on a robe, started a load of wash and threw the bra over a doorknob. It would come in handy tying up her tomatoes.

Right now she needed a glass of Pepsi with a lot of ice and two cigarettes. She was well over her daily quota but who the hell cared. It wasn't every day a person witnessed a ghost or spirit playing cat and mouse with Mrs. Earle and her organ and then conjuring up a storm that practically drowns everybody. It was too bad the pastor hadn't been electrocuted but Auntie guessed that even a ghost couldn't manage everything. Though Gertrude had managed a lot her first time out.

Ruthie took a cup of coffee into the living room and flicked on the television. She needed a little diversion after the second trip to the emergency room in less than twelve hours. This time they'd kept Daddy for observation. His vital signs seemed to be stable but you never knew with a man his age. Then there was the other news she'd received today. It was hard to believe she and Jennifer were related. They couldn't be more different than if they'd come from different parts of the world. That was undoubtedly attributable to Jennifer's mother's gene pool. No doubt Gertrude had seduced her father just as Jennifer had seduced Ruthie. She didn't believe for one minute what Auntie Potts had told her about Daddy taking advantage of the young

Gertrude. Daddy was a good Christian, a man of the cloth after all and should be given the benefit of the doubt. Not that there was any doubt in Ruthie's mind. And those diaries were just the fantasy ramblings of a young woman who'd allowed herself to be swept away and was feeling guilty for her sinful ways.

As for her father finding Gertrude's body and not notifying the authorities...well, that was unfortunate to say the least. He must have just panicked, made a poor choice and didn't know how to undo it. She would mention to Daddy that he consider retiring. Ruthie would make a point of visiting Dorothy this afternoon with her personal condolences. Now, there was a woman who could have been Ruthie's sister. They both had a flair for fashion and makeup. Perhaps, if the moment presented itself, she might be able to work TheWay into the conversation. Dorothy and her husband would be wonderful additions to Ruthie and David's team. TheWay was the perfect business opportunity for a nice couple with the good family values they seemed to have.

Ruthie felt her mood brighten at the thought. David would be so proud of her. She picked up the phone and dialed David's number at the Chrysler dealership. He wouldn't be too happy when he heard she wasn't going to make it home for a few days. But she couldn't leave Daddy and her visit to Dorothy and Jimmy Fifield was of the utmost importance. She'd make David understand, presentation was everything.

Estelle turned on the hot water tap full blast. Thank God she had some bubble bath in her toiletry bag. Days like today required a bath. Jennifer's mother had a great tub too. Long and wide and just made for soaking. She lowered herself, bit by bit, into the water, which was almost too hot.

There was a tap on the door.

"Yes?"

The door opened a crack and a hand snaked through holding a chocolate chip cookie aloft.

"Is that what I think it is?" Estelle wiggled her toes.

"Mrs. Lewkowski's famous Tollhouse cookies. Hot and gooey. Mavis just ran some over."

"Are you sharing?"

The cookie disappeared.

"Oh, come on, Jenn. You said yesterday I deserved the good girlfriend award."

Jennifer pushed the door open carrying a tray with a teapot, two cups and a plate heaped with cookies. She put it down on the bathmat.

"Wow. You really know how to treat a girl. Come on in, babe. The water's fine."

"Is there room for me?"

"There will always be room for you," Estelle said, reaching for a cookie.

EPILOGUE

If you had told me I'd end up at Dorothy's house after the funeral drinking lemonade and eating Cheez-Whiz on Ritz crackers, I never would have believed you. It's not like Dorothy and I became friends but we became friendly. I stopped calling Jimmy Goofball.

If you told me the Antichrist would survive his lightning strike, I never would've believed you. Though he did end up having a stroke and lost all ability to speak. I thought that was almost fair.

If you told me that I would end up inheriting the house I grew up in, I never would've believed you. The house had been in the Andersen family for years and it was in Bob's will that after my mother's death, the house would revert to Dorothy and me. In a twist of fate that almost defies belief, Dorothy became friendly with Ruthie and she and Jimmy joined TheWay and became very successful. They moved to Albany. Dorothy signed the house over to me. She wanted to leave Delicious far behind. A viewpoint I can understand and continue to toy with myself.

Herlick sold Healey's and became an antique dealer. His memoir about the funeral business became a bestseller. He sent me an autographed copy with a nice note inviting Estelle and me to his and Nathan's home in the Berkshires.

Auntie Potts gave up smoking and put a pizza oven in the repair bay of her garage and gas station. Delicious Pizza got third place in the West of Worcester magazine's "Best Pepperoni" contest. She says it's all in the crust.

I read each and every diary and burned them all. Reading them helped me understand Gert a little more though I can't forget how mean she was to me while I was growing up. I'm not sure I will ever be able to forgive her. I'd like to, if only to unknot my own stomach.

The Federated Church got a new minister, a woman with a husband and six kids who petitioned the church community to become a United Church of Christ congregation. She hasn't won yet, but she hasn't been fired either. That's progress.

Estelle and I can't decide what to do. She wants to turn the old house into a lesbian bed-and-breakfast. I have that love-hate thing going with Delicious. So, for now I rent the place to Mavis and her husband. They have twin baby girls and need the space. Mrs. Lewkowski loves having her grandchildren across the street.

Nana continues to give Estelle updates on Gert's adjustment to Eternity. The latest is that she's doing better since she's taken up Zen Archery. No arrows.

And me? I'm all right.

**Publications from
Bella Books, Inc.
Women. Books. Even Better Together.
P.O. Box 10543
Tallahassee, FL 32302
Phone: 800-729-4992
www.bellabooks.com**

CALM BEFORE THE STORM by Peggy J. Herring. Colonel Marcel Robicheaux doesn't tell and so far no one official has asked, but the amorous pursuit by Jordan McGowen has her worried for both her career and her honor.
978-0-9677753-1-9

THE WILD ONE by Lyn Denison. Rachel Weston is busy keeping home and head together after the death of her husband. Her kids need her and what she doesn't need is the confusion that Quinn Farrelly creates in her body and heart.
978-0-9677753-4-0

LESSONS IN MURDER by Claire McNab. There's a corpse in the school with a neat hole in the head and a Black & Decker drill alongside. Which teacher should Inspector Carol Ashton suspect? Unfortunately, the alluring Sybil Quade is at the top of the list. First in this highly lauded series.
978-1-931513-65-4

WHEN AN ECHO RETURNS by Linda Kay Silva. The bayou where Echo Branson found her sanity has been swept clean by a hurricane—or at least they thought. Then an evil washed up by the storm comes looking for them all, one-by-one. Second in series.
978-1-59493-225-0

DEADLY INTERSECTIONS by Ann Roberts. Everyone is lying, including her own father and her girlfriend. Leaving matters to the professionals is supposed to be easier! Third in series with *PAID IN FULL* and *WHITE OFFERINGS*.
978-1-59493-224-3

SUBSTITUTE FOR LOVE by Karin Kallmaker. No substitutes, ever again! But then Holly's heart, body and soul are captured by Reyna... Reyna with no last name and a secret life that hides a terrible bargain, one written in family blood.
978-1-931513-62-3

MAKING UP FOR LOST TIME by Karin Kallmaker. Take one Next Home Network Star and add one Little White Lie to equal mayhem in little Mendocino and a recipe for sizzling romance. This lighthearted, steamy story is a feast for the senses in a kitchen that is way too hot.
978-1-931513-61-6

2ND FIDDLE by Kate Calloway. Cassidy James's first case left her with a broken heart. At least this new case is fighting the good fight, and she can throw all her passion and energy into it.
978-1-59493-200-7

HUNTING THE WITCH by Ellen Hart. The woman she loves — used to love — offers her help, and Jane Lawless finds it hard to say no. She needs TLC for recent injuries and who better than a doctor? But Julia's jittery demeanor awakens Jane's curiosity. And Jane has never been able to resist a mystery. #9 in series and Lammy-winner.
978-1-59493-206-9

FAÇADES by Alex Marcoux. Everything Anastasia ever wanted — she has it. Sidney is the woman who helped her get it. But keeping it will require a price — the unnamed passion that simmers between them.
978-1-59493-239-7

ELENA UNDONE by Nicole Conn. The risks. The passion. The devastating choices. The ultimate rewards. Nicole Conn rocked the lesbian cinema world with *Claire of the Moon* and has rocked it again with *Elena Undone*. This is the book that tells it all...
978-1-59493-254-0

WHISPERS IN THE WIND by Frankie J. Jones. It began as a camping trip, then a simple hike. Dixon Hayes and Elizabeth Colter uncover an intriguing cave on their hike, changing their world, perhaps irrevocably.
978-1-59493-037-9

WEDDING BELL BLUES by Julia Watts. She'll do anything to save what's left of her family. Anything. It didn't seem like a bad plan...at first. Hailed by readers as Lammy-winner Julia Watts' funniest novel.
978-1-59493-199-4

WILDFIRE by Lynn James. From the moment botanist Devon McKinney meets ranger Elaine Thomas the chemistry is undeniable. Sharing—and protecting—a mountain for the length of their short assignments leads to unexpected passion in this sizzling romance by newcomer Lynn James.
978-1-59493-191-8

LEAVING L.A. by Kate Christie. Eleanor Chapin is on the way to the rest of her life when Tessa Flanagan offers her a lucrative summer job caring for Tessa's daughter Laya. It's only temporary and everyone expects Eleanor to be leaving L.A...
978-1-59493-221-2

SOMETHING TO BELIEVE by Robbi McCoy. When Lauren and Cassie meet on a once-in-a-lifetime river journey through China their feelings are innocent...at first. Ten years later, nothing—and everything—has changed. From Golden Crown winner Robbi McCoy.
978-1-59493-214-4

DEVIL'S ROCK by Gerri Hill. Deputy Andrea Sullivan and Agent Cameron Ross vow to bring a killer to justice. The killer has other plans. Gerri Hill pens another intriguing blend of mystery and romance in this page-turning thriller.
978-1-59493-218-2

SHADOW POINT by Amy Briant. Madison McPeake has just been not-quite fired, told her brother is dead and discovered she has to pick up a five-year old niece she's never met. After she makes it to Shadow Point it seems like someone—or something—doesn't want her to leave. Romance sizzles in this ghost story from Amy Briant.
978-1-59493-216-8

JUKEBOX by Gina Daggett. Debutantes in love. With each other. Two young women chafe at the constraints of parents and society with a friendship that could be more, if they can break free. Gina Daggett is best known as "Lipstick" of the columnist duo Lipstick & Dipstick.
978-1-59493-212-0

BLIND BET by Tracey Richardson. The stakes are high when Ellen Turcotte and Courtney Langford meet at the blackjack tables. Lady Luck has been smiling on Courtney but Ellen is a wild card she may not be able to handle.
978-1-59493-211-3